Stillborn

Stillborn

Diekoye Oyeyinka

East African
Educational Publishers Ltd.
Nairobi • Kampala • Dar es Salaam • Kigali

Published by
East African Educational Publishers Ltd.
Brick Court, Mpaka Road/Woodvale Grove
Westlands, P.O. Box 45314
Nairobi – 00100
KENYA
email: eaep@eastafricanpublishers.com
website: www.eastafricanpublishers.com

East African Educational Publishers Ltd.
C/O Gustro Ltd.
P.O. Box 9997
Kampala
UGANDA

Ujuzi Books Ltd.
P.O. Box 38260
Dar es Salaam
TANZANIA

East African Publishers Rwanda Ltd.
Tabs Plaza, Kimironko Road
Opposite Kigali Institute of Education
P.O. Box 5151
Kigali
RWANDA

© Diekoye Oyeyinka 2014
All rights reserved

ISBN 978-9966-25-969-1

First Published 2014

Dedication
For Prof and Iya ni Wura.

ACKNOWLEDGEMENTS

This book took a lot of time and love to come to fruition. I want to thank my family: Prof and Mev, you were the rock that gave me the courage to write, and the exposure to know how to write. Fola, Banke, and Kanyin, thank you for all the love and encouragement during the process.

For my aunties who loved and encouraged me with an almost blind faith: Aunty Yemisi, Aunty Cynthia, Aunty Tokunbo, Aunty Ndali, and Aunty Mariam – your stories brought these pages to life.

For friends who were more than just that: Simon Frey, for his encouragement and belief; Seye Olusoga, who believed in my dream before reading a single page; Naja Baldwin, my de facto agent, your support kept me from giving up many times; Mary Catherine Fixel, for making me put down the first words; Imran Bhaloo and Chloe Last, for saving my sanity in those difficult months; Moyo Odusola, for believing in my writing and pushing it to be better; Omotayo Adeola, for the courage to make those revisions; Osaretin, for a fantastic piece of art for the cover; Agatha, Nush, Charlotte, and Dolapo, for the random phone calls that kept me going; and the Good Guys and the House of OE.

I am very grateful to my publisher, and in particular Jane Mathenge and the rest of the EAEP team for bringing this long held dream to a reality.

Finally, for those who lived these lives I tried so inadequately to capture.

Thank you all!

PEAK LIBRARY

1. Secret Lives – Ngugi wa Thiong'o
2. Matigari – Ngugi wa Thiong'o
3. A Grain of Wheat – Ngugi wa Thiong'o
4. Weep Not, Child – Ngugi wa Thiong'o
5. The River Between – Ngugi wa Thiong'o
6. Devil on the Cross – Ngugi wa Thiong'o
7. Petals of Blood – Ngugi wa Thiong'o
8. Wizard of the Crow – Ngugi wa Thiong'o
9. Homing In – Marjorie Oludhe Macgoye
10. Coming to Birth – Marjorie Oludhe Macgoye
11. Street Life – Marjorie Oludhe Macgoye
12. The Present Moment – Marjorie Oludhe Macgoye
13. Chira – Marjorie Oludhe Macgoye
14. A Farm Called Kishinev – Marjorie Oludhe Macgoye
15. No Longer at Ease – Chinua Achebe
16. Arrow of God – Chinua Achebe
17. A Man of the People – Chinua Achebe
18. Things Fall Apart – Chinua Achebe
19. Anthills of the Savannah – Chinua Achebe
20. The Strange Bride – Grace Ogot
21. Land Without Thunder – Grace Ogot
22. The Promised Land – Grace Ogot
23. The Other Woman – Grace Ogot
24. The Future Leaders – Mwangi Ruheni
25. White Teeth – Okot P'Bitek
26. Horn of My Love – Okot P'Bitek
27. Without a Conscience – Barbara Baumann
28. God's Bits of Wood – Sembene Ousmane
29. Emperor Shaka the Great – Masizi Kunene
30. No Easy Walk to Freedom – Nelson Mandela
31. The Herdsman's Daughter – Bernard Chahilu
32. Hearthstones – Kekelwa Nyaywa
33. Of Man and Lion – Beatrice Erlwanger
34. My Heart on Trial – Genga Idowu
35. Kosiya Kifefe – Arthur Gakwandi
36. Mine Boy – Peter Abrahams
37. Return to Paradise – Yusuf K Dawood
38. Takadini – Ben Hanson
39. Myths and Legends of the Swahili – Jan Knappert
40. Mau Mau Author in Detention – Gakaara wa Wanjau

CONTENTS

PROLOGUE

I sit in Uncle's study, at his big desk with unfinished work. My thoughts are clouded, surfeited with unanswered questions. A strange stale breeze waffles in, suffocates the atmosphere, the air heavy, life recedes. Settling on the room, it shirks its proliferate potential. I wonder what next; I know Uncle's view – return home – is as unwavering as the finality of his death.

As I sit at the desk, I hear a faint distant drumming, the drummer unknown. It is a ghostly message, floating from an unidentified source. It gets louder and closer, overwhelming. Suddenly, an intrusion into my face, I am sure it emanates from within the room but from where, I cannot tell. Then I see them. They dance into the room, in their inchoate serenity: a voice within me whispers, "They are the dreamers of the stillborn child in 1960." They were surely mourners by all appearance, they had about them unseen tears of promise unfulfilled. They swirl, as apparitions; they float in the trapped capsule that is Uncle's study. Was this his legacy? Was this my destiny? I watch them dance to the tunes of the ghostly drums, to songs about my past and future. I watch them sway to the sorrowful beats. They beckon to me and I follow. My limbs are numb, uncontrollable and my mind is a quivering chamber of cacophonous inner voices. I am on the wings of a great eagle. The drums beat to a crescendo, speaking an ancient language, which though unlearnt and untaught, I yet understand.

In Uncle's voice, the music speaks to me as I follow its rhythmic dance beats. I understand its words but I do not comprehend all of its meaning. "You need a simpler tale to understand, you must speak with Emeka," it says. We are approaching a door that seems to open to all of space and time. The voice begins a trembling soliloquy.

At her beginning, I was there. I watched as she was entered forcibly, her insides plundered, her seeds corrupted. Her rapist is single-mindedly vile, he must execute his intention; he approached his mission with complete abandon, intent on a total violation of his captive, for that is what he is destined to do. Alas, no one could prevent the sordid act, no one knew what to do, how to stop it ... But now the seed is germinating. Some cautioned that we must abort. For her conception was an abomination, its consummation too violent and though her birth was seamless, the polluted seed forebodes the monster child. But the caution went unheeded, the fate of the child was sealed for its nativity transcends time; mere mortals cannot understand it. The child is born. Physically, she is a spectacle to behold. We laugh at the needless worry and fretting of the augurers. But it is years foregone and the legs refuse to walk, the hands refuse to work the simplest of enterprise and her words are incomprehensible and incoherent. The child is cursed by her paternity. She is named Nigeria, like her defiled mother. She is slow to mature, to grasp. She is premature. Her incubator is shattered and greedy hands reach for her supple flesh. Fingers of tribalism, bearing venal shawls of democracy and blankets of corruption invade her bed of affliction and debt. Even at birth, she is diseased. She was not washed as was customary, her navel was not cut, the child received no inoculation against the rampaging viruses that ate at the innards of her captors; she had no swaddling clothes and elements had their way in her. The child was stillborn. October 1960. At her birth, life was stilled.

But we have reached the door and the voice is suddenly silent. I am led to a grand room with a circular table at its centre. At it sit three men. There is an empty chair. It is mine. I sit and listen, ignored. But I am in the conversation. They speak words of substance. Their words are alive. Their utterances fill the room, spill past the door and beyond the present. Timeless words of immortals. I recognise them from hallowed frames and crumpled notes; they are the founding fathers I see Obafemi Awolowo, Nnamdi Azikiwe and Abubakar Tafawa Balewa.

Their conversation seems a monologue. A dignified trinity, their voices, weighed with a thousand sorrows of reason, is indistinguishable:

"But we did nothing wrong, we fought off the British peacefully
We gave them each autonomy through federalism
Yes, we had our faults, we made judgments, some erroneous
… but our mistakes should be their flashlights
We showed them the power of free education, taught them
how to build roads, how to cultivate nature endowed with cocoa,
oil palm, rubber, groundnut …
Then they found oil, the black gold, the curse of the land
Perhaps that is why
They drown in their greed
But who are they
The very ones we left behind to care for her
They are children trying to raise a baby
They are boys pretending to the status of real men
They refuse to grow up, to take responsibility
That is no excuse
There is no excuse
They fight about everything – religion, class, tribes, money,
power
They kill our dreams
They kill her dreams
She is like a stillborn
Her deformed heart has almost lost its beat
Yet, she stumbles on
As a zombie, blind, deaf, without ambition
They strangle their own dreams
But who are they
They are cowards
Their greed and corruption is not satiated by money
They never seem to have enough
Perhaps this filthiness of their mind does not stem from a love
of money but a fear of poverty
Even in their theft, they are inefficient
Foraging for seeds, they forget the fruit
They eat the seed and plant nothing
They should know what to do
We laid it out clearly for them."

Suddenly, as if noticing me for the first time, they turn to me. I am intimidated; they have the imperious stares of lions.

"Why don't they know?"

"Why don't they remember?"

"Why are they not reminded?"

I stutter unable to respond, until suddenly the drums begin to beat again. I am still cowering beneath their gaze, when I am again transported on the mighty wings of the eagle back through the door that conquered time and space to Uncle's study. The beats begin to quieten and the presence leaves the room.

And as Uncle's spirit passes away, I feel a slight shiver. A sentence, innocuous but consequential, has spilled from my reverie to the paper before me:

'The gestation period unknown, a C-section was planned. The day was October 1, 1960.'

The words sting my eyes with the cruelty of an arrow that pierces a baby's heart. I look out the window and begin to cry. Then I write with the violence of Uncle's frustrated fights and incomplete battles. The words pour with fury. As the lingering questions of the founding fathers assault my ears with the force of a thousand drums, my pen attacks and ravages the paper.

I could not stop.

PART 1

1960

I
Suffering & Smiling (South Eastern Nigeria, 1943 – 1958)

ONE

A romance turned tragedy is a most unfortunate affair. Emeka was conceived and born in such a calamity. His mother, too beautiful for her own good, ensnared Nonso at twelve and unknown to her, was already ripening into an object of unexpected affection; she caught the eye of Chief when she was only sixteen. The best end to a love triangle is one broken heart and the worst a Trojan horse. Unfortunately, luckily, this ended with neither.

At twelve, Nneka's young heart, untutored in the ways of the world, pledged its love to the boy that picked fruits for her from the village almond trees and brought her the little fish he caught in the stagnant pond. At seventeen, it stubbornly refused to betray that promise of first love. Neither money, nor prestige, the veiled incentive beckoning from a betrothal to Chief succeeded in swaying her iron-clad promise; nor could a mother's threats change her hastily made vow, instead, she became more resolute in her determination to actualise her word. This is the wonderful beauty of the female heart: at seventeen, it is convinced it understands love, a full five years before its male counterpart and it is willing to be pierced for this privilege.

Her mother stood in front of their mud hut, one hand on her waist, the other wagging furiously before her, the straw eaves causing a sinister shadow to fall across her animated face. Her voice thundered, "Only over my dead body will you marry that pauper farmer." The threat was not new, the words were still spoken with unbridled vehemence, but their effect was as candlelight at noon. She will not be moved.

"I love Nonso," Nneka passionately returned, "I will marry him," she proclaimed stubbornly for the umpteenth time.

"Love is the game of children; marriage the business of adults," her mother said with a tired laugh.

Nneka fled from the house to find her lover, the fountain of courage and solace. That night they did the unthinkable; they made love before their wedding vows. She knew it was impossible to snub Chief, especially since he had been travelling to Lagos to help form the new government. It was a full moon, as it always is when the eternal grand illusion of nature's orchestra is played; this is the season wolves howl and the day's beauty precedes a tragedy. Nonso waited at the usual meeting place, by the tall weeping willow that straddled the stream. Three years ago, they had sat on its lowest branch that tickled the water, the sunset at their backs, their toes towards the water, their hearts in the clouds. They had shared their first kiss. It was not magical; Nonso clumsily held a fishing rod in his hand, one end poking her ribs, their wet feet causing excited ripples. But it was eternal, a day never to be forgotten.

It was not as though Nonso did not have potential, he was a favourite among his peers and respected by the elders. He had taken over the family farm while still young after his father passed away; a life suddenly ended by a bout of typhoid. He was successful and by all measures, considered handsome by his peers. Yet, he lacked that all-important qualification, he was not Chief. He did not have a degree from London and he was not going to be part of the government of the new country of Nigeria. He was not going to make Nneka's family wealthy with two simple words: I do. One cannot seriously premise a life on handsomeness and human potential is nothing but a dew of the morning that can easily be licked away by sunrise. A successful life is built through sacrifice and nothing is sacred on its altar, not even young love.

Tonight he held her delicate fingers in his hands like he did three years before, like he would never let go. She kissed him with a passion that said, 'I will love you forever' and he sighed like a man

3

condemned. Neither said a word, but soon they were naked; they did what adults did but they were hardly aware of the consequences of their spontaneous action, the presaging of a calamity for them both. They lay on the bank of the stream in the warmth of the moon's approving glow. After all, how were they to understand the prognostications of the watching full moon, the day of the wolf. The wolf preys on the innocent, the wounded and young sheep, not the wise, strong and healthy ones. They professed to one another what they had known for years: I love you. Then they did not see each other for eight months.

She was pregnant but no one knew. Except for herself and her mother [of course], because mothers always know these things. She noticed the snappy remarks, the sneaking out early in the morning and the sluggish waddle. She was experienced enough to know the difference between a child's affectations to secret love and its inevitable consequences. Nneka tied her wrapper over her supple breasts, which were blooming in consonance with her 'condition'; they grew enough to hide her stomach that was yet to bulge sufficiently and reveal itself to non-medical observers. Her mother feigned ignorance and they remained in their silent standoff. Her mother reckoned the pregnancy was a month old when it was already in the second trimester. They could still arrange the wedding to the Chief quickly and pass off the unfortunate offspring as a premature birth in the lineage of the rich man. But fate conspires to expose the most well kept secrets of the naïve, for Chief was suddenly summoned to Lagos and he was to remain there for a whole year. Chief remained optimistic, however, thinking that good things come eventually to the patient. "No matter," he said, with his characteristic-rumbling laugh, "Nneka can only blossom more in that time."

And blossom she did indeed. The pregnancy made her glow ethereally. Nonso had been gone for three months. His mother had decided to return to her village since her husband was dead. Nonso was sure this sudden nostalgia for her past had much to do with his own present situation. But who can refuse the wishes of a widow, especially your mother. A hurried message to Nneka was never delivered by a younger brother who feared the spirits that danced in the dark more than the flames that would do likewise in his brother's angry eyes.

Three months later he was back, sick with malaria, possessed with a strange foolishness of feverish love. For a while, he had listened to his mother's passionate pleas for him to remain with her, but his heart was elsewhere and he had to find it. A man must not disobey his mother, even for love and on the day he set to go back, he was seized by malaria. He lay there thrashing and writhing on the straw mattress, his nineteen-year-old body oscillating between polar temperatures at high tempo like the tidal waves of the Atlantic Ocean in September. As soon as he was strong enough to stand, a week later, he began the journey. He stumbled through the thick forest along the lonely overgrown path that had been deserted by the villagers since the dry season had desiccated the river and created a shorter route. In his delirium his mind took a tortuous journey to a past hidden in the dark recesses of his soul. Suddenly Nneka was feeding him fruits and giving him water from a shoulder gourd. He was now asleep in her bosom in the shade of an old indulgent tree. But he was weak and what should have taken a week took two. He knew he was approaching his destination when he could hear the little boys by the shallow stream bordered by Iroko trees argue over whose premature fish was the largest. The strange smells from the lone hut at the edge of the village, where the one-legged man mixed potions with his three-legged dog assured him. He stumbled blindly past the prepubescent girls who played hand-clapping games with dusty legs and hair plaited up the middle under the mango trees with broad olive leaves. Soon he was in the village floating, unseeing and unseen, past naked children with protruding stomachs and running noses. He collapsed with feverish relief.

Of all woes, Nneka's aunt, retiring early from the day's farming activities would be first to come across his heaving frame. She took him to her house and fed him just enough to keep him alive, his delusions aided by special leaves she added to his meals. She was not going to let the tenacious young fool steal the family's golden goose. For five months, he was there, his farm overgrown with thorns, Nneka's heart with despair. But love is a powerful antidote and one day it seduced him from his prison and dragged him to the door of Nneka's house. She found him covered in sweat, collapsed in a heap. The warmth in his head spread convectively from him into her and gradually through her entire being, warming her lonely heart chilled from prolonged neglect, nay, abandonment. "I knew you would return," she said, holding his head against her stomach where the baby kicked to acknowledge its father.

She hurried Nonso to his derelict hut and nursed him devotedly in secret. And within a week, he was well, but as is well known, stolen joy is but fleeting. Nneka went into labour. They still operated under the erroneous assumption that no one was the wiser and when the soft heat of the early morning lured people to their farms, they stole from his house to the tree by the stream to bring forth the life they had created there. This time she shrieked and screamed. The baby came out quickly but painfully. It was tiny. Nonso kept tugging at the cord that accompanied the baby and Nneka's agony gushed from her mouth in strident torrents. The bleeding would not stop. It was obvious the mother would not make it and the tragedy of the realisation overshadowed the beauty of the birth. Suddenly a wolf howled in the dark of the night and Nonso suddenly remembered the day of the full moon when this deed was done. The day tragedy was conceived in the ecstasy of love.

Nonso finally severed the baby from the mother with a stroke of the machete. She was dead five minutes later, her head in his lap, the newborn bawling loudly in a nearby bush. The neglected boy remained exposed to the chilly October air while his father wailed over the corpse whose tears had finally dried. The child was only remembered long after it had stopped crying and was half frozen. Nonso picked it up and in a déjà vu that only fate found amusing, a woman would open the wooden doors of Nneka's hut to find a feverish male curled on the doorstep. This is how Emeka came into this world. His father whose soul was already strangled by grief would hang himself from the tree where he had first kissed the love of his life and by whose roots she now rested.

Nneka's mother scooped up the bundle on her doorstep. Loud wails rumbled from the depth of her being. For three days all she did was cry; sonorous screams, silent tears, deep moans, haunting howls. On the fourth, she shaved her head and named the baby Chukuemeka – God is great. Emeka was born in the most calamitous of situations, but he was to have a most remarkable life – fate always evens out its mistakes. God always takes care of widows and orphans.

TWO

Emeka's earliest recollection was of a bicycle and a radio. No one ever mentioned the tragedy of his true birth, but he realised he got away with things other children could not. Seldom did he abuse this privilege. He had a man he called father and a woman he called mother and his second memory was of the day they brought his brother home.

Perhaps his first memory was not actually one recollection but a medley of many occasions made singular by their regularity. Each morning his father would mount his bicycle with the boy on the handlebars next to the radio and his mother at the back. The father was very proud of both his possessions and he would dexterously hold one in each hand and manoeuvre to the farm.

The father would work on the yams, the mother on the cocoyam and the little boy would sit next to the radio that only got one station and play with Coca-Cola bottle caps in the dirt. The sounds were always the same. The impatient heavy strokes of his father's hoe, the measured shallow thud of his mother's and the heavily accented voice of the man on the radio occasionally interrupted by music. The heat stuck close to the boy like an unwelcome nanny, but he never got sick. A recalcitrant fly often stayed behind to dart at his teary eyes and mucous smeared nose even when the heavy air retired its drowsy compatriots.

There was no doubt he would have had a more prosperous life with Chief. His tragic parents would have afforded him more luxuries, but none could love him the way the Ogbonnas did. Not even his biological parents, for theirs was a consuming love that often forgot about the rest of the world and was fueled by a selfish obsession with each other.

Mr Ogbonna was quiet, like most men who had been childless for a long time and suffered many insults. He had been one of the first converts to the new religion and though childless, he had refused to marry again. People said he was greedy because rather than take a second wife, he bought a fan, a bicycle and a radio. When his sister died, he took the child and proved everyone wrong. Chukuemeka was a mixture of blessings and woes. Soon after he arrived, the farm began to flourish and Mr Ogbonna became the first man on their street to have a tin roof. A few months after Emeka turned three, Mrs Ogbonna finally became pregnant. Shortly afterwards, heavy rains came and wiped out all of Mr Ogbonna's harvest. No one else's farm was touched. The tide of joy and sorrow continued to sweep the household.

Five years later, another child would be added but only after a tragedy would claim the other young Ogbonna. Mrs Ogbonna, floored by the heartbreak, became unable to farm and barely supported Emeka and his sister. She always had a weak disposition and was widely known as an ogbanje because before her, her parents had had four children who had all died before they turned six. However, she never got malaria and it was only during those times when others were ill that she became active, her dead eyes sparkling for an errant week or two. But now she was inconsolable, lying on a mat by a tame fire that could not reflect in her teary pupils. Emeka's father simply squared his shoulders and worked harder on his farm, he went earlier and stayed later, coming home to bland dinners. This went on for a few years until one day a small insect darted at his left eye, its bite leaving it swollen. In his pride and ignorance, he would refuse to get it treated until it was too late and even then, it was all that could be done to save his life from a spreading infection, the eye becoming a mirror of his wife's demeanour. When the 'ghost' offered to take Emeka west with him and in exchange foot the medical bills, Emeka made the decision to go before his father could object.

THREE

The ghost was only a white man. He had sincere green eyes and tired hair that was crushed into his head by the African sun. He wore a short-sleeved white shirt and brown khaki shorts always. He carried a large black King James Bible with a gold cross and a lined notebook that he assiduously scribbled in with a black pen. He seemed to be constantly amazed and excited all at once. When he was not writing, his hands flailed around as they tried to comprehend everything and his mouth worked itself tirelessly. Then it would hang comically open, slightly too exhausted to shut properly and his left hand would rest on his sun-bleached hair, further grinding it into his weary skull.

His name was Father Patrick Grey and he was a priest. If the profession had existed, he would have called himself a sociologist. He was writing a history of the people of the Niger and its surrounding territory. He worked as a teacher, a priest and a self-appointed judge to whomever sought his counsel. When Emeka was twelve, he stopped paying his fees and instead made him his assistant. Together they walked from house to house and during the weekends from village to village. Father Grey alternated between floundering delirium and mouth-open fatigue. Emeka was generally quiet and withdrawn, but he had an ear for languages and was the only person who mostly understood the words that hissed from the Reverend Father's extraordinary red snout.

Four years into this tidy arrangement, Father Grey decided that he needed to go West to get a more robust comprehension for his book and wanted Emeka to accompany him. The following day, before the sun reached its zenith, before his father could awake to realise he had lost an eye and a son, while tears still flowed in the hut with the tin roof, Emeka set off with the ghost.

It was rare that an Ibo boy went to school in the West in those days. Emeka had longed to attend the Federal Government College in the East but his parents could not afford it. Father Grey quickly got a position with the Federal Government College in Ibadan and Emeka became the only Ibo student at the school. At sixteen, he was four years older than his classmates. His classmates regarded him with suspicion and amazement and at that age, these are not endearing attitudes.

He stayed in the dormitories, as all the boys were required to. There were four corridors of rooms bordering a sandy square with occasional tufts of grass. Each corridor had two rooms with sixteen bunks, a dank room for suitcases, a room with four holes in the ground that served as toilets and neglected flowerbeds that the boys pissed in under the cover of darkness. His bunkmate was a brilliant and reclusive thirteen-year old Yoruba boy called Dolapo.

It was a quiet evening. The approaching storm had made everyone restless during the day and now they all flopped down on their beds contentedly, rereading wrinkled letters from home. The moon was bright, almost full and the wind whispered soft lullabies. A dark cloud swallowed the moon and regurgitated it with a blind flash and thunderous roar. The sky wept with joy at the beautiful rebirth. It was the type of rain that fell as a continuous drop, reconciling the earth with its mother.

It was the type of rain that reminded little boys of quiet nights at their mothers' feet. It was the rain that had birthed the earth the day she left her mother.

"Emeka, do you want to hear a story my mother told me about the rain?" Dolapo tentatively asked, surprising his roommate. Dolapo almost seemed reluctant to speak about anything that did not involve schoolwork.

Emeka nodded in the bunk above, realising that his roommate could not see the gesture. Hearing the springs move but unsure of his response, Dolapo decided to proceed.

"One day an iridescent speck had appeared in the sky and it grew and grew. In those days, the animals lived in the clouds, there was no earth; the sky was home to all. But the speck grew like a fat leech sucking up more and more of the sky until it looked like it would burst and it did. It had never rained before, but it did so for fifty days and nights. When the rain stopped, there was an earth and a sky. The earth had trees, the seas and the animals. The earth had everything and the sky was just an endless blue mass, it kept only one thing – the sun. The sky was initially surprised but soon realised she liked her infinity – the depthless silence, the endless blue and the space that stretched to the horizon. She was happy until the earth began to mock and laugh at her. The sky wanted to grumble but had no voice, she wanted to cry but had no tears; she had nothing but the sun. So, she told him of her plight and they conspired to revenge. He shone in all his boundless glory and the waters began to come back to the sky. Soon the earth was a desert waste and the animals were dying in droves. They begged the sky to let them have the water back and she only laughed at the earth. Eventually, the stench of the dying animals became so noisome that even the sky could hardly bear it. Finally, the sky relented but first she took a picture so the earth would never forget what it looks like without her. So now, before every rainfall, there is thunder and a flash."

"I wonder why my mother told me this tale," Dolapo said, "but whenever it rains, I think of her."

They lay quiet and content in the scents and sounds of the September rain, inhaling the freshly washed sand and stirred vegetation. Frogs burped placidly from the edge of the forest and other sounds of a new spring sang out. The steady drum of a thousand drops on the slender almond leaves, the miserable chirp of wet sparrows and the hoot of an owl, which had been awakened prematurely in its unprotected roost.

As the rain began to abate, there was a stirring as the sound of a hundred beating wings filled the air. There were insects everywhere and while the boys ran around in the gleeful drizzle swatting them into wet shirts, Emeka quietly went about placing containers of water beneath the naked light bulbs. He sat on the cold cement watching the insects make suicidal darts into the reflected light. After a while, he began scooping them out, leaving behind the wet heavy wings. He spiced them with pepper and salt and roasted them in palm oil on a metal plate with the help of a heated iron. These ingredients were readily available due to the advantage of having a guardian who lived on the school grounds and had an infinite fascination with the local culture. He made a present to the dormitory prefect and to Dolapo who shared the bunk with him. After they had their fill, they handed out the rest. Suspicion turned into respect with Emeka and Dolapo becoming fast friends.

The incessant clanging of bells cut through the silent air. It was time for night prep. It was still the rainy season and the light drizzle and chilly air made Dolapo reluctant to go. He hid beneath the comfort of the grey blanket, shielded by a gauzy mosquito net. He decided the three strokes he would get on his behind the next day were worth it. Emeka's reluctance to leave the comfort of his bed was encouraged by the indulgence of his roommate. They decided to stay behind to eat some of the provisions they brought from home. It was rare for them to have the room to themselves, as there were always a few hungry mouths eager to indulge Emeka's generosity.

Dolapo was woken by the sharp sound of a palm across the face and someone poking his side. It was Emeka's delicate fingers. After the insect feast, the dormitory prefect had taken more than a passing interest in Emeka and it was not just for his ready access to palm oil. Emeka was fairer than most boys. He had long, feminine lashes and bright red lips in a permanent pout. He had unnaturally soft hair that made some wonder if the priest was his father. He had high cheekbones and was composed of delicate features. All the younger boys loved him. Half the older boys loved him. The dormitory prefect often called him into his room when he was in his towel and insisted on shaking his hands, letting the contact linger too long. Emeka had become accustomed to such unwarranted attention and had quickly discovered how to enjoy its privileges without its implied commitments.

Someone was sobbing quietly and there were rough voices from the centre of the room. Emeka's large eyes gazed patiently at him, interrupted occasionally by his thick lashes which fell suddenly and rose slowly like they carried a million weights. "Thunder is around," he said nonchalantly. Dolapo was immediately awake and sitting straight up. Thunder got his nickname because he habitually slapped younger students across the face and the sound it made was obvious. Thunder's aunt was the vice principal, so he had no fear of being disciplined. The last time Thunder had been to their room, five boys cried, one lost his tooth, half a tin of milk was seized, a whole packet of sugar and a box of cornflakes. Emeka seemed entirely unperturbed. "He wanted some gari, I gave him; let's eat." He was completely undaunted that someone was being slapped repeatedly across the face as he poured water on the concoction of milk, *gari*, sugar and groundnuts. It was desperately delicious and his confidence soon seeped into the food and into Dolapo. When they were done, without a second thought Dolapo marched past Thunder and the house prefect in the centre of the room and went to rinse the bowl.

Something was about to happen. The night told him so and he told Emeka when he reentered the room. "You worry too much," Emeka said with his easy grin. A shrill whistle echoed across the night and withered his inchoate smile. The metal barred gates began to rattle and shake, whistles were blown with urgency and voices began to jump in. The voices were drunk and incoherent. They were those of the security men who were to guard the students. Dolapo grabbed Emeka and told him to follow him; there was only one thing to do. They ran to the last room at the end of the corridor. Dolapo automatically began to climb the crumbling graffiti-covered shelves by the wall to one of the many large holes in the ceiling.

Every semester the ceilings were sealed and the walls were painted. It always took less than a month for holes to be punched into the ceilings to hide food from marauding seniors and invariably invite the rats. Emeka was deathly afraid of rats. "Look, we have no choice but to climb up there," Dolapo insisted, the terror evident in his eyes as he paused briefly with his hand frozen over a scrawl that said, 'If you mess with the best, you will die like the rest.' Emeka was unconvinced. Already, they could hear the padlocks being unlocked and the chain impatiently unwound. Without waiting to invite him up again, Dolapo hastened through the hole, the drunken shouts from below drowning out the frightened rats that were hurriedly scrambling away from him.

He heard the men stumbling around with intoxicated glee as they rounded up 'the spoilt miscreants that were wasting their parents' money and robbing their fellow students'; it was the excuse the guards would give the school authorities if any of the students reported the event. None would. None ever did and the guards knew this. It was the silent code of the boarding school, 'no casting': the code that encouraged the perpetuation of all sorts of unthinkable atrocities. That stimulated the boys to attempt whatever perversity entered their minds. When the belts, poles and sticks were rained down on the younger boys by the older ones, they nursed their wounds and painfully whispered, 'no casting'. "One day we'll be older too," they comforted themselves.

The guards continued blowing their whistles, yelling and beaming their torches even in the lit rooms. Dolapo crept to one of the smaller holes that overlooked the corridor and watched. They rounded up everyone, including Thunder and the house prefect. Even seniors and prefects tasted the occasional torment and even they were bound by the code, 'no casting'. Emeka had not gotten away, he was saying something to one of the staggering guards, when a long harsh whip extended from his hand and cut him short. Emeka's scream ran up the walls through the ceiling and hit Dolapo; he crawled slowly away from the hole. There were many screams and wails. It went on for thirty minutes, the old guards taking out the failures of their frustrated lives on the band of little boys. He stayed frozen for another half an hour after the sounds had died down before making his way slowly down the shelves and to his room. Emeka lay on his stomach and there were streaks on his back where fresh blood still glistened. Dolapo looked in his eye and saw the expression he least expected – shame. Emeka was gifted at convincing people to see his point or do things his way and it seemed he was most troubled by his inability to beguile the guards to his side. "They would not listen to me," he said slowly, as if shocked by the realisation that reason (whether true or not) was not always an option. "They refused to hear what I was saying."

"It happens," Dolapo said because he could think of nothing better to say.

"It happens," Emeka repeated in the sad knowledge that justice could not be done, as they were not supposed to be in the dormitories and more importantly, they were bound by the code.

Dolapo looked at him for a few moments feeling an inexplicable pang of guilt – the type that accompanied a preventable defeat. The next day, he placed under his pillow a book called *Things Fall Apart*.

Emeka was too consumed with his acculturation to miss his home. Unable to return East during the holidays, he listened to Dolapo's tales of his village with rapt attention. He wondered at his closeness with his cousin and laughed at the vivacity of his mother. He relived Dolapo's childhood as his because he had relinquished his to his personal tragedy. He asked for mundane details that initially surprised his bunkmate and was particularly consumed by the buzz that followed independence. When he could recount Dolapo's childhood tales better than he could his, he finally felt some release. And when Dolapo was gone, transfixed by his new hobby, he would transport himself to foreign lands with the books that Father Grey happily supplied.

II
Black Man's Cry (South Western Nigeria 1945 – 1967)

ONE

U ncle was born unto the cold raffia mat of his mother's dim candlelit bedroom and until his death, he never saw the white antiseptic walls of a hospital. His life began beneath the cool broad shade of an acacia tree – it was his first tangible memory. As tangible as a memory can be when one is merely five. He remembered the musty smell of his mother's green and white wrapper, the wide-open space of Oba's compound interrupted by shifting bodies and the harsh calls of the crows that circled above.

A childhood later, on October 1, 1960, the sky had many faces and the people had one voice. With post birth euphoria, the nation cried, independence! She had the fragile mind and greedy mouth of a suckling babe.

The summer vacations were extended and parents condoned the continued indulgence of their excited children. It was a night Uncle often recalled fondly. Of course, he was not known as Uncle then but as Dolapo Odukoya.

Dolapo Odukoya's days started when the sun shone through his paneless window and sliced the damp darkness of the mildewed dawn. He navigated his pen-sized chewing stick through his mouth, ridding it of the lingering taste of his vivid dreams. The cock had crowed already and he soon expected his mother's shrill voice to pierce the flimsy curtain that was his door – an exorbitant luxury that demarcated his nascent privacy. He found the first five minutes of every day jarring and grumbled about the tedium of the mornings.

17

In the living room, his father pensively chewed his stick, as a staccato honeyed voice whispered the morning news. His mother swept the dung-plastered floor, pausing at every tenth stroke to re-tie her wrapper, which refused to sit firmly on her slender waist. It would finally succumb to her nimble fingers once breakfast gave her more girth. After which she scrubbed Dolapo with a flimsy straw sponge, strong black soap and freezing cold water. It was his reward for the thirty-minute trek to the local stream with a small green pail. It was his punishment for still having the vitality of youth that made a trek to the stream at dawn an occasion to complain and skip rocks and bath with his friends before his morning scrub. Breakfast was always heavy, lunch was foraged from the innumerable trees and dinner was early. Everything for a little boy to do was done before six when the sun retired over the forested hills. But he found plenty to do in twelve hours.

The town of Ogbomosho was not blessed with an abundance of entertainment. Dolapo sat patiently on the verandah, waiting for the lizards to warm themselves in the sun. He stalked them from behind as he had seen his father do for antelopes.

"You must be patient Dolapo," his father would say. "If you wait long enough, they will show you when they are ready to be caught."

Now he knew when that time was. It was the moment after his impatience like an errant wave threatened to arouse his body into action without his consent and then subsided. He caught them as they tried to leap to safety. He tied them by the tail with fishing string to the big guava tree in the front yard, until they finally discarded their tails and fled; seven dangling tails was his record. Boredom was drowned in the shallow depths of innumerable pools chockfull with catfish. At first, he was frightened of their long whiskers, but Ranti once held one for five minutes. It was still alive and wriggled violently, opening its large mouth, gasping, initially terrifying, then sad. Anything Ranti could do, he [believed he] could do better and it was not because he was one week older, but because she was a girl.

Poverty snaked through the place, peeking its head through the shabby clothes and austere houses but politely keeping its distance – barely. Dolapo in his occasional Western garb was in complete bliss.

Dolapo remembered his tenth birthday as the first time in three full moons that he had not spent at least an hour running around the village, using a short stick to propel an old, worn bicycle tire ahead of him. His curiosity taking him from the well-trodden grassy paths that led to sparse farms to the hard mud lanes that ran through the town centre. After breakfast, he would head back to the stream for a morning swim with his cousins – all girls, unashamed by their nakedness. Then with the solemn hills as his distant companions he would set off on his solitary wanderings.

The glowing furnace of the smith's chambers was always his first port of call, the dancing flames as innocent as his unbridled thoughts. The smith was a talkative young man with an unrepentant smile. "Ah Dolapo," he would say, "look at this your father's hoe, how has he broken it again?" But before Dolapo could reply, he would continue, "This time, I'll make sure not even your father can break this one."

"You said that last time," Dolapo returned.

The smith laughed, "You're right, but this time I mean it, I am going to smelt …" And he would go on excitedly about different things he intended to try to make the farming instruments stronger and sharper.

Dolapo could not always understand him, but he liked his infectious enthusiasm. The last time Dolapo saw him was the week before he began going to the secondary school in Ibadan. Since he ceased patrolling the streets with his tire almost three years back, he had been by only twice. The smith was even more excited than usual.

"Dolapo!" the smith practically shouted when he walked into the hot chambers with its shadows that danced even at noon. "I am going to make a plough," the smith said.

"What is that?" Dolapo asked.

"Well," the smith paused, "I'm not too sure myself, but soon we shall be independent. Independent smiths make ploughs and independent farmers use them," he said, sure of his last statement.

"What is an independent?" Dolapo asked. He liked the smith because he let him ask as many questions as he liked.

"Well," said the smith, scratching his shaved head with stained fingernails, "independence means you can make your own decisions," he said firmly, attempting to stretch his muscled back that never seemed to be fully erect.

"What is a plough and why is it connected with independence?"

"Well," said the smith scratching his scarred bare chest that was black with heat and soot, "a plough is the greatest farm tool invented."

"And independence … ?" Dolapo was asking.

"Wait, I'll get to it," the smith said and for a brief moment his smile was absent as he thought about it. "Well, a plough is better than a hoe, right?" he asked.

"I suppose," Dolapo responded.

"And if we're independent, we make our own decisions right?"

"That's what you said," Dolapo answered.

"I know that's what I said," the smith responded impatiently. "So, if we make our own decisions, we will decide to make a plough because it is better," he finished. His smile was back, bigger than ever. The thought of independence made him happy. His answer made him happy; he felt it was the right one.

Dolapo smiled as well. It was impossible not to smile with the smith.

After an hour of conversation, the smith would teach him a new tune to whistle. The smith was a terrific whistler and Dolapo was not bad. With a tune and smile, he would continue his journey, weaving through the scanty huts that clustered the main street, chasing chickens and ambushing lizards. His final destination was always his mother's elder brother – the Oba's house, to see his cousin Ranti and share a furtive lunch. On his way, he talked to the shiny black goats that ate the discarded yam peels and watched the toothless, old bowed woman talk to herself. Each day he made this most fulfilling journey round the village, spending many blissful hours with his bouncy circle.

"Dolapo my darling," Mama Ranti called out, a soft smile spreading across her chubby cheeks, muting the severity of the six prominent tribal marks that adorned her face like exclamation points. She was a rotund woman and her fondness for her nephew was manifested in a tight hug that swallowed him in her ample bosom. He found the gesture overly effusive, particularly as Ranti always rejoiced in his discomfort, but was willing to endure it for the reward that followed. Daily, at noon, Mama Ranti set a huge bowl of steaming amala on the floor of her hut. Clustered on woven mats in a rough circle, Dolapo's cousins gathered and he fought with them for the stockfish that floated lazily in the thick gbegiri soup.

His mother gave him a thorough beating when she first heard of his gluttonous pastime, her shrill chastising voice punctuating each stroke.

"Poverty" – whack!

"is" – whack!

"the destination" – whack! whack!

"of the greedy." – and here the whacks assumed the rhythm of a drum roll and the crescendo was tears for both.

His father walked in on the commotion and calmly asked, "Why is everyone crying?"

"He has been eating at Oba's house, robbing those poor girls of their meal," his mother sputtered out angrily.

His father frowned briefly then said, "And this is why you want to kill him? You could not just stop him?"

"If you spare the rod, you spoil the child," his mother spat, reverting to the scripture – her immutable defence. His father said nothing, but he walked out of the house and returned with a large stick, which he put in front of her and said, "Okay, kill him."

There was mirth in his hard eyes as Dolapo's body went rigid with horror. "Leave me and my boy," Mama Dolapo retorted.

"No, kill him," his father repeated again placing the large stick in her hand.

"Leave my baby alone," his mother said, "don't you know his body is a holy temple." At this, his parents exploded with laughter and his mother hugged Dolapo. She rarely hit him from then on, instead, resorting to prayer for the preservation of Dolapo's body and soul.

Ever since, after each indulgent visit, Mama Ranti would give him an agbalumo and he would walk into his house, eating the small, round, orange fruit with its sweet acrid taste, spitting the dark shiny seeds at the placid goats. When his mother would invariably ask him, "Did you eat something at Oba's today?" He would respond coyly, *"Mama Ranti funmi ni agbalumo"* (Mama Ranti gave me an agbalumo), avoiding the answer or a lie that carried even greater consequences.

One day, he and Ranti had stayed at the stream too long. It was the first time he caught a fish and his pride resulted in a sluggish, dance-inhibited stroll. As they approached his house, his excitement gave way to fear, he was late for dinner. He said a hasty goodbye to Ranti, hid his fish in a bucket in the backyard and climbed into his room through the small window. He tore his shirt in the process but barely noticed; he was more frightened of his mother's fury if he was caught. Just as he lay on his mat, his mother burst into the room.

"Where were you?" she asked, "I called you for dinner ten minutes ago. It is amala and you cannot eat it cold."

"I was here, I did not hear," he said hesitantly.

His mother's eyes were suddenly ablaze, "Dolapo Oluwatobiloba Odukoya," his mother said resorting to his name in its entirety to fully express her anger, "do not lie to me."

He sat up on the mat, his voice was beginning to waver, "I am not lying …," he was saying, when his mother crossed the small room in three brief strides. She slapped him twice, once on the face with both hands and another on the back as he doubled over crying. He ran outside and cried beneath the guava tree, streams running down both his swollen face and left leg. He cried for twenty minutes for the pain, hurt and injustice. "I am her only child and she does not love me," he cried to himself.

When he got back in, his cold amala sat on a mat in the living room. His mother ignored his tear stained face. "You will finish your dinner, or you will not leave that spot," she said firmly and walked out. He cried again silently to himself, the tears running into the soup, the amala was hard and unpalatable. He poked it

22

with his fingers and cried some more. He was consumed by self-pity; he wished he would die so his mother would realise how much she truly loved him. He wondered why he had not died on the spot when she slapped him across the face – that would have taught her. He contemplated jamming the rock hard food down his throat and suffocating himself. He sat there for half an hour moving the hard food around the plate, unable to place a single bite in his mouth, which was full of the caustic taste of despair. His mother walked in with a plate, whose contents faintly carried the whiff of fried fish.

She paused at the door with the plate in her hand and a smile on her face. "My baby, my hunter, my love, my crowning joy, you are not angry with your mother, are you?" Dolapo shrugged his shoulders and looked at the wall. His mother laughed, "My heart, my darling, my warrior," she continued walking towards him with his fish, seasoned and fried. Dolapo was fighting hard to resist the faint smile that threatened to colour the corner of his lips. She had gotten to the mat, she put the plate down and scooped him in her arms. "You're almost too heavy to be picked up now and certainly too old to be crying." She showered him with kisses, which he pretended to fight. "Who is making you cry, who is making my brave warrior cry?" she asked with mock incredulity. Dolapo was determined not to be won over so easily; he was going to beat her at her game.

"My mother beat me for nothing," he said beginning to sob again.

"What," his mother said feigning surprise, "I know your mother very well, she loves you too much to do such a thing. What did you do to her?"

Dolapo knew there was no way around it, he had to admit his crime, the evidence was right in front of him, waiting to be consumed. "I lied," he said reluctantly between sniffs.

"Why would you do such a thing and to your darling mother?" his mother asked. "Okay stop crying, eat your fish and we'll forgive each other." His mother put him back down with the plate of fish and began to do a dance and sing his praises.

"Dolapo is a good boy, Dolapo is a good boy, Dolapo is a good boy, I know, I know, I know," she sang, swaying her slim hips and swinging her slender neck from side to side with each line. She repeated the song as he ate, using other adjectives like 'brave, fine and strong' to describe her son. By the time he finished the fish, which unknown to him was salted by his mother's remorseful tears, the caked amala and earlier sobs were long forgotten and she told him a bedtime story. She rarely told stories.

His mother was not cruel but was often overly serious in a way that prohibited others from thoroughly enjoying themselves. Her light frame and lighter voice gave her the air of a chastising angel that sat on your shoulder and disapproved of everything. Her husband had a better disposition but was too engrossed in his work. Everything about him was strong – his hands, his voice, his will. He never had to reprimand Dolapo because his instructions, so forcefully stated, were never disobeyed.

Emeka would roll with laughter at Dolapo's tales, choosing not to dwell on his childhood that had ended with the premature death of his brother. There were some joys and many tears, but his parents seemed to lack the necessitous strength of character to properly indulge either. And when the tragedy came, although he was never told of his birth, he began to suspect that something more was amiss and it blunted the heights of pleasures and depths of sorrows.

TWO

October 1, 1960 was an atypical day. It was almost midnight, but no one was asleep – not even the children. They stayed up, boggy-eyed, six hours after the sun had retired, excited by their parents' chatter. A few of them, avowing stamina, ran around and tumbled on the dry, cracked earth. The entire town of Western Ogbomosho had gathered in the compound of Oba Oguntoyinbo, where a small, black and white television set sat stacked next to four radios – even the ancient widow whose age had long been buried with every one of her eleven children. Sixteen large gourds of palm wine had already been consumed. They feasted, talked and danced. There was a pulsating wrestling match during which Kunle Kolawole threw Dada, his elder brother and reigning champion; and Fagbayi the drunkard entertained the crowd with his liquored tribute to the sweet, milky, nectar of the palm tree. And in the intimate comfort of dusk, strapping young men flirted with bashful ladies on hushed walls. An approving silver smile sat high in the sky and the elders huddled in corners, conversing in serious tones. With their modern technologies, they had an ear for each corner of the globe and an omnipotent eye. They had predicted the Time.

Five minutes to the Time, quiet swept the area. The only audible sounds were the turning up of the radio volume dials. WNTV, the first African television station, was emblazoned proudly at the bottom right corner of the screen. The Queen's envoy began to speak, his voice muted on the television, brought forth by the quadruple echo of the radios. Although most of those assembled did not understand a word that was said, they kept their eyes glued to the flashing pictures from the national stadium in Lagos. One hour later, Dolapo's uncle joyously proclaimed – "We are free!" And the men from Ile Alapo echoed this on their talking drums. After twenty minutes, the impromptu dance session ended as abruptly as it had started and the swaying hips of the youths were replaced with the wizened words of the elders.

At fifteen, Dolapo could only partially grasp all this but he understood something great was happening. During his two years of secondary education, he was taught 'Nigerian' history, however, it mostly involved names like Lord Lugard and Hugh Clifford and he could not relate to the joy that made his uncle's legs shake with excitement. Dolapo was the only boy in his age group and returning from the Federal Government College in Ibadan to find that he could no longer play with the girls the way he formerly did, had assumed an air of melancholic isolation. So when people began to dance and sway with tired legs, drunken minds and overflowing hearts, he was determined to outdo them all. He mirrored the weaving moves of the young men, his fatigue substituting for palm wine.

When the crowd gathered again by the television, Dolapo excitedly wedged himself between his uncle's elephant-trunk-like legs. As the Oba's only nephew, he had the best view of the undertakings. He tried valiantly to keep his large brown eyes open but he nodded in and out, his ears only half absorbing the rumble of voices that drifted around his head like a comforting blanket of wisdom.

"Dolapo ti sun lo," Ranti said to her mum, her head barely balancing on her neck.

"You should also be asleep," her mother returned.

"But he's going to miss the biggest day in our history!" Ranti said. She had a strong neck that extended prominently. The length was inherited from her father and the strength from her culture.

Dolapo would have had a similar neck but for the nascent commencement of adulthood. When they both turned ten, Dolapo's mother declared him a man and as he exited the house, she handed him the large steel bucket. He was initially excited, imagining his morning trek, which had doubled with the purchase of the bucket two months ago could again be halved. He imagined that he would no longer have to do the trek with the small green pail he habitually balanced on his head twice each day.

26

"You're a man now," she said, "you won't have to go with the plastic ike two times to fill this one up."

Dolapo walked to the stream with brisk steps, he was a man now. Ranti was already there. The wrapper she wore around her chest was folded neatly on the low branch of a willow tree.

"I wonder what you're covering," Dolapo used to tease, "it is too long for you." But Ranti was proud to be the only girl her age that had her own wrapper and she would hold her head high in disdain as the seams of the wrapper dragged along in the mud. Every evening she would wash it diligently in the stream and it would be just as dirty by the next day.

"Dolapo, let me race you," she said as he approached the banks.

"I don't have time for games today," Dolapo said, full of his budding manhood. He held his bucket high. She noticed.

"Ranti, where is your bucket," he said with as much authority as he could muster.

"Over there," she said pointing at the bucket and swimming towards it. Dolapo picked up the small orange pail and filled it with water from the stream.

"I think you should only do half until you're used to it," Ranti said. Dolapo ignored her. He filled the bucket again and once more dumped the contents in his larger metal bucket.

He lifted the bucket with some trouble and set off. "I don't have time for games," he called over his shoulder, his body slanting dangerously to his left as he strenuously clutched the metal handle in his right hand. His left hand extended, was trailing tiny droplets of water on the path that ascended the hill. After just ten metres, it was sweat that stained dark patches on the white sand.

Ranti hurriedly tied her wrapper around her chest. It had belonged to her mother. Ranti had not begun to blossom and she had to wrap it three times around herself. By the time she was ready Dolapo had disappeared over the hill. "Dolapo," she called, but there was no reply. She balanced the bucket on her head, cushioned by her hair and an old shirt made into a mound. She walked briskly up the hill, following the trail of water Dolapo left behind. She got to the top still calling his name. She stopped and smiled. He was at the bottom, a wet trail culminating in a large puddle around his feet showed how he had swayed down the hill. She caught up with him quickly. Without saying a word, she dumped the contents of her bucket into his. It came up to three quarters.

"Maybe, you're right, this is just practice, I should not fill it up," Dolapo said out of breath.

Ranti laughed. She started to sing 'Jack and Jill went up the hill'. "I'll catch up to you," she said turning and running up the hill. "Just don't hurry and spill almost everything again," she said over her shoulder.

"I'll slow down so you can catch up," he said. Ranti laughed again. She caught up with him 200 metres from his house. Both his arms ached and the bucket was down to half. He would pick it up with both hands and walk about five metres at a time with rapid wobbly steps, the water splashing around the inside of the bucket and occasionally edging over to douse his muddied feet. Ranti walked beside him patiently, stopping when he did with the bucket still balanced on her head.

"Why don't you just carry it on your head, like a normal person," Ranti said.

"Because that is for women and children," he retorted shifting the bucket from his left to right hand every five steps and spilling a good amount of it.

"And you're a man," she said mockingly.

"Yes I am, as a matter of fact," Dolapo said firmly. They were quiet for a few steps. Dolapo was covered in sweat.

"Do you know why the tortoise is bald?" she asked. Dolapo smiled. Mama Ranti told good stories about Ijapa, the mischievous tortoise, to her children every night. Ranti often told them to him the next day.

"One day, tortoise wanted to marry, so he went to his in-laws' house to ask for her hand in marriage."

"Who is her?" Dolapo interrupted, grasping her meaning but feeling rather moody from his task. He did not feel very adult any more but believed he should act like one.

"His betrothed, of course," Ranti said, remembering what her mother had said when her younger sister had asked the night before.

"What's that?" Dolapo asked.

"Will you let me finish my story?" Ranti snapped, she did not know what it meant. She had nodded when her mother said it and just realised she still did not know what it meant.

"Someone you marry I guess," she continued.

"Anyway, as I was saying," Ranti said. She often said that. She was often interrupted. She spoke a lot.

"Dolapo, my warrior, my strong man," it was the voice of his mother. They looked up; they had not noticed her approach.

"Good morning, ma," Ranti said kneeling slightly, with the bucket still balanced on her head.

"Ranti, my darling," Mama Dolapo said, "have you seen the new man in the house?"

"Yes, ma," Ranti said in the same sugary tone, "he is so strong, he has carried a metal bucket like a man."

"Yes oh, don't joke with my man," Mama Dolapo said. "Dolapo, here, bring that one," his mother said, taking the large metal bucket easily in her hand and handing him his usual plastic one. "Hey Ranti, see our man, filling two buckets in one go."

"He is our superman," Ranti continued with delight. Dolapo could almost weep from exhaustion. He turned and wordlessly walked back to the stream. When he saw the hill, the tears streamed down his face and he let them. He encouraged them saying to himself, 'It's the last of my childishness.'

On the way back, his wearied arms hoped his mother would again come to his aid. But as soon as he saw the house, he wished against everything that she would not. His arms were straining at the sockets, but he continued resolutely, his eyes not wavering from the front door. He walked into the kitchen and placed the bucket delicately on the floor without spilling a drop. He looked at his mother. She smiled. He smiled as well and held his head up, knowing he had made her proud. He went to his room and collapsed on his mat.

Dolapo slumped to the ground and was abruptly awoken as his uncle suddenly leaned towards the television; Jaja Wachuku the Nigerian House Speaker had stood up to formally accept the deed of independence from the Queen's envoy.

"Go on my son!" Oba shouted, his fleshy fist raised, though the rest of the town was shrouded in anticipatory silence.

Dolapo lifted his head drearily from the forest of legs and pulled his weight up with the help of the Oba's trouser legs. At his tug, Oba Oguntoyinbo glanced down quickly.

"Ah! I'm sorry Dolapo!" he chuckled and helped him back to a seating position.

The Union Jack was being lowered and in its place, the green, white, green standard was raised, fluttering with pride and hope at the top of the flagpole. Dolapo eyed the hoisted flag from his upright position. The 20,000 spectators at the stadium roared with joy through the television and the villagers echoed their sentiments, their voices united by the magic of independence. It was a victory for Nigeria; it was a victory for Africa. The free population of Black Africa had just jumped by fifty percent.

And so she was birthed: a large country rich in diversity, an emerging elite and an abundance of resources – all ready ingredients for a tasty tale. If only they knew the story, if they suspected the tale, then maybe the shouts would not have been so loud or the dancing so free. Or maybe it would have, because freedom is freedom no matter how reckless.

The rainmaker, Ojo, executed his duties to perfection. As the last of the revellers were retiring in the frosty dawn, a heavy storm beat down on the village, washing away the telltale signs of the festivities from Oba's sandy compound.

Dolapo woke up later than he had ever risen before. The hens had laid, the cock had crowed, the sun had risen. His mother had stumbled out of bed. The pap had been ground, the akara had been fried, the sun had reached its zenith. His father had followed suit. The sun had set, the moon was glowing, the dogs were howling. Dolapo finally stretched his tender limbs surprised his mother had let him sleep the entire day.

He tripped over their mangy dog and greeted his parents the traditional way – body prostrate on the ground. Scratching his left thigh and moving like a sleepwalker, he went to his favourite tree and started to urinate. It was then he realised that it had rained all day. He realised wistfully that he had missed the orange pools that flowed through the muddy streets sweeping them clean of corncobs and the broad leaves that had housed mini feasts of akara and eko. He always won the paper boat races he held with the other children when they nonchalantly played in the dirty waters, ignoring their open wounds. The skinny yellow dogs would watch miserably from beneath the scant eaves and uncooperative trees that missed more than the occasional drop, unable to seek refuge in the houses that had recently had their floors plastered with cow dung. The air had the refreshing aroma of freshly washed earth. He reached down and scooped some of the wet ground into his mouth. A smile of satisfaction spread across his lips, it tasted like the air, like all the parts of the tree, bark, branch, leaf and root. Like the thousands of flowers and their wandering pollen. Like the sweat of a dancing crowd, the piss of a little boy, the shit of a mangy dog. It tasted like earth and his childhood before he went off to boarding school and he found it wistfully delightful.

His parents were deep in conversation when he went back in. They had been consumed with politics, conversing in hushed tones for the past month. He did not fully understand the gravity of Independence, of Nigeria owning a television station, of his town having paved roads and running water. He did not grasp the importance of the man in the round spectacles. Dolapo would sit at his father's feet barely absorbing what they said.

Some farmers had rioted because of taxes ... they were burning government buildings ... they had kicked out the British ... that man with the round glasses had made a whole television and a space station ... his uncle had bought the television ... Awolowo!

The conversation crashed around his head like his old rotating tire. He liked his father's deep calming voice and his mother's excited shrieks, so he listened. He still preferred the stories of Ijapa that Fagbayi told after his second gourd of palm wine. And sometimes, he still fondly reminisced about when Ajike the woman who made the local beer used to let the children sit in a corner of her food shed for an hour and give whomever told them an entertaining story some of her burukutu for free.

When he got home on those days, his mother would accost him with, "Where have you been?"

"At the stream," he would say.

"And," she would probe suspiciously.

"And Oba's house."

"Where else?" she would ask.

"Under the big tree opposite the market."

At this point, her impatience still insatiate would retreat, because he would state every place he had been in its banal singularity withholding the actual answer she sought with wide-eyed mischief.

His parents' marriage had always been happy but they had settled into the comfortable rhythms of many years spent together. Then independence changed all this and suddenly, his mother was giggling again like a shy virgin and his father was giving her inappropriate pinches when she bent over to stir the soup. Nine months later, Dolapo had another sister.

THREE

Destiny is the collusion of significant events in the lives of others to form subtle changes leading to substantial conclusions in the life of another. This is the case for everyone and this was the case for Dolapo. Luckily for him, the machinations of destiny were favourable. When Dolapo's first sister was born, five years earlier, after another of Oba's jamborees, he was required to stay home and help his mother. By the time he regained the freedom to whistle with idle birds, he had lost interest in chasing tires along muddy streets. His uncle had spent most of the previous party with a man from the next town who had been to school in Lagos and had been induced to begin a feverish campaign to educate the children of the village.

Mr Gbadamosi, the new teacher who always held up his trousers just below his chest with multicoloured suspenders that clashed with his short polka dotted tie, had barely overseen a week of classes before an outbreak of cholera desecrated the entire student population. It was in this chaos of diarrhoea and vomiting that Dolapo reemerged into the pedagogic atmosphere. He marched into class on the first day to see Mr Gbadamosi standing at the front of the class with a large cane in his right hand and a thick book in his left as if he were addressing a roomful of children. Dolapo looked doubtfully at the only other living being – an agama lizard that nodded its bright orange head on the far wall – unsure of what to do when Mr Gbadamosi's voice jumped out high and authoritative.

"Young man, sit down. What do you know about Mary Slessor?" He had a very dark complexion that contrasted with the white socks he wore under trousers that were very much afraid of his dusty shoes.

"I can tell from your blank look that you know nothing. Do you know anything about anything?" he continued, barely waiting for an answer; his bald, shiny head starting to show beads of perspiration.

"You know nothing about nothing. I can tell from your expression, you just don't know," his voice had the quality of a circus magician, "Young man, I will teach you everything of something and something of everything."

"Yes sir," Dolapo finally said.

"Yes, young man, until your friends stop shitting and vomiting, it is you and I. Not me and you, you and I: write that down." He said the last sentence in English and smiled with delight at the face of confusion turned to him. "We have much to learn, young man, much to learn."

They continued their private lessons even when the other students returned to the class. Mr Gbadamosi had a habit of adding and dropping the letter 'h' and when he tried to teach the class about Asian Geography, he would say 'Shout Korea' instead of South Korea and look with fright as 'Korea', would jump from their small mouths in a deafening roar. He had eyes that blinked too often and in those moments, they would seem to stammer out an SOS. Mr Gbadamosi showed up at Dolapo's house an hour and a half before dinner and demanded, as compensation for his trouble, only a large portion of Iya Dolapo's delightful cooking. On the days when they studied Mathematics, he gave himself a bonus by assigning Dolapo problems and foraging through the many fruit trees that littered the compound, surprisingly agile in his strange outfits. At the end of each day, when Dolapo turned over his perfectly added figures, Mr Gbadomosi would look with pride and say, "Now, now, young man, we must call a spade a spade not a fat spoon. You have a brilliant mind!" and then add with a juicy smile of satisfaction, "And your father has the best fruits in all the land." His eyes also seemed to nod rapidly in assent.

Over the years, Dolapo continuously proved to be a great student and the intense schedule led to an accelerated acquisition on his part. He possessed the rare quality of ingesting everything he was told and adequately parrot it back, unflawed, with an effortless flourish. His parents and uncle began contemplating sending him to the Federal Government College that had opened up in Ibadan. Once again, fate was decided in the form of a disease, this time in the solitary form of malaria. Dolapo was engaged in his new private hobby of rock skipping after dinner at the village stream when he happened to disturb a pair of mating mosquitoes. The male was soon entangled in a spider's web and the vengeful female left a noxious bite on his upper right arm. He thought nothing of it, he barely noticed. His nascent mind was too caught up in trying to make the rock get a fourth bounce. A few weeks later, he had a high temperature and his entire body was contorted with feverish spasms. This moment he was wrapped in mountains of blankets, the next he was soaked in sweat. His mother was in hysterics, his father solemn. Luckily, the district commissioner had sent a health inspector to monitor the recurring cholera outbreaks and Dolapo's fever began before he left. The inspector, a little man with thick spectacles, was anxious to prove his worth as he had once again arrived too late to attribute the eradication of the disease that was already on the wane to his infallible knowledge of superior medicine. He promptly bombarded Dolapo's fragile body with the potently bitter Chloroquine and a host of multivitamins, postponing his return trip to personally oversee the recovery. Dolapo was soon well and with a ferocious appetite to the delight of the self-congratulating health inspector. It was then decided that Dolapo would go to the Federal Government College and then to the university to become a doctor.

During his time, Dolapo realised he had a greater affinity for statutes and law than medicine and won his first case with an impassioned plea to his uncle and parents to allow his sisters and female cousins to go to school and take up the mantle he was relegating.

He knew he had made the right decision when he visited home in his final year of high school.

Oba Oguntoyinbo had many eccentricities; it was what made him such an adept politician. He conjured occasions out of nothing and showered those around him with gifts much to their adulating delight. Dolapo's father, whose ethos was work and honesty, often clashed with his unwarranted extravagance. After Baba Dolapo had returned innumerous gifts sent over by Oba after he first married his sister, they had eventually found an even ground for gratuitous joviality. February 29 intrigued them equally, a day that did not exist for three years and suddenly unheralded, a whole day appeared to do as they pleased, it was the only day Baba Dolapo restrained himself from waking at dawn and toiling until he retired with the sun. Dolapo remembered those days fondly, as always a gift appeared from Oba that his father consented to retain.

His mother recounted often the time in the fifties when he was still very young, Oba sent the electrician over with a ceiling fan. Dolapo stood beneath it for hours staring at the blades as they whirled round in circles. His father was uncharacteristically buoyant, suddenly, he had picked him up and said, "Do you want to see it up close?" and Dolapo nodded.

"Promise you will not touch it," his father continued and strangely, of the entire incident, it was this sole caution Dolapo remembered. As his father brought him closer to the fan, a solemn awe spread over the boy, his body went still and his eyes wide. His mother was hysterical, but his father was laughing. Baba Dolapo was infected by his own jollity, he let out a strong laugh again as he lowered the boy, but it was not sufficient. He looked at the boy, at his large eyes that betrayed the fear the rest of his body refused to show, he was proud. He whispered in his ear, let us show your mother how brave you are and Mama Dolapo who was approaching to snatch her son from this happy man who was barely her husband almost fainted, as she saw her son's nose headed again for the blades of the fan.

Baba Dolapo was gently singing a Sunday School favourite as he took his son closer to the whirring blades of the fan, 'Be bold, be strong for the Lord thy God is with you,' he was singing it softly, so it was barely audible over the noise of the whirring fan. Dolapo's face was only two inches from the fan, his eyes were saucers, his body as rigid as a corpse, his mother was crying on the floor, unable to look, unable to approach her newly possessed husband. It was barely a couple of seconds but Baba Dolapo would swear afterwards that his boy stared death in the face for an hour without flinching. When he finally lowered the boy, there were tears in his eyes, he was proud. Wordlessly, he handed the young boy to his mother and went to his room. They did not speak for the rest of that day, but the next day Baba Dolapo took Dolapo with him to the farm for the first time. He carried the boy on his shoulder and walked him the entire length of the expansive farm like a conquering hero. You will not do this, he kept saying to the boy softly, you will be greater than I, you will be greater than your mother and you will even be greater than Oba. He whispered the last part gently like he was afraid the palm trees would steal his wish and nullify it with their errant gossip. Baba Dolapo had said that to the infant many times but now he believed it.

On February 29, 1964, Dolapo returned home from school unexpectedly. Although uncertain, he guessed something was amiss at home. His mother had sent a note saying she would be unable to visit as she usually did every last weekend of the month. The walk to his compound told him something was awry, there were no signs of festivities, not even a hint of joy in the air; it was unlike Oba to relinquish a chance to celebrate. His father was in a heated conversation with the electrician and his two assistants who looked uncomfortable as they held unto a large black and white television.

"You cannot bring that in here," his father was saying with vehemence.

"But we cannot return it," the electrician was saying with traces of fear, "you know how Oba is, he believes in shooting the messenger."

Dolapo was an astute eighteen-year-old and it did not take him long to figure out what was happening. He had noticed the broadening rift between his father and his uncle and he knew it had only been a matter of time before a conflagrated ego caused the straining relationship to break. He knew the cause and he supported his father, not because he was that, but because he was right. He swallowed his agitation as he got to his father.

"Ah Dolapo," his father said in surprise, he had been too wrapped up in the argument to notice the approach.

"*Baba, e fi won le, e je ka soro* [Leave them alone and let us talk]." Since, he began going to school, it was rare that Dolapo spoke to his father in Yoruba, so his father did as he said with barely any hesitation. There was a frown on Dolapo's brow as he thought of the words to say. It was the first time he had not spent his first moments at home with his mother, his sisters or Ranti.

They strolled slowly through the town. Dolapo was neither tall nor particularly handsome, yet every eye turned naturally towards him. He seemed to have an evident quiet intelligence that went ahead of him like the talking drums of ancient time proclaiming his presence and achievements. This was what made adults listen to him and other youth revere him. When he was in the village, he seemed almost distinct from everyone else, as a man set apart for exploits, as a prophet of the people.

They walked in silence for a while and Dolapo finally knew what was bothering him. The town seemed split in three, some parts had amassed large wealth, others were retrogressing, but most heartbreaking were the parts stuck in time. He had noticed that the many projects launched with much fanfare for the independence celebrations remained unchanged. The large tap that was to nullify the need for the daily trek to the stream was testament to the lack of progress, its faucets standing as a ten-headed parched statue. The road that had been dug on the sides to make drains remained as muddy mounds that impeded the sparse traffic. The cocoa and palm trees were yielding less while the farms got more arid and all the improvements that were to have heralded the birth of a new Nigeria remained frozen, as they had been in 1960. It seemed progress had died with the birth of the nation. It seemed her dreams and ambitions were stillborn.

Yet, Oba's house was doused in opulence and Dolapo noticed that the wealth was seeping out in tight rivulets, flowing to the pockets of incompetent men who had adroitly navigated the transition, ingratiating themselves to Oba and the new government. Men that in the days of prevalent farming could not afford a bicycle now drove cars to Ibadan and Lagos, unashamed of their ineptitude, unbowed by the decrepitude of their people that was made more blatant with each corrupt purchase they imported to the town.

"Why is this happening?" Dolapo asked his father and before he could answer, he added, "is it my uncle?"

His father remained silent for a moment and responded, "Myopic eyes are blinded by the rings on their own fingers, myopic eyes do not see beyond today," he paused, "do not blame your uncle, his eyes have been stolen by unscrupulous men and his sight substituted with the voice of sycophants."

They got to the southern hills overlooking the farms and plantations. His father stopped him and said, "Dolapo, look at us, we have been blessed with a lot of things, more than your uncle and his friends can misuse; soon it will be your turn to make a mark." He thought his father would say more but he was silent, they turned around, looked over Ogbomosho for a few minutes and then began to walk home.

When they arrived, the television had been installed and a brief anger lay on his father's forehead. "Dolapo, it won't be easy, the pleasures of this world are seductive and the chances to be enticed are numerous... Corruption only takes a second, they don't require your consent but they need your assent. Decide what you want to do with this, you're a man now." His father said gesturing at the television set before retiring into his room.

Dolapo tried to turn away but the box beckoned to him, he turned it on just for a glance, perhaps only to see if it worked. A football game between Nigeria and Ghana at the new Liberty Stadium in Ibadan was showing. He turned down the volume so his father would not hear, he wanted to turn it off but the enchantment of the little figures kicking the ball enticed him. It felt luxurious and he enjoyed it. Slowly, a feeling began in the pit of his stomach. He felt sick, he felt like a traitor and was ill at ease. It became so overwhelming he could not focus on the television set. He rushed outside but even the cool air could not suppress the feeling of discomfort. He realised he was running. He ran until he got to the house of the electrician. He banged on the door, noting with disgust, the signs of extravagance that littered the cramped room when the electrician opened the door. An old conversation with his father echoed in his head, 'A lack of vision hobbles such men; they would cram their small rooms with big objects instead of spending the money on acquiring a larger place. They can never hold onto the money long enough, they reason in spoonfuls.'

"Come and remove it now," Dolapo said it with so much force that he frightened himself and the electrician.

"Yes sir," the man responded, confused even though he was almost three times his age. Dolapo was embarrassed and did not wait for the man, his feet began to move again, but instead of heading home, they took him to Ranti's favourite spot under the acacia tree where she used to go to avoid petulant younger siblings.

He was panting when he got there and was halted by a brooding presence sat at their usual spot. Mama Ranti always did Ranti's hair in an elaborate plait that was held up with string. It was the most expensive hairstyle of the time and Ranti was proud of it. She had an erect posture to match her pride. The figure sat there had disheveled hair and was slouching. Ranti was religiously strict about appearance. He knew something was wrong. He knew the threads that held his family, his community, his nation were unraveling like the yarn that usually held her hair in place. "I did not know you were back," her unmistakable voice said, but she did not look behind her.

Dolapo was angry with her and did not know why, yet he sat next to her and held one of her small hands intimately the way he would a girlfriend and she laid her head on his shoulder. Frozen in their intimacy, he felt his heart thaw, he heard his fears and dreams jump around his mind. She knew before he spoke what he was to say and she was afraid. Her heart hurt, "I can't pick sides," she said simply.

He lifted her face, looked into her eye and caressed her right cheek. He ran his thumb over the scar that he had put there when he had misplaced a throw of his rock and it had grazed her cheek. He knew how much she loved her father and how much the Oba loved her in return.

He paused, he thought of how much he loved her father and how much the Oba loved him in return.

Already, victory was claiming its victims. Even his mother, sure and upright, was bowing to the pressure, her shrill voice was hollowed, less believing, but there was no bitterness yet. "Nothing is new under the sun," she would say heavily, sadly to no one in particular and Dolapo knew she thought of her misguided brother in those times. It was her assurance.

He remembered once when he was younger he had asked his mother if he could marry his cousin. She had laughed at him, long and hard and finally, she had said, "She is not strong enough for you, the life you're going to lead, you'll need a very strong woman." Then, she had laughed at him again.

He said nothing to Ranti's comment but held her hand again. He pondered on his mother's words and her laugh. His thoughts were interrupted by the sound of Ranti's voice, "Dolapo, I am transferring to the Queen's College. It will set me back a couple of grades but it's the best I can do; it is how I know to protest."

"But won't you be old for your year?" Dolapo asked with a frown.

"Yes, but I don't care, I'll still be far from the oldest, we make the sacrifices we can, I can't school in Ibadan anymore, it is too close to here, to what my father is allowing to happen."

"But is that necessary?" Dolapo was saying.

"Dolapo, enough of your buts," she cut him off. "If we cannot do what we must do, then we do what we can do," she finished looking at him. He was proud of her, perhaps his mother was wrong.

"Roses that bloom at dawn don't often last till dusk and the night flower is still a bud at noon," he said suddenly, quietly; unwittingly recalling his mother's eternal caution.

III
J'En Wi T'Emi (1961 – 1967)

ONE

Emeka's plan was simple – he would become a businessman, he would become rich, he would return east, he would get married. It all became apparent the day Mr Chukwura came to give a speech at the school. His accent had been so thick, Dolapo sometimes turned to Emeka to interpret. He wore bulky glasses and had a dense beard that sat inches ahead of a solid neck. He was barrel-chested with hefty arms and pillar-like legs. He had no understanding of proportion; his clothes clung to him, his cowboy belt buckle was the size of a fist and jewelery dripped down his stout fingers. His wife was tall and inelegant. She was wrapped in too much rich fabric of a bright red that was visible down the road. Her hair was permed and done in a winding tower that made her perspire endlessly. Save for a visible moustache and a few strands of hair peeping from her chin, her face would have been beautiful were it not bleached – giving the impression that it was borrowed from a much fairer person. Strings of gold weighed down her much darker neck and she could barely lift her arms. She had the careless grace of a village beauty queen. They would have remained caricatures for a humorous anecdote, had not the man the noble solidarity of an Igbo heart. Emeka was summoned after the speech.

"My son," he said with his heavy accent and weighty smile, "they say you are the only Igbo boy here. It cannot be easy, I salute you." The words fell out quickly after each other like soldiers falling into formation.

"Yes sir," Emeka returned, unsure as to what to make of the encounter.

"What do you want to do?"

Emeka was about to say, "I don't know."

But the man continued, "Business? Yes, you must want to do business or you will not be here in the West, haha," his laugh was like mortar on concrete. "When do you graduate?"

"In four months," Emeka said.

"Don't bother with the university," he said, "I only went to the primary school and look at me," thick lips supported by a heavy jaw parting. "When you finish here, come and find me," he said, handing him a card. "Okay, my son, God will keep you, eh!" he finished, handing him more money than Emeka had ever seen. Emeka had not even contemplated what to do after graduation, but now he knew without a doubt where he was headed.

Four months and five days later Emeka said his byes to Father Grey and was in Lagos. Mr Chukwura had a busy electronic store at Ladipo in Mushin. He would look with contempt at the Lebanese and Indian merchants that had remained behind after independence and say to Emeka, "They must return to their country or we will chase them out."

To which Emeka would respond, "Yes sir".

Mr Chukwura was convinced that car accessories were the future and Chairman's store was stocked with many Peugeot parts, for that was what everyone called him, including his wife.

"The secret is to know what people want before they want it and if you're wrong, convince them." That was Chairman's philosophy and that is what Emeka learnt from him. Chairman believed there was only one thing for a real man to eat – eba and he ate it three times a day. For the past twenty years, Chairman had eaten the exact same thing at the same times, three times a day and each time with as much relish as the last. The only variance was the choice of the accompanying soup.

Chairman got to the office at seven and Emeka began to arrive at six thirty so he could do an inventory of Chairman's large stock in those thirty minutes. Chairman did not really need to come anymore, but he did not trust anyone, especially not the Lebanese who were just a few stalls down. He took a great liking to Emeka because he had come to Lagos on his own and gotten into the prestigious Federal Government College, Ibadan. Emeka had a head for numbers and languages and was rigid about routine. Soon, when Chairman went on his bi-weekly trips, he would leave Emeka in charge and invite him to dinner the night he returned.

Emeka never had the desire to travel but he gained a curiosity for foreign places from Chairman's rigid stories and the books he assiduously devoured. Chairman liked instability everywhere but in Nigeria because he said it was good for business. He would return from a trip with a heavy satisfied smile and say, "There will be a coup in our neighbour's garden soon." It was his sole attempt at humour. The only other time he did something for amusement was again after a very happy trip that accompanied the news of multiple coups d'etat.

"It is even better because it is military men overthrowing other military men, which means they will get rid of everything from the previous regime in a show of austerity." He explained this nonchalantly to Emeka because it was a well-known fact that military coups were beneficial for connected people, among whom Chairman was.

"Then they will need upgrades," he said, attempting a mischievous smile that did not quite work with his large lips. "We will buy their yesterday's goods and sell them as today's here, then we will buy today's here and sell them as tomorrow's there," he said gesticulating towards the general direction of West Africa just as his wife was bringing over his dinner. He had all three of his boys (which was what he called his employees) over. He was in such a jovial mood that he challenged them to an eating competition when his wife had dished out their food. He looked at their polite portions, laughed and said, "Is that all?" he doubled over in laughter. "Nwanne," he called his wife, "put all their own together and put more for me."

"Chairman, you wan kill yourself?" Musa asked.

Chairman laughed in response. "A python will never die from swallowing a goat. Its stomach will only stretch to accommodate," he returned.

In fact, his stomach was so stretched that two hours later, Chairman was hungry again and had a snack of boiled plantains stuffed into a loaf of bread. Emeka enjoyed those days; he enjoyed the bustle of Lagos and its promise of wealth. Chairman never knew what to do with his money so he gave his boys generous allowances. The other two spent most of it in the nightclubs where high life seeped out seductively. Emeka did what he had seen his father do all his life and kept his in a shoebox under his bed. The other two boys were Ikenna and Musa.

Ikenna always wore a singlet to show off the muscles he was proud of. He listened to soul music continuously, singing along in a strangled voice and attempting to dance like James Brown – dreaming of going to America to meet his idol. His sole distinguishing feature was a prominent scar on his nose, which he got when he decided to smell an iron to determine if it was indeed hot: as he was occasionally inflicted with brief periods of inexplicable unintelligence. Unlike the others, Musa was Yoruba, but he was an opportunist, which made him a great businessman. When he saw the women come by to make passes at Emeka, he would say, 'You should come out with us later,' and the women thinking us included Emeka would say, 'Okay'. Musa loved Afro Juju and listened to Ebenezer Obey and King Sunny Ade on the highest possible volume, to the chagrin of Ikenna. He would brush his wavy hair in twenty precise strokes and then set off for the local joint with Ikenna to meet the girls. After furnishing them with three bottles of Star, he would say with regret, 'It seems Emeka cannot make it,' at which point they would be too drunk to care. Emeka would be oblivious to all this, his sole transport out of his lonely room being the pages of innumerable books.

One day, Chairman came to Emeka looking troubled, his big lips like an overripe upturned banana.

"Emeka, come here," he said so sadly that Emeka almost assumed he was dying.

"Yes sir," he responded, maintaining his habitual answer.

"Have I taught you well ... Do you trust me?"

"Yes sir."

"Good," Chairman said, nodding slowly like he needed that exact answer.

"There is going to be a coup, there is going to be a war."

"That's great sir, whose garden?"

"Ours," Chairman replied with a solemn voice that frightened Emeka.

"Sir, are you sure, sir?"

Chairman gave him a sharp look like he wanted to chastise him but instead said in the same gentle voice, "I've been watching for these things too long to not know when it is about to happen to my own people. How much is your life worth to you?" It was a question so unexpected, Emeka could not think of an answer.

"Until you find out, don't lose it. Remember that, don't lose it till you find out." Then he broke out into his habitual smile that made the last five minutes even stranger.

"I see you don't party with the others."

"No, sir"

"Good. Do you know the parable of the talents?"

"No, sir"

"You must read your Bible, very important, you'll find out how much your life is worth."

"Yes, sir"

"Is that all you will say?"

"No, sir."

He chuckled briefly but was suddenly solemn again. "I know what my life is worth; I need a favour from you."

"Anything, sir."

"Remember you said you trust me, now can I trust you, too?"

"Of course, sir," Emeka said, a little hurt that he even had to ask.

"Good, my son, I know I can. Listen carefully, I am leaving for the East in two weeks and I will not return. I want you to sell everything we have in the stock. Send half the money to me. Don't worry; I will contact you. Then keep the rest for yourself," Chairman paused, "and take care of the other boys," he added almost reluctantly. Then he finished with emphasis, "But yourself, most importantly."

"Sir, what are you talking about? Where are you going? I can't keep half of your money …"

"You will do as I say," Chairman interrupted, "Now, if you are smart, you will listen carefully. Find one of your Yoruba friends that you thoroughly trust, change all that money into dollars and tell him to save it in a bank for you."

Emeka was going to ask another round of questions, but Chairman put his heavy paw on his right arm and said simply, "Trust me, my son, I know," a wan smile spreading on his weary face that finally told his advanced age.

TWO

It had been eight months since that conversation and Emeka was beginning to imagine that perhaps Chairman had just been paranoid, when the coup was announced over the radio. Emeka had sold most of the merchandise during the munificent ease of the Christmas rush and was in a buoyant mood. Even after paying Musa and Ikenna generous bonuses, he still had a significant amount of money left over. His initial fear at the doom that Chairman's conversation had implied seemed exaggerated as despite numerous speeches and proclamations by the new military leaders, nothing changed. He sat in the almost empty store with Musa one slow evening. Finally, he was beginning to notice the ladies that stopped by their store and lingered too long unsure of how to entice an uninterested man.

"Do you think there will really be secession?" he asked Musa.

"Obviously!" was the prompt response, "Everyone knows that Ojukwu is power hungry. If Awolowo was not so stubborn, he should join the Igbos, then we will have the brains and business savvy. What do those mallams bring to the table?"

"And you are not worried?" Emeka said, ignoring the blatant tribalism of the remark.

"Haha, not at all. Nothing can happen to Lagos. What did the coup change? The wahala is between the North and the East. At worst, we will have to kick you out," he finished, giving him a slight wink. "That is why I have been telling you to taste these Yoruba girls before you are sent back to your village. Me, the last six months, only nna girls, only your fair skinned sisters I dey touch oh!"

They both laughed, but that night Emeka went to the bar with them for the first time. He was handsome and had a lot of money so the girls were excusing of his two left feet. He bought drinks freely and drank none of it for the first couple of hours. He was more amused than interested by the scene. But true to his word, Musa showed up with the fairest girl in the club who was obviously Igbo and this got Emeka thinking of their earlier conversation. It put him in a pensive mood and he did not pay attention as he drank bottle after bottle that Musa gleefully sent his way, until he suddenly had to use the toilet and realised how intoxicated he was. He sat swaying gently with his head in his hands and barely realised when he was joined at the table. He did not remember conversing with the lady for half an hour or crying on her shoulder because of his neglected past, as images of his ignored family replaced the rowdy revellers. He did not recall getting in a taxi with her and her taking him home and assisting him while he vomited violently in a pale plastic bucket. He did not remember taking her address but he woke up the next morning with a headache determined to outdo the previous night's band.

The sun was too bright, his mouth was dry and he felt like he had been attacked savagely. It had been a long time since he had tapped palm wine with his father and he had never drank anything in that quantity. There was a bucket to the side of his bed and a glass of water on the nightstand. There was a cheeky note written in the fat curves that were unmistakably feminine saying, 'Hope you feel better, take this,' and a pack of pain killers next to it. He took the medicine and was disturbed by loud bangs on his door. He crawled over to it and turned the key. Musa burst in with shouts of "My brother, I hail thee!"

"Please be quiet, I'm dying," he whispered harshly. "Can't you see I'm dying?" he whispered again at Musa's excited face.

"How you do am, I tried all night, Ikenna tried all night, everyone tried all night, aje butter girl, I wonder wetin she dey find for place like that."

"What are you talking about?"

"The babe you left with of course, she dey talk from her nose, excuse me, excuse me, just like that she dey give every boy isho!"

"Ahhh, the written note, the written note," everything echoed in his fragile mind.

"She leave note, make I see, my guy! I tell you she be correct girl, look at her address, Ikoyi! You bagger! How you do am?"

"You're making too much noise, I did not do anything, I did nothing," he repeated unsure of his night. He had woken up still in his shoes. He had no clue who she was and he finally managed to get Musa to leave with more, "My brother, I hail you, we must go out again." To which he had muttered an agreement he did not intend to honour.

She was tall for a girl and studied in London. She had soft skin the colour of milk chocolate. She had never permed her hair. She was an only child and was here for the summer holidays. Her father was the education minister. She wanted to be an architect. She liked to be in rowdy crowds because only then did she truly feel alone. These were the things he should have remembered from the previous night but all he knew was that she lived in a very wealthy part of town and wore a guava-scented perfume. He thought about her all through the weekend but was too afraid to visit the address.

On Monday, at about noon, a chauffeured Mercedes parked in front of the shop. The man walked up directly to Emeka like they were old acquaintances and handed him a note. He stood politely to the side indicating a response was expected. It said simply, 'Time for our lunch,' and he recognised the handwriting and the sweet smell that had lingered in his room all weekend. Unthinking in his curiosity, he jumped into the car, beside the driver and was cocooned by the smell. The car pulled up to the Ikoyi country club and he was ushered to a table at the back by a man in a maroon waistcoat who identified him by name. He found it very unsettling that everyone else seemed to be expecting him despite his ignorance of the occasion. An elegant lady sat at the table. She wore a light, flowery dress that kissed the top of her crossed knees. The legs that protruded beneath that were long, hairless and ended in shoes he had never seen the likes of before. Her hands sat in her lap and a smile on her face. There was a large pair of glasses on the table next to a bottle of water. She said nothing and made no motions but her smile broadened as he approached the table. A dazzling smile that conveyed instructions. Sit down, they said and he did. Relax they said, but he could not. She let out a conservative laugh – one intended solely for her and her company.

"I knew you would not remember me, now is this because someone had too much to drink or because someone keeps the past in an abandoned safe?" she said lightly, leaving him completely disarmed. He had used that exact phrase many times in his head, 'keeping the past in an abandoned safe', but had never once remembered uttering it aloud.

"You are an interesting fellow, even in your state, you said things that still echo in my mind, but firstly, will there really be a war, my father says no, but I suppose it is his job to be reassuring ..."

"What's your name?" he asked and her quick blush gave him some temporary confidence. But she recovered and raised a perfectly arched eyebrow.

"You should not let strangers into you apartment or allow them to tuck you into bed," she returned with a cheeky smile on her slight lips.

"I shouldn't let myself drink so much or honour lunch invitations from strangers"

"Oyefunke."

"Delighted to meet you," he said in mock exaggeration and they shared a cautious laugh.

It was strange banter. She was normally conservative, he was always reserved and they both knew they were meeting on borrowed moments. She knew she would be back in London in two months and he knew he would be forced to go East soon after. They enjoyed the intense, carefree relationship that fits snugly in restricted time – the type that encouraged strong opinions and unusual habits. They talked about love and war, they talked about dreams they did not know they had until they slipped out from their lips in gay conversation. Two months later, Emeka would tuck her in the safe he put all his best memories, the ones that threatened nostalgia when visited: like his family, Father Grey, Chairman. But it was during one of their many lunches that he realised his destiny was bigger than his ambitions and it scared and thrilled him all at once.

"You are an unusual guy," she began.

"Really," he returned, the mockery in his voice annoying her slightly.

She looked him squarely in the eye. "You have the remarkable habit of being immediately liked by everyone you meet."

"So?" he asked flippantly, the same indulgent smile tugging at the corner of his red lips.

"So," she echoed incredulously, "we live in the most populous country in Africa at its most divided time and you ask so?"

"And who am I?" he asked in a pointed way that insinuated many things about her privileged status.

"That's for you to find out," she said with a tight smile, for the first time exiting the lunch before he did.

He thought about that many times, but the next time they met, she acted like nothing had happened and he was afraid to revisit that topic.

She refused to tell him when she had to return and when it came, it was as sudden as their meeting. At lunch, she said simply, "It has been a pleasure, you were wonderful company." And he said, "You, too." They made physical contact for the first time since she helped him into his bed and it was a brief hug that forever engraved the sweet scent of guavas in his mind.

Initially he had intended to wait out the war somewhere in the less troubled southwest, he had enough money to live inconspicuously in an indifferent neighbourhood. Instead, he sold the store and all that was left of it the next day, his time in Lagos was winding down and he knew because the streets had too many buses laden with pots and mattresses – goods that indicated a journey of finality.

Dolapo worked in a law firm and Emeka decided he should be the custodian of his small fortune. Over the years, they had sporadically kept in touch through letters, the last one being over a month and a half back. Emeka made his way through the endless traffic to Ikoyi like he had done thrice a week for the past two months and walked into the law office of Sullivan and McGregor. An overly efficient secretary promptly summoned Mr Dolapo

Odukoya. There were conservative hugs, the kind only shared by close friends who mostly guard their affections.

"How are you? I went to the university, they said you were interning here," Emeka began.

"Yep, one more year of school, but I'll be done in May and back here in September for good," Dolapo returned.

"I need a favour. I'm sure you've heard of the rumours."

"My friend, abeg they are just rumours."

"Maybe," Emeka said with a pensive pause, "anyway, I want you to put this in an account for me," he said placing a large suitcase in Dolapo's hand that was full of dollars.

"What are you doing? Don't be silly," Dolapo said, taking a peep at it and hesitant to handle such a large amount of money.

"Please, it is a favour. Look, if this rumour is real, I don't think my money will survive the war and if I don't survive the war, it is yours to keep. You should start your own firm and stop working for these oyinbos."

"Never, I can't use your money. I see it did you well to skip the university," Dolapo said with a wide smile. "Look at you after just three years," he continued.

"To each his own, to each his own. I've finished the first phase of my life. I'm waiting till I know the next. Just promise me if I don't return, you will use the money."

"What! Are you going to fight as well? You don't seem like the type, you are still a small boy. We're in our early twenties, abeg don't throw away your life."

"I'm not, I'm trying to find it, but first I must ..." There was a pause, "I must go, take care." And Dolapo was left with a black suitcase and an uncompleted sentence.

PART 2

THE WAR

I
Water No Get Enemy (South Eastern Nigeria, 1967 – 1969)

ONE

A year later, when the late rains of May fell, producing sweet scents in Ikoyi and floods in Mushin, Ojukwu – Governor of Nigeria's Eastern region – announced the secession in his honeyed baritone.

Emeka sat in shock at his till in Leventis, his mouth agape, his mind blocked, staring at the innocuous looking radio with its message of war. Still unaware, or perhaps simply unconcerned, customers hurried from aisle to aisle, scrutinising stacks of Nestle corn flakes and tins of Peak milk. Emeka knew it was coming, forewarned by Chairman, he had prepared for it, yet he was not ready. The lady in front of him impatiently tapped a set of well-manicured red nails on the counter bringing him back to the present. He quickly stuffed her products in a plastic bag and mechanically did so for the rest of the day. Arriving at his flat in Apapa, which he now shared to save costs, his brooding roommate held similar forebodings of doom; they knew they had to leave.

"Conductor say make I pay am double, he come slap me for face," his roommate said revealing a prominent black eye.

"Omo, our time don come oh," Emeka responded with a deep sigh, "be like say na tomorrow we must commot!" He had also been jostled at the bus stop on his way home, his fair face and accent giving him away as Igbo. Without bothering to resign, they left early on the first bus heading east. It was obvious their jobs would not be waiting for them. The announcement that had passively leaked

55

out in the afternoon had agitated latent lattices of discontent, like a large drop in a nigh empty bowl, reverberating ripples accumulated bias into social fracture.

Chukuemeka arrived at his parents' house to ebullient hugs and effeminate kisses. His father stood a respectable distance while his sister and mother fawned over him. They finally shook hands and managed a brief hug. There was obvious worry written in his father's seeing eye and even the habitually tranquil surface of his blind orb was marred by anxiety. Emeka had lived the last few months in limbo. He had taken a job that kept him in Lagos and just paid his bills because he was afraid of coming home. He did not want to see the excitement on his sister's face or worry on his mother's because he did not feel the same. It was his nature and they could not understand it. But mostly he did not want to look his father in the eye, because he was the only one who truly knew how he felt: that despite leaving the house too hastily and never looking back; that having never visited since, but sending as emissaries, envelopes with scant notes and thick wads of cash; that despite all this … he had no regrets about his decision. They talked about the only safe topics – the present and the future.

It was never a question of whether, but when he would join the Biafran army. His mother and sister reported promptly to the local centre to help sew uniforms. His father sent ten percent of what he produced on his farm. The first couple of months, Emeka's help on the farm sufficed; but then the leaders of Nigeria declared all out war on their errant brethren from Biafra. Even before the declaration, he could sense some unease in the heavy air that bespoke of a held back reproach when he sat together with his father in the evenings. Despite his wish for his son to promptly join the army, Mr Ogbonna was restrained by a quiet shame that was kept in sharp focus by his unseeing eye. Because although he had not overtly agreed, Mr Ogbonna was convinced Emeka had made the decision to follow Father Grey because he had wavered when initially asked permission by the priest. In his mind, he shouldered the burden of Emeka's decision to venture into the unknown for his family. A father is allowed to request of his son one impossible decision and his ledger was already red. It was obvious Emeka did not share his enthusiasm for an independent nation at all costs.

Mr Ogbonna still listened assiduously to the radio, straightening up with pride anytime Ojukwu's smooth voice trickled out. He even occasionally attempted a few dance steps when the local music came on and he had drunk enough palm wine. His blind eye seemed to twinkle when the announcer said, 'This is Radio Biafra.' Emeka knew it was simply a matter of time before he had to enroll and he walked around like a guest who had overstayed his welcome but had no place to go. The day Biafra also declared full-scale war, his father could barely look him in the face.

The moon was as glorious as the day Emeka was conceived. Mr Ogbonna had drunk more palm wine than was prudent. He sat by himself, at the end of the bench listening pointedly to his radio, which was giving updates on the status of troops and recruitments. He had not spoken a word to Emeka since the announcement the day before and only communicated his hunger to his wife. The tension was as heavy as the clouds that had threatened to burst all evening. Emeka sat with his sister at the other end of the long wooden seat, telling her about Lagos and occasionally about Dolapo.

"What do you miss most about Lagos?" she asked innocently.

Emeka was silent for a few minutes, "The life," he said finally, "the place is full of so much life."

Suddenly, his father's bitter voice hurdled his mother who sat in between them and said, "So we are dead here abi? That is why you won't come home, that is why you won't fight abi? There is no life here to fight for abi?"

The venom of his questions struck Emeka, but he chose to ignore them. He felt like a Nigerian, he felt they were all Nigerian and he had a quiet suspicion that his father could read his mind. At length, the uncomfortable silence diffused sufficiently and Emeka was practically panting from the strangled air that was finally reentering his lungs. His sister looked very sad, so he pulled out *The Lion and the Jewel*, by a young activist playwright named Wole Soyinka and began to read it to her softly. They were so caught up in the book, they did not notice his father had unsteadily made his way over and was standing over them. Suddenly, he snatched the book from out of Emeka's hands.

"What is this poison?" he asked in anger.

"It is not poison. It is by an intelligent Nigerian activist," Emeka responded springing to his feet from the force of his suppressed fury.

"Intelligent! Nigerian! Activist!" his father spat out each word like they should never belong in the same sentence. His cloudy eye held the force of an approaching storm. "You ungrateful boy, you will not corrupt my daughter. You will not take her away like you did my son. My only son." The last three words fell with weight of a bomb and the war he fled seemed inconsequential to the battle that raged in his mind.

"Mother, what is he saying?" The question came out in a mild strangled voice and the look on his mother's face confirmed what he had long suspected and what she could not voice.

He fled to the solitary comfort of his room. He crept out at the first sign of light and saw his sister curled on the floor outside his door. He picked her up, gave her a hug and a kiss and placed her in his bed. His mother sat at the house entrance and they shared a quick silent hug. He walked away from the house quickly without looking back.

TWO

Emeka looked out of the window; there was no moon and the rain was falling in blinding sheets. It was not good weather to be a sniper, it was not a good gun to snipe with and he was not a good sniper. He crouched below the sill clutching the old hunting rifle tight to his chest and saying his prayers. He could not see past the deluge or hear anything over the rain's thunderous roar. His eyes darted furtively around the room, which was strewn with debris and rubble. The remnants of his dinner from two days ago sat at the centre. He had not eaten or slept since then. His excrement and vomit lay in the top left corner but he did not notice them anymore. His mind was on the body slumped against the wall and the other corpse sprawled across the doorway. A spray of blood was the only other adornment on the cracked cement. A frantic couple of minutes had resulted in the dead Nigerian by the doorway, the loss of his partner and hot blood and piss wetting the right leg of his trousers. He had not had time to attend to his leg, move the bodies or even think about them. The gunfire was incessant. The Nigerian troops were closing in rapidly and their crude weapons were not keeping them at bay, as they had been told they would. He kept repeating to himself that the war was necessary, he kept praying, he kept crying, he kept cursing Ojukwu and Gowon – the Nigerian military head of state.

He woke up to the sound of boots on the floor. He fumbled for his rifle but it was too late, the gun was already pointed at his head. They recognised each other; neither of them said a word. He lowered his gun and they stared unblinking at each other – both too numb to portray their shock. The Nigerian sat down on the floor as well, away from the bodies. They both stayed that way the rest of the night, the air heavy with death, their minds heavy from war.

The gunfire died away slowly, neither of them hastened to follow it, secluded in their solitude, they silently sat. The rain stopped and the sun came out, but there was no rainbow to be seen. He dozed off again, the injury to his right leg was bleeding through the hastily tied rag and it made him drowsy. He looked up, the Nigerian was staring at him and their eyes met for the second time since his entry. They both wished they were not there and their eyes said so. He tried to open his mouth but his lips were too cracked, his head lulled from the attempt. He wanted to tell him not to go out just yet, the place was littered with ogbunigwes, but his mouth would not even open wide enough to say 'mines'. He attempted a tired smile to show gratitude for his life, but the Nigerian remained statuesque. He reached into his bag and pulled out a book with well-worn edges. He could barely stretch it out, but it elicited the first smile from the Nigerian who took it back wordlessly. He fought with his eyelids and willed his mind to stay awake but to no avail.

His whole body was sore; his head was pounding and his leg felt tight when he awoke. He looked down and saw that it was bandaged. Not with a rag but a real bandage and some iodine. It really hurt; he suspected the bullet must have been pried out. The Nigerian was gone. The helmets of the dead soldiers had been filled with water and left by his side and he drank from them greedily. One of them was only half full; it had a hole in it. There were the fried remains of a small animal he could not identify but he wolfed that down as well. A final present from an old friend.

A light drizzle fell outside, but a chorus of frogs did not punctuate it the way he remembered from his childhood. They had all been eaten. For the first time in his life, he reminisced. He thought of his parents and his sister. He tried not to think of his brother, the memory was too painful.

That day, the rain had come in warm waves and they had raced ahead of it all the way down the muddy uneven street, they just made it through the front door of the house when it cascaded down loudly on the tin roof. Emeka quickly stripped to his tattered underwear and ran back out, his naked little brother in tow, their excited shrieks drowning out Mrs Ogbonna's protests.

They ran around the house, singing songs and shouting in delight. Their mother told them to come in so they would not fall sick, but they only giggled in response because they were having too much fun. The rain got heavier and louder until they could not hear each other, still they kept running. He did not initially realise that his little brother was no longer behind him, but as he rounded the corner, he saw him there, splayed on the floor. There was a huge gash in his head. It was bleeding intensely, a bright pink ribbon extending from his head and disappearing rapidly.

He started to scream, but no one could hear. He picked up his brother and staggered to the front door. When he got there, he could not say a word. His mother screamed and cried until she was hoarse. Even though he was dead, she cleaned the wound and bandaged the head gently. Emeka could not speak for a month after that and everyone thought the experience had made him dumb.

Emeka wondered why a battle of such intensity had ceased so abruptly. Two things suddenly became apparent; he had been incapacitated for almost an entire day and had lost his sense of smell. Perhaps it was the shock of being holed up in a room full of putrefying bodies. What he thought was fog, was smoke. He was grateful for the rain. Most of the trees and buildings around him were scorched. He switched trousers with the fallen Nigerian and boots with his slain Biafran comrade and then set off through the blackened forest foraging for animals that had escaped the soldiers to be caught by the fire. Their charred remains would be welcome food. He ambled along painfully and slowly. He wondered how many bodies lay in those scorched buildings, quickly forgotten in an endless war.

He came to an area mostly preserved from the ravages of the fire. Clustered together were a clump of barely burnt palm trees that had been aided by the merciful rains. He heard a bleat; it was the painful, drawn out bleat of a goat with a heavy udder. Emeka was convinced he was losing his mind. He thought if he ignored it, it would go away, but it was unrelenting. He unwittingly began to meander towards the sound. There was a crudely made goat pen. They were the goats brought along by the Nigerian army to provide milk and to lure defectors. They were abandoned in the fire. The first three stalls were full of scorched carcasses, but there was still a goat in the last one. The fire had miraculously stopped short of its pen. He lay tiredly in a mound of black pellets and milked its bursting bladder into his thirsty mouth.

He filled the empty can he had in his backpack and set to devouring the first of the roasted goats. It was a feast to his senses. For a second he imagined there was no war. He was back at home, in the brief years between the mourning for his brother and his leaving home.

Emeka had to learn how to speak again, slowly, like a small child. At first, he could only utter Ibo words, but eventually whole phrases came to him. He used to teach his brother English and he did not regain the language for a whole year. One day he was conversant only in vernacular, the next he woke with his vocabulary as intact as before the accident.

Emeka was the only one the Ogbonnas could afford to send to school, even though his brother was smarter. So everyday he came home, sat him down and taught him everything. At least he used to. After the death, he could not stand the thought of school anymore. He could not do anything he did with his brother — he could do nothing. One day he sat mopping in the house but an incessant fly buzzed in his ear just out of reach of his hands so he could not slap it away. The room felt stifling, his mother was sprawled almost comatose in another corner. The whirring fan was doing nothing other than create a screechy distraction. He went into his room, picked up his book bag and realised he was walking into the classroom.

The teacher blinked his sincere green eyes in surprise but said nothing. After the class, Emeka marched to his desk and told him he did not want to pay the fees anymore but he was going to keep coming to classes. Before the teacher could object, he marched back out of the door. When he showed up the next day, the teacher said nothing. He called him on the third day and said he had a job for him to do. He returned every day after that. That was how Emeka came to be Father Grey's assistant.

During this time, he had remained sullen and his parents melancholic. Even his educational prowess could not lighten the mood in the house. There was no laughter in the house until his sister was born. She did not take away the pain, but she brought with her new smiles. His father stopped listening to the radio in the solitary confines of his room. His mother began to sing again when she roasted the goat for the annual New Year's celebration.

He packed as much of the roasted goats as he could, wrapping them in palm leaves and placing them in his bag. He hobbled for a long time with his bandaged leg and goat in tow. He did not know what to do, but he was convinced he did not want to return to the frontlines so he headed into the forest. The first week he was very tense and afraid. He was constantly scared he would be caught and labelled a deserter and his goat eaten. It was his sole companion, a new friend, a listening ear and supplier of nourishment for days on end. He would walk for miles, dragging his injured leg behind him, clasping the rope that held the goat firmly in his hand.

Initially, he did not notice that the leaves of the trees were getting greener and the air was getting fresher. Scent still eluded him and his mind was tormented by a bloody wall and fermenting corpses. The timid bleats of his goat provoked panic; afraid it would be heard, but grateful for its humane distraction. He did not like the sounds of rain. For him they represented death and war.

There was an abundance of grass and puddles of water from which he filled his can and his goat was content. He constantly contemplated killing the animal and savouring a final feast, but he could not. The fear of loneliness was the animal's security. So they trudged on, man and beast. At night he would climb into a tree with low branches, carefully pulling up his companion with him.

He got to a part of the forest where the trees were exceptionally dense. Not a single streak of the moonlight that was the cheeky smile of a small child hit the tangled weeds and foraging roots that lined the floor. After stumbling through for half an hour, he decided to turn around and find a way around it. His leg was throbbing and he was finding it more difficult to navigate with the goat. Just then, he saw a shaft of light seeping through ahead of him and he struggled towards it. He had not realised how disheveled he was until he saw the clean serenity of the compound before him. Even the chickens that pecked at the ground seemed to bob their heads and scratch the brown earth in unison. The trees around the enclosure were tall and unwavering like soldiers in formation.

Towards the far end of the space, to the left of a towering pawpaw tree stood a thatched bungalow with mud walls, its exquisite craftsmanship giving the impression that the choice of material was deliberate not necessitous. The rest of the clearing was covered by low vegetation with evenly spaced out trees. He saw the green shoots of the tomato plant, the mound of yams and wide leaves of pineapples. He was just wondering which juicy fruit grew in the broad trees closest to him when a movement caught his eye.

He yelled in fright when he saw that the brightly coloured mound at the centre of the compound was a woman bowed in prayer. Except for leaves and blood, he had not seen colours that bright in a long time. He realised he was practically naked and suddenly felt ashamed. His nails were long, broken and black. His hair was a tangled mess of twigs and leaves. His shirt was now a bloody piece of rag bandaging his thigh. He had discarded his boots and socks a long time ago and his pants had become ragged shorts held by a bit of string. She seemed as an apparition, sacred and normal. His reverence and shame kept him rooted to the spot.

Her head bobbed up and down, her forehead kissing the mat, her fingers pointing to him then to the sky. She was completely unperturbed by his presence even though he was sure no one had made their way through to this clearing in years. She finally looked straight at him with a big smile on her face as she got to her feet. Her dress was bright and flowing, like her hair, like her aura. She spoke with a soothing voice that caressed his tired mind and stimulated his fatigued legs to buckle.

He woke up in a sweat with a pounding head from a nightmare in which he ate his goat. There was bandage around his head; he must have hit something on his way down. Someone else was there; she was talking to the person. She was telling the person not to eat the carpet and then to produce some milk and lay an egg. She was speaking in the same soothing way he somehow remembered and he began to imagine he had damaged something in his head. Her voice was like morning dew as she entered the room, seemingly originating from nowhere, but settling life unto everything. She was taller than he recalled from before his fall, taller than her voice.

She was a melee of contrasting features. She had cloudy grey eyes like a retreating storm, large ears that lay flat against her skull, a thin upper lip that sat astride a full fleshy bottom and a fair slender nose. Perhaps just one of these would have stood out on a regular face, but they all colluded to make her look almost ordinary. She was neither ugly nor beautiful. But she was not unpretty; and her features were as unsettling as the only phrase fit to describe them.

Although it had slipped away unnoticed, it returned in overwhelming waves. The long forgotten aroma of frying eggs, the raw smell of manure, the refreshing scent of fresh grass, he fell into an uncomfortable coughing fit. She hurried out of the room and returned with a calabash of water and a kind smile. Her teeth were perfect pearls demarcated below her upper lip by a precise gap the width of half a tooth. It gave her smile an air of reflected serenity and when she was twelve she had had it carved in. He quaffed it thirstily; he had had mostly creamy milk for three weeks.

Her smile remained in place. Her hair was silver. Her face was unlined. Her age was impossible to tell.

THREE

She was a twenty-three-year-old widow. She had not spoken to a human in two years. Her memories had faded from colourful narratives to grey pictures, like a favourite dress worn too many times. She carried the outside world as a collection of concise notes. She was Igbo. She was a Muslim.

She noticed the cross on his neck and remarked: "I see you follow the religion of love. I follow that of devotion, there is not much love these days, I follow the times," she said with an easy smile.

But her actions betrayed her words. There was no one else in the house. She had been talking to the chickens and his goat. Perhaps afraid she would lose her ability to converse, she kept up a running commentary, often about the books she read. On the sole shelf, by a corner of the room, stood about a hundred volumes. An impressive amount for the period and circumstances, particularly as the house was practically bare. He began to notice other oddities adorning the room, the grandiose radio, the pile of records next to the gramophone, the exotic pictures … He wondered where he was.

She left to say her prayers in the glow of the setting sun and returned to find him on his feet fingering her books, his hand resting unconsciously on his bandaged thigh. He had turned on the radio because it was the only familiar object. It was a broken faucet of propaganda, leaking patriotic phrases that he barely heard. A book had caught his eye and it conjured up a much stronger image. It was of a haggard face that bandaged his leg as he drifted in and out of consciousness a few weeks back. The rain had been ceaseless that night; it fell in sheets of lead and sorrow. Then it was the same face, much younger, wearing the same earnest look as he gave him the book, *Things Fall Apart*. He had never read a book outside of the classroom before then, but love of great literature can be contagious and it had been so with him. Rain, whips and sorrow had also marked that night. Finally, he understood why Dolapo gave him the book that night. It had not been because of Okonkwo, but the foreigner in his home.

It was a strange house – a type so inexplicable you grudgingly fell in love with it. There were a surprising amount of handmade objects and Emeka suspected this was how she passed her time. He remembered he did not know her name. There were handwoven cane chairs, knitted blankets and crudely constructed frames that held the exotic pictures and paintings. All the contents so bizarre, they clustered comfortably in the strange small hut. A fat brown hen sat watch on an open window and his little goat stood guard by the door.

The well-read books arranged on the clustered shelf brought a contended smile to his worn face. He found many books that had titles with strange names like *Lolita*, *The Master and Margarita*, and *A Hundred Years of Solitude*. He did not even bother with the authors' names. The same King James Bible that the priest used to earnestly read each day with his solemn voice sat there. There were other Bibles, a Koran, a book on Hinduism, another on Buddhism and all sorts of spiritual texts, but it was not until he saw the name 'Wole Soyinka' etched into the spine of a small book that he fully felt at ease. He was itching to know her story and where he was, but he was a guest – an invader and had to be patient. She came back in with her smile and aura. He was holding a picture frame that held the portrait of a man whose expression said he had seen many things. But before he could inquire who it was, she said, "You must be starving," and laughed at a joke that he did not understand. "First we eat, then we talk," she said.

She brought in things that were familiar to him, made in a very unfamiliar way. The chicken, potatoes and vegetables all sat in a happy mash in a bowl. His hunger placed the first spoon in his mouth and he was surprised at how delicious it was. She gave him a few more rounds and he felt sick from eating so much. They sat outside and while they ate, the darkness fell suddenly and completely. With it came the bygone evening sounds of his childhood and he forgot completely that he was in a war. A chill had come with the darkness and they made a fire and sat around it in knitted blankets. She seemed unwilling to talk and he had forgotten how to. They sat in silence staring at the fire and unexpectedly he puked. She looked at him in surprise; she still seemed often startled by his presence even though she was attending to him. The same hurried laugh that had emerged earlier peeped out like a bright moon on a cloudy night and was again swiftly swallowed. She got him some water and he sat in his shame, grateful for the attention. A plane flew over too far away to be seen and soon they heard the deadly bombs that had sat in its belly fall like soft knocks on a stubborn door.

She started suddenly, unprompted, "He was very intelligent and beautiful – he was a beautiful man." Her eyes matched the clouds as she stared up at them and seemed lost in a distant time that could have been yesterday. "His father was hardworking, he travelled often and they owned the first motorcycle in these parts. He was quiet, intelligent and rather strange. While the rest of the children played, he would crawl among the tall grasses catching grasshoppers and crickets. He barely spoke. He just seemed to work and study like his father. Even at that age, when all girls are beautiful and boys fall in love, he brooded in juvenile solitude." Then she must have seen something in that portal of time for her voice trailed off and she stayed silent for a while. Emeka remembered the nights when he was a child and his mother told him stories around the fire. He wept. "Well, we must be off to bed now," she said unexpectedly and Emeka realised that even the crickets had been momentarily quiet and the hens in the trees had not clucked or fluttered all that time. The world had waited in enchanted bated breath for her soft voice to reappear.

She led him back to the room, where the hen and goat still sat dutifully. He collapsed on the bed with many questions that turned into distracting dreams. When he woke, the room was bathed in white light and he was temporarily frightened. The hen had laid an egg; it was the first thing he noticed. Soft animal noises lay around and he noticed a cat was sunning itself on another window that faced towards the clearing. He went over to stroke it and the woman was once again praying with her head to the floor. He looked over the room, his mind confirming the inventory his brain had registered the previous day. When he returned to the window, the woman was contorted in a strange shape that was so unfamiliar to him he shouted, "Chineke!" All his forgotten superstitions rapidly returned and he briefly thought she was about to turn into some sort of animal. She untangled herself at the sound of his shout and approached with her usual smile. He was not soothed.

"Yoga," she said. "Do you read?" she asked walking past him to the shelf and pulled down two books. One said *Yoga* simply, the other was one of the books he had looked at the previous day and had a large black cat on its cover. "We'll eat and then we'll farm," she said.

They spent a month like that. They ate and farmed. She said her prayers and did her contortions. They both read. As soon as he was done with a book she would give him another. He enjoyed reading, but these books were strange and had strange ideas. One of them talked about equal societies and he could not imagine a village functioning without the chiefs and elders, in another, the devil changed shapes and jumped around. Sometimes she knitted. She took care of the animals and seemed to often forget that he was there. He got used to the life, to the quiet evening sounds, to her soothing voice, to the queer simplicity of his room. The place had a kitchen, a bathroom and two rooms. She stayed in one that had a bed and many books and he stayed in the other that also had a bed, a couch and the windows with the hen and cat. He once asked her why there had been another bed and she replied in case someone came along, as if it was the most natural and expected thing. And then one day unexpectedly a storm came and fell unhindered for three days, opening their two lives to one another.

She sat on the couch in his room quietly knitting as he read *Animal Farm*. She wanted to test his alliances. She remembered there had been a movement beginning in the university before her self-imposed exile. A movement that had made her husband nervous and talk about the stirrings of war. In those times, he was haunted by another war, a greater one that had recruited from far and wide and thrust men together in ways never before seen. Perhaps that is the beauty of war, if fought for a noble cause, irrespective of outcome: some good can be moulded with the ashes. But who can predetermine what is noble, the cause is carved from the contents of the ashes.

Emeka was burning to discuss these notions of equality with her but she was always reluctant to let her sparse voice escape its curious capsule. The rain had been cascading down for a day and a half and she walked purposefully to the wooden cabinet in the kitchen that held foreign delights they rarely indulged. She returned with two cups of spicy chai in her hand and continued recounting the tale like there had not been a five-week break. "My mother told me all that," she suddenly continued. "I was not even born," she muttered under her shy laugh.

"The first time I saw him, he was so exotic, he had been everywhere. He joined the British army, he saw the Chinese, the Indians, Egyptians, he was even in Europe. He brought back things that no one in the village had ever seen. He talked of strange things, he had strange pictures, he was peculiar to everyone. He had a box that spoke and another that sang," she said motioning at the stereo and gramophone.

"I was an outcast because of my strange eyes, they thought my Chi was half dead, but he did not care. He was old, much older, but we found comfort in each other. I thought he could have an answer for me. When Ojukwu came onto the scene, talking about his revolutionary ideals, he became withdrawn – he could not bear war anymore. He told me there would be one soon and we had to get away. My parents were happy to get rid of me, so he paid my bride price. We wandered for a long time and found this," she said gesturing at everything.

"We built it over three years. We brought over most of the possessions." She handed him his cup and sat back on the couch.

"During that time, I asked him once why he did not mind my strange features," she paused here and smiled because she knew that Emeka had also wondered about the same thing.

"He said he believed our features were legacies from our ancestors. Then he said personality was a combination of inherited traits shaped by environment. He called them the features of the soul. He said I was unique externally and he was internally," she paused again. "I like that explanation," she said mostly to herself – "we fit."

He must have been cursed, Emeka thought to himself and was upset she kept invoking superstitious thoughts in him. She was quiet again, but this time it was more of a shared silence. She looked up and it was suddenly like the shadows of the past that had veiled her soul were laid to rest and she saw him for the first time. She looked at him with large grey eyes full of shy curiosity and he fell irretrievably in love.

The next morning, as he placed the book back in the shelf, she asked unexpectedly, "In an unchanged failed system, do you think new leaders are bound to perpetuate the disappointing cycles of their predecessors?" Her voice was like nectar, sweet and smooth.

It threw him off and he only uttered a stutter in response. There was something different about her. She had a twinkle in her eye that was at once serious and mischievous. "I am referring to the book you are reading … and the country," she added, like he did not know.

"I think there is hope," he said finally, "it is our own country, ruled by our own people."

"Are you referring to Biafra or Nigeria?" she asked in a mocking voice that made him feel small.

"Either one," he said offhandedly, disliking her sudden interest in stimulating conversation. He was angry she finally chose to relinquish her silence at a time he was unprepared. He could not think of intelligent things to say and was unconvinced a woman should be debating such topics in the first place.

He was still thinking of that discussion later that night when he turned on the radio. A song with plenty of local pipes and the ogene played out rhythmically repetitively – unmistakably Igbo and for the first time he really thought about her question. He wondered if it mattered if he were Biafran or Nigerian. He had lived half his life in Lagos and had jumped with joy when the green white green replaced the Union Jack: he had been proud to be Nigerian. His memories were Nigerian. He had happily listened to Dolapo's stories of how it was celebrated in his village and he had watched the changing of flags with the priest as well. The priest had been silent, but he had been glad. Now, he was a deserter in a war he did not want to fight in a place unfamiliar to him. His musings were interrupted by the distinct voice of Ojukwu and he was listening attentively without meaning to.

For two years we have been subjected to a total blockade. We all know how bitter, bloody and protracted the First and Second World Wars were. At no stage in those wars did the white belligerents carry out a total blockade of their fellow whites. In each case where a blockade was imposed, allowance was made for certain basic necessities of life in the interest of women, children and other non-combatants. Ours is the only example in recent history where a whole people have been so treated. What is it that makes our case different? Do we not have women, children and other non-combatants? Does the fact that they are black women, black children and black non-combatants make such a world of difference?

Our struggle has far-reaching significance. It is the latest recrudescence in our time of the age-old struggle of the black man for his full stature as man. We are the latest victims of a wicked collusion between the three traditional scourges of the black man – racism, Arab-Muslim expansionism and white economic imperialism. Playing a subsidiary role is Bolshevik Russia seeking for a place in the African sun. Our struggle is a total and vehement rejection of all those evils which blighted Nigeria, evils which were bound to lead to the disintegration of that ill-fated federation. Our struggle is not a mere resistance – that would be purely negative. It is a positive commitment to build a healthy, dynamic and progressive state, such as would be the pride of black men the world over ...

... Since in the thinking of many white powers a good, progressive and efficient government is good only for whites, our view was considered dangerous and pernicious: a point of view which explains but does not justify the blind support which these powers have given to uphold the Nigerian ideal of a corrupt, decadent and putrefying society. To them genocide is an appropriate answer to any group of black people who have the temerity to attempt to evolve their own social system.

72

The voice was chilling and chocked with emotion. Emeka was not entirely convinced. He remembered his week posted at the war front, when the soldiers diverted the food meant for the civilian population. He remembered the flimsy justifications: are we not fighting for their benefit, should we not be strong in battle? But then, he thought of his family. The charismatic voice had dodged a thousand trees and pierced his armour of contempt and his shunned memories stripped him bare. For the second time since his desertion, Emeka cried.

A week later, a pale moon still clung obstinately to the sky even as a soft gold illuminated the horizon. A palm tree stood tall in the enclosure and on this romantic morning, Emeka attempted to climb it. He thought briefly of the last time he had tapped the sweet nectar, the day before the announcement of the war. His sister had been the only person at ease as they had sat around the fire slowly sipping from the bowls. She was the only one who could ignore the fact that the present is simply a waiting period for the future. And the future was war. He made a belt that encircled him and the tree and used that to shimmy up. He cut a precise incision in the flower and fastened a container to collect the sap that flowed out in milky purity. He was surprised at how well he remembered and softly whistled a song to himself about the palm wine tapper, noting with pride that he was he. She seemed to tie up his tongue and he was determined to be eloquent that evening. With childlike glee, Emeka placed the container under the shade of a broad leaf and thought about it excitedly all day. In the evening when he returned to his little treasure, his goat had drunk most of it, spilled the rest and was staggering around bleating miserably. He was at once disappointed and sad remaining in a sullen sulk for the rest of the evening, his fierce features enforcing a quiet dinner. The next day he tried again without the easy success of the first day and ensured to put the meager sap he got in a safe place. She only gave him a wry smile when he handed her the bowl leaving a hooked eyebrow suspended. She took a gentle sip and made as if to say something, thought against it and let it hang. Emeka had many good thoughts flowing through him but before he could let any of them out, they were both fast asleep. Emeka woke up in the middle of the night, she was sprawled on the couch, a faint grey light, the colour of her hair floated in through the window and caressed her svelte neck. He draped a blanket over her and she gave a gentle smile.

The next morning, when he arose, she was in the courtyard doing yoga. She offered him breakfast, muttered a timid "Thank you," and rapidly walked away. They avoided each other all day with the unspoken agreement of people who had shared a tacit secret. He was sitting upright in the bed with a novel in his hands. He had been staring at the same page for the past hour, his mind anywhere but on the book. Perhaps it was the din of the rain on the tin roof, or the air pregnant with questions, or her grey eyes that clouded like the sky had done earlier in the evening.

"Where is your family?" she asked, putting down the knitting she had only pretended to engage.

It was an unexpected question. "I don't know," he said. He looked uncomfortable and she knew not to ask him any more questions from before the war because a man who would not talk about his family has voluntarily relinquished memories of his past.

"I used to hate this place whilst we were building it, it was like running away, two outcasts chased away by society," she said, a false laugh masking her pain and cynicism. He had never seen her so vulnerable, her eyes almost looked brown – almost ordinary. "He died during those uncertain years before the war truly began. He slept and did not wake. I think he was just fed up."

Emeka stopped stroking the cat in his lap. He felt strangely elated she was slowly opening up to him but he also felt choked – as if her memories were eating up the space – and crowding the room.

"Then his relatives showed up with their unbridled greed masquerading as tradition. I was a witch to them obviously. I was mourning my husband and they were asking why the house was empty and where I hid all their brother's treasures. They shaved my head, washed his body and asked me to drink the water to prove I did not kill him. I left that night, my mind shrouded in sorrow, blinded by grief," the same morose laugh.

Emeka finally understood the long contemplative silences, he imagined her crouched on the floor, bald, in black, her mind trying to escape, her heart masked in confusion trying unsuccessfully to mourn, while cruel cold fingers pointed accusingly. He imagined a bit of that was forever frozen in her and would always return uninvited. He went to the couch and sat next to her but she did not notice.

"I got lost," she continued, "I wandered around for a long time and when I was convinced I would finally join him, I realised I had unwittingly walked to this shelter we built to hide from the war. When my hair grew back, it was this," she said pointing at the grey on her head, which she kept braided in varying local designs. "I guess our battles started the day he died. You're the first human I've seen in three years. In three years," she repeated. "Good night," she said calmly.

They continued like this, long periods of silence sliced by shards from the past. Mostly hers, Emeka still found it difficult to reminisce.

Then the war ended.

The voice of surrender came through the radio, but one month later, they realised nothing in their life had changed. Neither went hunting for lost idyllic pasts. They lived cautiously around each other until one day, three months later; they realised their trepidation was the fingers of subdued affections. They began a strange courtship – Emeka picked her flowers, he made her blush, but he was sufficiently disciplined to only display restrained affection for five years.

One day, he sat on the couch in the fading sunlight, finding it difficult to concentrate on one of the many copies of The Bible she possessed when a page dropped unto his lap. It was a poem titled *A candle in the sun*:

In dim corners they snivel
Minds wretched, diseased and feeble
In their miserly existence together they cling
Bowed together by life's damning sting

In the misery of others they rejoice
My grief their pleasing choice
Their dominant power I can't fight
I'll retreat and be my own light

In their corrosive light I lost significance
Their scrutiny eroded my importance
My obscurity is my solace
I will run to my hiding place

My limbs fatigued, my brows creased
I strained and yearned to glow brighter
All my efforts it mocked and teased
My body not soul got lighter

In obscurity I was born
You're merely a candle, I am the sun
…
Till at last extinguished, with it I was one

He could guess quite easily when she wrote it. She walked into the house with a harvest of plump tomatoes and he was so excited, he asked her about it before she had a chance to set them down.

"You read it," she said it like it was neither a statement nor question.

"Yes."

"Mmhhh," she said dropping the tomatoes in the sink and rinsing them carefully.

"Why the unfinished line?" he asked.

"Because then it would be complete," she said with her smile.

"So?"

"Then you miss the point," she said with tired finality.

"What point?" he asked persistently.

"It's a poem about relativity and significance. If I finish it, then it becomes a finished poem comparable to other finished poems and then it loses significance."

"But now, it is simply an unfinished poem like many unsuccessful poems."

"Why did you desert?" she asked lightly in a way that implied, 'Why did everyone else not desert.' A question that asked: 'Not where were you running from, but where were you running to?'

"I was fighting a war that was not mine. I realised my life was more sacred than my belief."

"Selfish now, aren't we?" she said mockingly.

"I only joined the war because my father believed in it so much … and I thought with my involvement I could hasten it and also prove myself to him." It was the first time he had mentioned his father.

"Until a match sees the sun, it believes it is king of the dark," she said finally. He was not convinced by the answer, but he was satisfied.

"Marry me," he said and she smiled in response.

FOUR

He was reading the book *Immortality* by Milan Kundera and in its vast poetry, he realised the simple truth 'that life is not elongated by the amount of seconds added to the first but the value given to each extra one'.

He finished the book two days later, at a time when the fierce noon sun had already blazed for a couple of hours. The air was as thick as soup and he fell into a daydream. The walls were covered in it, the floors were made of it; it was an endless room of clocks and they all ticked gently and in unison sounding like the mechanical purr of a contented lion. They all proclaimed quarter to two o'clock – in figures, roman numerals and every other representation of the number and he awoke. It was not the startled jerk that releases one from a nightmare or the serene arousal from a sweet dream, his eyes opened and his mind was clear like he had not been asleep just a second ago. It was a strange dream but he felt no alarm.

He had asked her six months earlier and she had smiled without a response. But the words were not futile; with the passivity of her smile, another layer of hurt was stripped away. One quiet dusk, she had looked at him intently and said, "Let's do it tomorrow," and her wish was evident. The next day he tapped some wine and she cooked. They passed the day like every other but at night, they said their vows with the full moon, the goat and an old cat as their witnesses. He touched her tenderly for the first time, she kissed him for the first time and they consummated their love sans the wolf, sans the innocent avowal of his progenitors. The silver moon reflecting in her silver eyes had transfixed him and he became forever subject to the whims of the heavenly globe, unable to get an erection without its ethereal help.

But as he walked into the room to tell her of his daytime reverie he felt the blood rush between his legs at the sight her endless ebony legs, the soft curve of her lower back that suddenly blossomed out into the twin bridges that linked the two and he realised that the dream indeed had a meaning.

II
Alagbon Close (Southern Nigeria, 1985 – 1997)

ONE

It was fifteen years and nine months later. Development had slowly eroded the seclusion of their forest enclave and a daughter now invaded the privacy of their love. The university, short of able professors had accepted his wife despite her dubious credentials. Emeka was a writer with the regional magazine, his riling comments typed out tortuously with two fingers pointing accusingly at the keys of his mechanical *Underwood Five*. The morning he woke up to find his ten-year-old daughter busy at his completed article decorating it with random words like clock, moon and rain, he shed a happy smile and said two things, "It is never too early to begin to rebel," which she instantly forgot and "it is good to learn everything, because you will be paid to do tomorrow what you enjoyed learning today." She always treasured the last statement because even at that tender age, the Igbo business gene was already manifesting.

The many years of isolation had bred a culture of habitual routine. Everything was done in a certain way at a certain time. In the mornings, his wife got up and said her prayers facing the same direction everyday, where she thought the Qibla was. Then she would collect the eggs and Emeka would milk the goats. She would make breakfast and he would do a bit of farming. She would head off to the university after the meal and Emeka would type slowly on his typewriter with his back to the window. They had begun homeschooling their daughter initially to pass the time on rainy days but she was so far ahead of her peers when the time came to enroll her in school that they had decided to stick to it. Emeka would put her in his lap and make her recite the ABCs until she became too big and he watched patiently as she solved arithmetic problems two feet away from him. The only sounds to be heard were their measured breathing, the occasional strike of the keys as each letter was forcefully recorded and the soft scratch of her pencil on paper. Her name was Nneka; she looked like a plain version of her mother, lacking the startling features. Emeka had unknowingly given his daughter the name of his birth mother. She had the natural smells of a child who spent her days reading novels, playing with animals and gardening. Emeka had fallen in love with the sharp minty taste of TomTom. Always, he had one of them in his mouth sucking thoughtfully on the small black sweet with white stripes. They sat in the living room that was practically unchanged except that the occupant was now Nneka. In the afternoons, they typically read to each other until his wife returned. Dinner was prepared from memory of local dishes or the pages of foreign cookbooks.

Emeka only went to town twice a month. Often, his wife went by his newspaper office before and after work, dropping off his recently finished pieces and returning with new articles in a thick brown envelope. He rarely slept, "Make hay while the sun shines," he used to exclaim to his wife in the early days when worried, she awoke with him. But the real reason had a more sinister source. His true motivation was the need to forcibly exorcise the collage of bloody, mangled bodies swimming before his eyelids, forcing them open. Instead, he often spent the night reading and rereading everything that was sent to the magazine. On the days he went to town, he would have endless meetings and although his boss did not like the arrangement, he was excellent at what he did.

He went the mornings after the moon was at full or half strength. On those nights, he would make a fire outside and he and his wife would alternate telling stories to Nneka and Bingo, the dog they got when she was born.

Early the following day, he would rise even before his wife's prayers and tap some palm wine. When he returned, he and his wife would share a sloppy calabash and the conversation was most heated on those nights.

"They have all been criminals! Gowon, Obasanjo, Shagari, Buhari, Lord help us, what these men have done, even this Babaginda is a thief! I am sure of it!" Emeka would begin.

"But Murtala was not so bad and Balewa was a noble man," she replied.

"Exactly why they killed them, they don't want the people to see that things can be done right, so they can keep stealing until the country is robbed blind. And I know this Babaginda is going to finally put the nail in the coffin!"

"Darling, you must not be prejudiced, everyone must be given a chance to prove their worth."

"I don't trust leaders who wear glasses at night, look at Charles Taylor." At which, they would collapse in helpless laughter, turning politics into comedy because it was more bearable than the tragedy that was the reality they both knew so well.

"How was your last article received?" she asked suddenly.

"As predicted, the government is silent. Babaginda is an evil genius, he has arrested more people than he released in those first few days but he would always point to that to show his tolerance."

"I'm so proud of you, darling. If men are being arrested for fighting for the plight of their people and everyone remains silent, then we commit a greater sin. It would be spitting on their legacies."

"Exactly," he said with a satisfied smile. He looked at the starless sky and was pleased. He had finally found a way to contribute, even if it was just through melancholic musings from his pensive pen.

TWO

He could not remember the interior of the Black Maria. The journey was a medley of boots and whips. He did not see his blood run down the corrugated floor of the van and drip through rusty crevices leaving a trail that no one would follow. The laughter of the guards would echo in his head – even after the sound of the gun that would mistakenly go off soiling his feet with his editor's cerebral cortex, bouncing gleefully around the void of his unconsciousness long after his left eye would be cemented shut by dried blood. He would be dumped out unceremoniously; the only thing marking his stint in the diabolic vehicle being his third molar neglected by a tired crack that had drank too much blood. He did not know how long the ride had been, his mind had fled to a frozen moment in the past after the butt of the gun silenced it. The ground was hard mud, coloured by blood, baked by the sun and shaped by the stamping of heavy boots and the impact of light bodies. He was at the infamous Kirikiri Prison in Dodan Barracks, Obalende. He kept thinking of his dead editor who had been dumped carelessly to the side like a sack of spoilt potatoes. He kept thinking of their last conversation and how the editor had been right about the crackdown and how he had not believed it. He refused to think about his wife and Nneka or to soil their memory by projecting them into his current surroundings.

The day had started like most at the end of the month but the night had been different. The tales by moonlight had gone on later than usual and Emeka had worked until three in the morning when fatigue had flung him unto his bed. As soon as his head hit the pillow, he was again consumed by a dream of ticking clocks. Once again the clocks ticked in unison although, this time, its hands were stuck on the second before it became two. He walked around the room at ease, unperturbed by the strange sight of frozen, ticking clocks until he arose refreshed two hours later. He looked over at his wife because he knew something was about to happen but she slept soundly and he decided not to bother her. He walked out to tap palm wine for the evening revelry and was swamped by the scent of ripe guavas. He remembered his conversation with the daughter of the education minister so many years ago and smiled because she had been wrong. His destiny had not been bigger than his dreams, he had not bridged cultures; he was a contended recluse with a happy family and he was pleased with his life. By the time he had put away the calabash full of sweet liquid froth, he had long forgotten about her and his dream.

When his wife dropped him off at the office in their old 504 Peugeot, he once again had a strange feeling of foreboding that he at once dismissed. He kissed her on the lips and said, "In a bit," like he always said.

When he walked into his office, it was obvious something was amiss, everyone was nervous, even his habitually unflappable editor, who kept swallowing phantom spit and adjusting his tie.

"The government is cracking down hard on journalists," his editor said.

"That's not new," Emeka said, trying not to be infected by the fear that gripped everyone else.

"But this is different. Did you hear what happened at *The Guardian Newspapers* in Lagos?"

"Yes, they arrested all the senior staff, but we are different, they left themselves open to harassment by not properly picking sides. If you are going to condemn the government, you can't half-ass it: it means you are open to intimidation."

"Emeka, you're obviously not in touch with reality," his editor interrupted. "Yes, we have received nothing but threats, particularly after we started writing about the disappearances, but they are using letter bombs now. They are not being subtle anymore! We are risking our lives for the memories of dead men."

"And is this not our job?" Emeka asked defiantly, looking his editor in the eye for the first time. "It is why we are safe, you worry too much," he said trying to ease the frightened look that he saw.

"The eye of the world is on us. This is the time to shout our ills and discontent from the rooftops. Babaginda's hand is most restrained against his real opposition now."

"Emeka, they arrested those journalists for writing a much more watered down version of what we published. How do you think we are going to get away with this?"

"Don't worry," Emeka was saying when the sound of a gunshot interrupted his words.

They both looked at each other in panic and suddenly the other rooms seemed to explode in screams. The sound of crashing furniture could be heard and the crude words of bloodthirsty soldiers hovered above the bedlam. "Where are they? They are bastards. Do they think they can slander our honourable government?" Different voices all spouting the same venom. Emeka looked over and saw that his editor had pissed himself and was covered in large beads of sweat as he tried to fit under the desk of his office. Emeka remained frozen. He watched from behind a curious smile as the soldiers came in and asked, "Who is Chukwuemeka Ogbonna and where is his useless editor?" He watched his editor stutter and break into tears. He watched the hands slap his face repeatedly and the boots make contact with his sides. He watched until he was slapped across the face with a gun that would loosen his third molar.

"Move here! Move here!" jarring and harsh, like shards of glass on a baby's skin, it was the imagery that came to him as the words assaulted his throbbing head. He realised his body had resumed without him; he was marching in a single file naked and wet. There were people ahead and behind him all looking resigned and miserable. Just as he realised no one was tied or handcuffed, he saw a fresh corpse a few feet from him. He looked up to meet a guard's bored gaze, his sneer daring him to run. They were stuffed into a dank, dark room where the sun had died. More and more bodies were piled into the already cramped space until the foul breath from fifty bloody mouths polluted the air. They were tiredly wedged in like insignificant cogs in an abandoned machine. The gates slammed shut and miraculously, slowly, spaces began to appear, not much, but enough to take away the morbid hope that they would in fact suffocate and die on that first night. Their clothes had been returned to them without shoes, belts or other accessories.

"All new inmates must fast for three days," the harsh voice of a guard said. Five days later, some had died, all had shrunk and now there was enough space for them to sink tiredly to the ground. In his dim consciousness, held up by the proximity of everyone, the voice of the man next to him floated gently in his ear, the audible delusions of a wearied soul, muttering repeated curses in many languages.

The voice was refined, his skin was soft and by the end of the week, his young face was covered in large red welts – the mosquitoes took an exceptional liking to him. The guards liked him, the other prisoners liked him, he understood the three major languages and spoke another fifteen local dialects; he kept everyone thoroughly entertained. His father had participated in one of the earlier coups d'etat. They had been brought to the prison together and when on the third day the guards came to announce that he had been shot, the boy had replied simply. "That thief, you don shoot am, chai!" And although everyone had appreciated his crude comedy, he was quiet for the rest of that week.

On the first morning, at seven, a man with a shaggy beard issued a call to prayer and someone else recited some psalms from memory. No space was too limiting for the battle of religions. The guards armed with whips watched calmly for thirty minutes, then the new inmates were led into a sandy courtyard with the chilly fingers of dawn reaching down to massage their open wounds and sore bodies. They were asked to lie down in the sands as the guards urinated on them and buckets of cold water were dumped on their backs and then they were told to roll around. The grains of sand stuck to their backs and when the whipping began, it felt like a thousand nails hammered in with individual care.

On the fifth day, a guard finally came by with food. He walked calmly and talked soothingly. His voice was quiet, his features were quiet: nothing about him was spectacular. He asked softly for the bucket in which the prisoners urinated. He emptied it of most of its content and then poured the first meal they had been offered in five days into it. He handed the bucket back with neither sneer nor smile. His face was almost serene – it showed no emotion. For the first time, Emeka saw grown men cry in the company of others. He was so thoroughly disgusted he reached into the bucket of stone dotted beans, grabbed a handful and stuffed it into his mouth; forcing himself not to gag on the acrid, sour taste. Emeka was looking the guard in the eye and for a brief second he noticed the right one flutter like a sharp gust of wind had been blown into it. Immediately, the guard's impassive stare returned for a few more minutes, then he turned and walked away. When he was out of earshot, the charismatic boy made a comment about hungry Igbo boys, but the respect was evident in his voice and Emeka was glad he had done that.

The next morning, they were served stony beans again with stale bread and everyone silently cheered when the beans came in the proper containers. In a matter of minutes, all the food had been devoured, causing many to keel over and vomit. Two more men died, but nobody mourned because it meant more space when their bodies were removed. The silent guard from the previous day reappeared at the front of their cell with another guard whose teeth all struggled violently to escape from his small mouth. He followed his silent companion with too much efficiency and called out six names from a list in a grating voice. One of the men on the list was already dead; he was not missed and the rest were marched deeper into the prison. Four of them were told to enter a cell that was much smaller than the last but given that it was formerly uninhabited, it seemed like an expansive space. There were four narrow cots suspended from the wall with rusty chains. The silent guard of the previous night continued to march down the hall and Emeka was shoved roughly after him.

Soon they were consumed by screams. There was a corridor of cells and in the first, a man with an erection was being held down as a stem from a broom was shoved into his penis. The silent guard continued his walk unruffled. Even when the penis was forcibly bent breaking the broom stalk into tiny shards and taking the screams to inhuman levels, he did not break a stride. In the second, a man was strapped to a chair and his faded moans showed he had been there too long and had been electrocuted too often. The third cell was dark, empty and tiny. Its doors were not barred like the others but instead were made of smooth slippery metal. A musty smell, like old swamp water and rotten corpses oozed out. The guard turned the keys of a rusty lock and the door swung open. He shone a torchlight into the darkness, revealing a large cavity where the floor should have been. At the opposite edges were narrow ledges large enough for the feet of a little girl. Emeka was told to place his feet on the ledges and the door was slammed shut so hard he almost fell off his precarious stand. He stood with his shaky legs pressed against the wall, he felt faint from fatigue, hunger and the overwhelming smell that was the space. Suddenly he heard a faint sound like a heavy hand moving through water. He looked down in fright; his eyes slowly began to adjust to the rotten light of his cell. The darkness was almost impenetrable and for a long time he remained oppressed by the quiet sounds of the unknown. Finally, he made out the sharp ridges, the coarse scale and the patient teeth of a large alligator. Emeka stood, unknowing, for three days above the jaws of death, not sustained by memories of a past he hoped to once again revisit, but by the conviction that a man goes through travail to become great. But soon even that was not enough and just as his legs began to buckle, the door was opened and he, blinded by light, lost his footing. The silent guard grabbed him just as he was about to slouch to his death; he weighed so little; he was easily dragged out.

Emeka woke to the fair puckered face of his old cellmate. "You don wake!" he exclaimed, "I was starting to think I was wasting all this good food on a corpse," he finished with a harsh laugh; a new laugh that bursts out when you sleep in a bed made of feathers and awake in one of stone. "You are strange, you've been muttering about clocks for two weeks. They must have shown you something in those three days, my god." Emeka looked down at his emaciated body, his mouth felt empty – a metallic spoon protruded from it, but he could no longer taste.

For a month, he stayed in bed, only moving slightly so his muscles would not atrophy. The voices of his cellmates ebbed over his head like a depressive mantle. O.C's came through the most. He was even fairer than Emeka and if it were not for the dents on his face, would have been more handsome. Before they had been arrested – he and his father – in the middle of the night, they had lived as kings. His father had come to power with the Obasanjo military administration.

The hollow, dead laugh would ring out, "I hear that officer gives those boys a whipping every morning, twenty-four strokes and then stuffs them back in that cell."

"Why were we moved?" someone asked, a fearful priest with a sharp squint. When he was not concentrating, his eyes had the unfocused glaze of one whose glasses had been purposely stepped on.

"We're political prisoners," he said with a laugh, "they can't torture us too much, in case, there is another coup tomorrow and we are suddenly somebody again!" he said, flinging his hands casually to mean any of them in the cell. "Quite simply, we have to hate the people that put us in here more than the guards torturing us here, so that if God willing fate reverses some roles, we send them here instead of killing the guards. But that man there is lucky, when they take you into the chambers, they don't intend for you to be anybody ever again!" he responded jerking his head casually at Emeka.

"How do you know all this?"

A smile came upon his face, "They shot my father as soon as we got here," he said calmly, "do you know who I am?" a dead caustic laugh rang out. "He was a greedy man sha. You see there are some people whose hands are so dirty they must forever remain in the dark. My father wanted to see light: he wanted recognition. He was a utility man. He did the things that needed to be done and was well compensated … very well compensated," the laugh rang out again.

Emeka looked at the boy through his fog, he could not have been older than twenty-one. In the empty echo of the boy's laugh, he knew what the boy intended to do when he came out and he began to form a backup plan. For he realised that even though Nneka and her mother had been his life, when he closed his eyes, they were not there.

The priest was permanently nervous, jumping at shadows, seeing nothing. There were three others in the cell; two were normal, or as normal as one could be in place like that – they spoke quietly, ate quickly and slept fitfully.

The last person was a thin man with an angular face who had refused to say a word since they had been there. He had old scars on his body that showed he had been previously acquainted with the same tormentors and one wondered what someone could do to be thrown in this hell twice. In the first month, he was constantly led from the room and returned with fresh scars and tired blood. He barely ate, he hardly slept, yet the guards treated him with deference and almost awe when they were not beating him to the point of death.

When Emeka was finally able to sit up in his bed, there were just four of them left in the cell: the priest, the fair young man, the angular dark man and himself. There was no light from the corridor and they only knew it was day when eight rectangles from a corner of the high back wall fell on the floor like bars of gold. Everyone had settled into their private routines. And Emeka realised faith was the most personal element in the composition of a man. It was during this time he became fluent in three more languages. It was during these eleven years, eleven months and twenty-seven days that Emeka lost religion and found faith.

O.C was never quiet. He did not know how to be; he knew too much about too many things that they spilled out of him. It was difficult to believe most of what he said but impossible not to.

"You know the alligator well you stood over?"

"Yes," Emeka replied weakly, wondering with horror how he survived.

"There's a whole pond at Aso Rock, they just disappear people there ... full of those creatures!" he always spoke like he was telling a fairy tale with appropriate hand gestures and facial expressions, but when he was done his face would be serious, like he had just revealed a personal secret. Five minutes later, his puckered face would have a big gash across the bottom and his teeth would peek out playfully behind cracked lips. His favourite companion was the priest whose large ears were always willing to listen to these tales.

"Let me tell you about my last week before I came here," O.C would begin. The priest had finally been given glasses and his eyes would expand with wonder behind them as O.C told his tales.

"I woke up and took a stash from the dresser."

"What do you mean took a stash?" the priest asked.

"During holidays, like now, there is a dresser in my room and it is covered in bills. About three by four by eight and whatever I spend is filled in by the next morning," he said it with the offhanded arrogance of a boy who still took great pride in wanton extravagance. At this point, everyone was listening, which was his initial plan.

"What?" the priest shrieked and O.C only smiled.

"My dad did the pick-ups from the bank."

"The pick-ups?"

O.C looked at him like he was from another planet.

"Yes, everybody knows the top generals force the Central Bank to print money and send it to their houses. They had a rotational system on who gets what batch."

"Jesus Christ!" the priest said.

"My dear sir, isn't that blasphemy," O.C said with a cheeky smile. "Anyways, for every batch my father picked up, he kept a bag, they use large duffel bags," O.C said matter-of-factly.

"The things these people do to us," the priest said looking around.

"There was a change of regime, recently, as there always is and my father wanted to run for Governor or something. They needed a fall guy, a scapegoat, but mostly he stepped on the toes of a certain godfather, so …" There was no remorse on his features. He looked the way one looked back at an exciting ride at an amusement park: like he was a bit sad it had ended but he knew there were still many more to hop on.

O.C spoke many languages; it was a hobby he had picked up to put fathers at ease so he could take their innocent daughters on dates. He realised Emeka had an ear for it as well and began to teach him. While the priest said his prayers in a dark corner and the other man sat in brooding silence, they would be hunched together repeating phrases and words. They did it initially to entertain themselves, but after a few months, when the priest and the musician (for that was what the silent man was) were gone and it was just the two of them left in a much smaller cell for many years, they did it to protect their sanity.

The musician had his first and only conversation twenty months later, a week before he was released. His repeated tortures were halted. An uneasy calm had settled over their cell. The only thing worse than solitary confinement is the enforced solitude of a crowded cell. The mental erosion of other tortured beings ate at the soul in places its mind could not have imagined on its own.

On that day, it must have been morning, for the oppressive darkness was being quietly chased away by a few strands of grey light. It must have been a Saturday because there was the sound of shuffling as the guards came to work still drunk and heavy limbed. And it must have been between the months of April and July as the cell was freezing from the chilly harmattan winds. Suddenly, the soft voice of a lonely bird escaped into their cell. It was not a happy cry, for the bird was forlorn, but it was the first humane sound they had heard in many weeks. The priest had a misty look and said, "God is great." O.C began to laugh and Emeka softly sang 'Three little birds' – the anthem of perseverance.

"You like Bob?" he asked suddenly. His voice had the falter of an abandoned vocal chord.

"Yes," Emeka said, surprised.

"He's good, he's lucky. There are only three things to sing about: God, Love and Revolution. He has the luxury to sing about all three," he said it sadly, with the heavy air of a man that had chosen a path with no options.

O.C suddenly interrupted, "You mean you don't speak for all these months, you do not talk about your twenty-seven wives, or let us grieve with you for your mother, you don't even entertain us and this is all you say?"

The man looked thoughtfully for a while and finally said, "You cannot think of yourself during a tragedy such as this, because you will be weakened by self-pity, instead you must ponder the plight of others so you can arise with greater strength. Do you know why Nigeria is still the same, no progress, bad governments?" he asked. He never said a word so the whole room was intrigued by his sudden outburst.

"Because we adjust to the situation. Look at all of you talking as if this is normal. Until we hate the situation, until we can't stand it, until we act abnormal in abnormal situations, until we stop 'making do' with each successive government and their worse policies. Nothing will change. Nothing! We must start a movement ... a movement of the people!"

"I don't agree with you," the priest said in a quiet voice.

"Yes," O.C said, "think about others, that's ridiculous." Emeka wondered why he prefaced or followed every statement with a dry chuckle and he decided it was the only way his young mind could bear the miserable realities.

"No, I mean earlier, what you said before," the priest cut in, interrupting the laugh. "God is love and love is revolution. You cannot sing about one without the other."

"Which God? Allah or Jehovah?" O.C asked with a mocking sneer.

"There is no Allah or Jehovah, they are made up by the white man to exploit us!" the musician spat it out with contempt.

"The one that transcends religion," the priest said.

"I don't believe in anything that cannot be proven," O.C said in his pretentious display of wisdom.

"The sole necessitous proof is our ability to equally doubt and believe even in the sneering face of brutal reality," the priest returned quietly.

Emeka did not believe in God sufficiently to blame Him for his misfortune or plead for deliverance. He had approached the Bible as a book of great historical and poetic narrative – nothing more. To him, it was a collection of fascinating stories and stringent moral codes. Long after the conversation had died down and the musician and O.C were asleep, he watched the priest pray quietly at the other end of the cell. A faint, silver light crept through the window, haloing his baldhead. When he was done, Emeka approached him and asked. "So you believe in God ... only one God?"

"I believe He is the way, the truth and the life."

"What if you are wrong? What if Jesus was just a prophet or there are indeed many paths to get to God?" Emeka asked, thinking of his wife who bowed to Allah.

At this, the priest was momentarily silent and then he said, "The Americans believe in Capitalism, the Russians believe in Socialism, both believed only one would work. Only one did, perhaps the other was just applied erroneously. I believe we are called and our path is shown to us. Sometimes we follow, sometimes we don't."

"Predestination?"

"That implies a lack of choice. I believe we are all assigned a path that helps us achieve our fullest potential and all shall be accorded to us if we follow that path. But we can choose to deviate to our own detriment."

"My problem with religions is they all make up these rules that confine you to hell or ensure paradise. How is everyone so sure? Do you believe morality can be subjective?" Emeka asked with a troubled look on his face.

"No," the priest said slowly, "but I believe judgment is personal."

THREE

When Emeka awoke the next morning the Bible that had come with the priest's glasses lay by his head but the priest was gone. Even O.C did not know if he had been released or sent into the chambers. Six days later, the musician was set free and O.C and Emeka were dumped in a smaller, mustier cell that never got any light. The space was too small for O.C's mind. Mostly, he talked incessantly about nothing substantial and those were the hardest times for Emeka. But other times, O.C told him about the intricacies of politics, about godfathers, zoning, contracts and kickbacks – topics that were initially repulsive and boring but O.C's intense interest finally won him over. It was during this time that he really taught him languages and gave him intricate details about the people in power because as he said, "All you see in public is just a huge charade; it's the same faction permanently in power." And he taught Emeka about the cabal.

Everyone knew where they were, but no one knew where they were. Such was the nature of Kirikiri Prison, the political prisoners who disappeared were assumed to be there, but no one really knew for sure. The outside world had no information on them, but the guards liked them and gave them old newspapers so they knew what was happening outside. They knew of the opposition to Babaginda's Structural Adjustment Programme (SAP), they knew of the incessant fuel scarcity, they knew of the permanent crises and their ill thought through solutions. They knew of the elections that were cancelled and rejoiced when that unpopular decision finally led to the end of Babaginda's regime. They read a year after the annulled elections how the winner was arrested for declaring himself president. They knew when Shonekan came into power, but did not know of the billions that disappeared in those brief three months until much later. They knew when Abacha seized office as the prison quickly swelled to bursting capacity and the marching of inmates to the chambers became a regular occurrence. They knew when the unions went on strike and Lagos ground to a halt in protest. There was a riot in the general wing of the prisons and the din went on for a whole day when Frank Kokori and the other labour leaders were alighted from the Black Marias. O.C laughed aloud when the man that got his father and him arrested was also thrown into prison, "The cabal carousal," he said, shaking with laughter. And once again, the country was in an uproar when Ken Saro-Wiwa was killed with the other Ogoni leaders. And when Emeka realised that the world went on because Nigeria had too much oil, he began to pay more attention to O.C's future plans for them.

O.C and Emeka were released on August 1, 1997 because no one remembered why they were there anymore and, more importantly, because there was no more space for them.

The silent guard entered their cell and a mirthless chuckle that only moved his right shoulder slightly was the only indication it was not a normal day. O.C's request to know their destination was ignored. They were blindfolded and felt the air get less heavy as they were led towards the entrance of the prison. They heard the engine start and felt the many potholes on the road as they endured a bumpy ride with no destination. Suddenly, they were tossed on soft earth and their blindfolds harshly yanked off. The sunlight was assaulting, the air was intimidating and the heat was oppressive. But they were all so welcome that O.C screamed in delight. Before they could ask questions, the van drove off in a billow of dust and smoke clouds.

"We must be just outside Lagos," O.C said tiredly.

"How do you know?" Emeka asked fatigued.

"Let's start going," he returned, a determination in his step. But it did not last, their legs were not used to such exertions. Tiredly, half limping, they trudged on as the sun fell, through the night and finally just before the sun came up they saw the sign 'Welcome to Lagos'. O.C tried to whoop in delight but only a dry croak escaped, cracking his tired lips. They approached many okadas asking for a ride to an address O.C produced and were permanently ignored.

Finally, a man agreed for a price that was ten times the regular. Tired and smelling, they clung unto the motorcycle as it weaved through traffic. They turned into a street of high walls and barbed wire that shielded expensive cars and imported houses. "Wait here," O.C said, at the top of the road. He went down the street with renewed hope that almost brought back the confident walk he used over a decade ago. He stopped by a tap protruding from a wall and cleaned himself as best as he could until a cursing guard chased him away. He pressed the bell of a house with black gates. He stood nervously looking up the road. Emeka watched as the gates were opened cautiously and a guard emerged. They conversed for many minutes and the gate was shut. The okada driver who had been muttering beneath his breath was beginning to more loudly voice his displeasure when the gates were thrown open again with another figure – a small woman – standing next to the guard and continuing the inquisition for many more minutes. Suddenly, they heard a loud yell and saw a well-jewelled hand reach out and drag O.C into the compound. They waited for such a long time that Emeka fell asleep only to be woken up to find he was leaning against the driver with O.C's content face beaming at him with a bag over his shoulder. "Aunties are essential," he said, "let's go welcome ourselves to the world, tomorrow we plan." The driver took them to the Eko Hotel and O.C gave the man what he would have made for a day's work. Any hesitation on the part of the hotel clerk to let them in was quickly banished when O.C dropped a small bundle on the counter. They ordered huge meals that they could not eat and took infinite showers and for the first time in many years slept a sleep void of nightmares.

They arose long after the sun had reached its peak and begun its gradual descent. The rumours had made the rounds enough times that the city was already shrouded in black before his brother made the formal announcement on television that Nigeria's greatest musician, Fela Kuti, had indeed died of AIDS.

"Where is the room service?" O.C asked impatiently. The air was heavy like the Earth had stopped rotating on its axis and this agitated him. He had jumped out of bed at three o'clock in the afternoon excited at the prospect of a new life but the air was strangely dead and he could feel it. He took a shower but could not shrug off the feeling and eventually his fretting roused Emeka.

"Where is the room service?" he asked again looking around impatiently.

Emeka had not thought about them in about a decade but a picture of his wife floated before his eyes as he lay in the bed. "What?" he said looking unfocused.

O.C picked up the phone and dialed the desk but no one picked up. Finally, he stormed out of the room. Emeka used the time to reflect on his next move. He was overwhelmed by an urge he had never felt – a longing for the past. He began playing scenes of the reunion in his mind forgetting that everything changes over time.

O.C came back into the room with a stricken look on his face like he had seen a ghost. "Our cellmate is dead … the musician," he continued when he saw the confused look on Emeka's face.

Emeka continued to stare blankly at him and finally said, "I'm going home. I'm going home now."

"No, we have to bury our cellmate, then go see my uncle. Your home is not as you remember and you are definitely not who you were. It is best to leave them in peace than have them go through this trauma. Trust me, I've seen this happen many times." He spoke with the absolute confidence of one who knew he was right and Emeka hated that fact.

Emeka lay in bed and wept, but the vitality of the city and the unbounded hope of the Nigerian spirit seeped through the window to comfort him. Grief knows the seductive song of the sirens and it was exactly what Emeka needed in his present state. He was slightly pacified by the singularity of numerous cries raised for the same cause. They descended the unlit stairs of the hotel and were immediately encircled by a multitude. They marched and cried with a million others but Emeka's grief was private. He mourned the death of his past – the burial of his soul. The mourners carried candles and lanterns and placards of Fela as they thronged through the streets of Lagos. The only pity was that if the corpse in the coffin at the head of the procession were breathing, the revolution that he had called for all his life would have been a reality that night. They were dragged along by the procession whose head and tail they could not find. And then O.C made a careless statement that made Emeka realise he had to go home, he said, "It's a shame there would be no genuine tears at our funerals." And just before Emeka disappeared into the darkness, O.C gave him a stack of bills, an address and a patronising smile because he was sure he would be back.

It was the confidence with which O.C spoke the words that frightened him. Although Emeka erased the faces from his past, he knew that he wanted to be remembered. As he journeyed towards the East, expectation swelled his heart. He remembered the delicate caress of his wife, the soft smile of his daughter and the cool that had always welcomed him to his austere house because of the canopy of palm trees. They were the sorts of memories that always have the same outcome and Emeka could barely sit still with joy. The bus dropped him at the spot it had dropped him a hundred times in the past. Nothing had changed, the bus was still old and rickety, the conductor was still a dirty young man with a mouth full of curses and stale breath and the road was still only lit by the fickle flicker of kerosene lamps sighted through mud windows. Then everything was different, the path was overgrown, the door hung on its side, the farm was overgrown and the animals were gone. The ground was covered in dust, the beds were stripped, the cupboard was empty and his family was missing. And he realised what he should have realised many hours ago – that he was on a fool's errand. He was no longer the same person and it was not just the lies of the mirror – his soul was profoundly buffeted by the hydra-headed assaults of terror past and present. Again, he wept – for the last time, for a past that was no more and for a future forever altered. When he was done, the most extraordinary thing happened – he looked again in the mirror and saw a most ordinary face. In the eyes was no laughter, in the smile no joy, in his mind no hope and in his heart no pain. And since emotions are a summation of our past, we could say he was amnesiac because with his last tear had been lost his ability to feel.

Seventy-two hours after Emeka set off to find his family, he knocked on a door many miles north of where he wanted to be. O.C opened the door like he had only stepped out to buy bread, the brief hug the only giveaway that something more had transpired.

"Just in time for work," he said casually, "I went ahead and told my uncle you would take the job." His face already looked fresher, his smile broader.

Emeka nodded sadly in return. He had known after their fifth year in jail, when they began having conversations strictly in Hausa that this was his probable future but he had hoped – and now no more. He finally noticed the confidence with which O.C strolled across the floors of white marble and asked, "Whose house is this?"

"Mine, well it was my father's, it's mine now. A pre-advance from my uncle you can say, isn't that funny, getting your house back as a gift. I'll take it … I'll take it." Determination was written in his every movement and Emeka knew everything would be just fine. It was not the life he wanted, but it would be a life. Emeka began conversing to distract his mind.

"What exactly are we doing?"

"There we go. That's what I like to hear. First, we'll start with transport, we'll distribute diesel. We'll end up in politics and in between we'll do everything else." His voice was trailing by the end and his eyes were far in the future. He looked at Emeka and let out a short laugh. A laugh to cover the fact he had mistakenly shared his ambitions.

"We would expand rapidly," O.C continued with a smile. "So you have a more discreet," he paused, "important job," he finished carefully. "You will sort out everything behind the scenes for the company."

Emeka understood he would be filling the old role of O.C's father. They both smiled tightly at each other. The implications were obvious, if things went awry; Emeka took the bullet. He did not mind. He did not care.

It was a very lucrative job. Initially, he worked primarily for O.C's uncle – a retired general, who believed that the nation owed him and was rewarded handsomely. So daily, he transported money from the bank, from white executives in quiet bars, from Nigerian politicians in opulent offices, to the general's house, who would allow a lazy smile and say simply, "My dues." Emeka was given a number of suitcases every week. One was his share. A couple he quickly distributed as bribes for the company. The rest he kept in large plastic bags and placed in large freezers in the basement of the general's house. Emeka had come up with that idea six months into the job and that had elevated him to the magical role of special advisor/ personal assistant/ right hand man – depending on the setting. Emeka's quick mind meant he was in high demand and this was how he met a certain man called Muktar.

PART 3

AISHA

I
Upside Down (South Western Nigeria, 2002)

ONE

She was covered in blood and the man with the axe was about to deal another blow. She awoke with a jump – it was the same nightmare: the same memory. The dark, unfamiliar room was not comforting and though she was fifteen, she began to cry. The bed was wet. The family was nice, but she would rather they did not know, she had been there only two days. The girl that had brought her over had left the morning before and she disliked having the room to herself. She quickly took off all the bedclothes and put them in a heap by the carved wooden frame. She struggled with the bulky mattress but finally got it to the balcony of the room and laid it on the banister. She set it down and looked about her.

It was a densely cloudy night, but just at that moment, the moon came out. It was full and its light calmed her. It was one of those big silver moons that induced werewolves in American forests and tales by a communal fire in African villages. There was a huge weeping willow in the garden and she knew she had found her favourite spot. She looked over the high fence that separated their compound from the neighbours. Like in hers, there was a security man dozing next to a large dog. The dogs began howling at the moon and she found this strangely soothing. The guards continued in their slumber. She sat there and listened to the racket, her gaze on a blue bicycle in the next house whose spokes reflected the silver from above.

She stared intently at the bright moon to erase the indelible, expanding red stain that seeped out of her dreams. The howling drowned out the screams and shrieks. Aisha sat there until the clouds again swallowed the moon. Then all the bad memories returned and she stayed on the balcony, crouched and sobbing.

II
Who Are You (Central Northern
Nigeria, Late 1990s – Early 2000s)

ONE

*A*isha was born in the late eighties but in a part of the country less prosperous than the rest. Her father was a man with a silver tongue and an insatiable libido. He was on a grand quest to find the love of his life and in the wake of this he had left behind two fatherless children, two aborted pregnancies and Aisha and her twin. Five discarded lovers.

Muktar – her father – had been born in a polygamous home. One day, while eavesdropping outside his father's door – a strict Muslim, who only had four wives because he could afford to – he heard Mama Ahmed, mother of his best friend, his father's second wife talking in a low voice. She was asking his father to deprive him of an education so her son could go to school in England. His father was protesting, but she was his favourite wife so he succumbed. Muktar hid behind the curtains, tears running down his cheeks. Mama Ahmed came out of the room, a smile on her face and on that of Ahmed, too. He could not believe it: his brother, his best friend was part of the conspiracy. The brother whom he had taught the rivers of Africa (Nile, Niger, Senegal, Congo, Orange and Limpopo, Zambezi) song to pass Geography? He knew he would never trust again. He quickly developed a glib tongue and a steely heart; his best defences against a treacherous world. He vowed he would be successful but never polygamous.

Years later, he had a cousin he already called wife and a soon to be mother-in-law he called mother. The stage was set for a harmonious wedding. It was an arranged marriage, yet the soon to be husband and wife already loved each other. Unfortunately, the devil that jumps into the pants of young men with too much money visited our young groom to be and he found himself fathering *a child with another woman. Muktar was not going to be in a polygamous marriage so he absolutely refused to marry the woman. Shame and dishonour followed. "For a man that would not fulfill his duty is also not fit to marry our daughter," his to-be mother-in-law categorically stated. The young lovers were torn apart.*

Muktar, tormented by the ghost of a foregone love, moved from state to state in the North, seducing young women and fleeing when they got pregnant. A mistake became habit – a mishap a character flaw. The destiny of his father had cast a long shadow over his life – the past became him. The only positives were that with his calculating mind and alluring personality, he set up a string of necessary contacts and sound businesses – accumulating vast wealth and dubious prestige across the region.

Three ruined young women later, Muktar found himself in the bed of a young firebrand. A Marxist feminist Pan-Africanist, with fire in her eyes, wisdom in her head and magic in her loins. Yes, fate had been kind enough to give him a second chance. But she refused to convert to Islam. He could not understand it; it was the religion of her family, of her lover, of her ancestors. But with her coy smile and seductive wink, he would find himself naked and spent but the argument unresolved.

She went by the label of Christian even though she was anything but. On a cold harmattan morning with a pale sun, Muktar agreed to marry her in a church. In the magic of the ceremony, she found herself somehow drawn to the cross and started attending Sunday services. Fighting the malaise of being tied down, Muktar allowed himself to be dragged along. They were happy years. They were young, in love and wealthy. They had a lovely white house with prominent flowerbeds that were maintained through the year despite the droughts that often desiccated the region. He even taught her to drive in that first year, fighting during each session and making up happily later. Then she got pregnant.

Muktar was ecstatic but much as the wedding had lit her religious spark, the pregnancy did the same for him. Muktar began to attend prayers on Friday. Then he stopped going to church on Sundays. And though he could not coerce her to the mosque with him, he forbade her from attending church services. Then cracks began to appear in their marriage because though love is everything, it is not enough. The nine months were up and a pair of beautiful twin girls arrived.

Seven years of frayed harmony followed, but one day, the family drove up to the house and there was a woman with an eleven-year-old boy that looked unmistakably like Muktar. It was then she found out for the first time that her daughters were his third and fourth children. Muktar was a shrewd man but he was not wise. He knew if he simply sent the first woman away, he would lose his wife too, so he stupidly invited them to stay with him in adjacent rooms.

Slowly, the curse of the polygamous life he had so haughtily shunned was stoutly planted. The new woman shared the kitchen and Muktar. The wives, rivals, cooked on alternate nights and he shared their rooms with them in turns. However, the new inhabitant was a bitter woman whose cantankerous spirit snuffed out the atmosphere of joy. On days she was not to have Muktar, she would wear her best clothes and do herself up in the way he most liked. She would sit demurely on a cushion by his chair while the other wife, Mama Aisha, worked in the kitchen. With seductive winks and suggestive hips, she would go about pampering Muktar and his brooding ego.

Fifteen months into this unhappy arrangement, Mama Aisha cooked and Muktar slept with the wrong wife. The next morning when he awoke, Mama Aisha was gone with her twin daughters.

Initially he was almost relieved, but the mere thought of being jilted could not be accommodated by his proud soul. He could not condone such a slight. His mouth adopted an initial sneer as he hunted them in his quietly obsessive way. But it was not for them; it was a self-obsession that could not stand being shunned. The same obsession that gave him a pensive silence; made him visit the barber every week; meant he dry-cleaned all his clothes (even his underwear); inspired a house covered in reflective surfaces. The type of obsession that ensured that he always knew what was happening on the streets and in the seats of power. An obsession that meant he could never truly love anyone because they were never half as important as he was. It was this insatiate obsession that invited a sadistic and triumphant smile on his full pink lips when he finally discovered they were living quietly in Jos.

It had not been too difficult finding them. His wife was compulsively enticed by the good life and he knew her epicurean bent of mind would draw her inexorably to one of the larger cities where she could get a well paying job. His first instinct had been to check in Abuja but none of his contacts had heard of or seen a tall, slender, dark woman with an unmistakable mole on her left cheek and an unbridled tongue. After several other cities, he was beginning to believe she had headed south and was about to give up. But, a stroke of fortune pointed him to Jos, where there was a new teacher at the Hillcrest school who fit the description and had twin daughters. It was actually Halima's uncanny likeness to her father that gave them away. She had the same honey eyes and voice, the same refined nose and fair skin, the same delicate fingers and small ears, the same thick crimson lips. He still had his boys blundering around Kaduna when the call came in. Muktar smiled to himself: it was time to return home.

He stayed seated in a dark corner of the well-hidden bar. His eyes were his sole visible feature and could belong to anyone – they were spectacularly normal. The overeager driver, one of the men he paid to eavesdrop on their bosses, walked in and sat down nervously opposite him, disconcerted by the dispassionate eyes.

"Nagode sir," he said hurriedly.

"You have news?" it emerged in a soft neutral voice from the endless darkness that was the rest of him. He failed to acknowledge the greeting.

"Yes, sir, I tink I pind them, sir," Mutu said mixing up his fs and ps and dropping some hs and ws.

"Where?"

"You see, sir," he began, trying to emphasise his competence, "at the school where my master's son goes, he says there are tu new girls, twins sir, walahi tallai, he says one of them is so beautiful he tinks he is in love, the way he describes her sir, she is the one you pind!"

An invisible smile briefly played beneath the turban that covered his face. "Good work," he said curtly. He got up and left, leaving an envelope lying nonchalantly on the table.

He made the call to Muktar and simply said 'Jos'. Two days later, as they sat in the cold comfort of the car observing the woman and children from a distance, he knew Muktar was going to make a mistake. But it was not his job to advice, he simply executed. Muktar briefly glanced at Halima, a young, female version of himself, he almost let a proud smile slip, but he had to banish such limiting sentiments as he intended a fitting payback for his humiliation. His wife walked with purpose in her stride, the bounce that had made him fall in love with her – eliciting lust and hate. But it was Aisha that captured his steely gaze, he looked at her with contempt, she had all the qualities and features of her mother but in her young teenage body, they seemed disjointed and unattractive. He imagined her mother must have looked just like that as a child and was irritated that someone that had once looked so unattractive would have the audacity to leave him. She held her mother's hand and her quiet, generous, bookish nature was almost evident in the way she gently placed her feet, as if unwilling to hurt the ground. Her dark skin shone like an ill-fitting suit and her thin lips seemed inadequate for the large nose that hovered above them. Her features lacked the finesse that made her mother beautiful and Muktar was disgusted he was the father of such an ugly child.

"You know what to do," Muktar said.

"Yes," he replied in the same neutral voice.

TWO

Tat-tat-tat was the sound of the rain on the metal roof. There was a slight drizzle and most of the passengers were asleep. The girl seated next to him was plain, but not many people usually sat by him voluntarily – he had one of those too eager faces that made people stay away. The bus rumbled slowly over the pitted road. It had to swerve occasionally to avoid potholes and mounds of burning tyre. They drove by a graveyard of torched cars and scorched houses. The bus came to a crawl to navigate some obstructions. The head-tie in front of him flew forward and he heard something splash on the rusty floor. A faint acrid smell wafted up – she was throwing up. Then the thick pungent smells lurking around the bus squeezed their way in through the sealed windows and a number of people fainted. A woman screamed and others began to wail. To their right lay the burnt remains of a woman and her daughter. Her blackened skin had slid off in some places exposing pale flesh. Her innards had spilled out engulfing her child like a pink, protective blanket. He turned away and switched off his mind. The rest of the journey he sat staring at the Bible in his hand, unable to read a word.

The girl next to him was crying softly. She had been doing so for a while now. He wanted to comfort her but his soul was desiccated. It's okay, was all he could think to say but it was so sadly inadequate. He continued to nonchalantly run his finger over the cross engraved on the Bible. "Why?" she finally choked out. "It's okay," he replied. The rest of the trip her head leaned against his shoulder, shaking it gently with her sobs, wetting it lightly with her tears.

She was a Corper, just like he was. She had been sent from Enugu to serve here in Jos. At a time when Ibos were emigrating the city en masse, it was an unfathomable decision. "I'm from Lagos," he said. Her name was Nneka and she was an only child.

Nneka wanted to be posted to Lagos. She had tried everything except the right thing – she had refused to pay a bribe. So, she ended up in Jos: the cauldron of ethnic tension, to serve her country.

"I'm Daniel," he said, "where do you work?"

"I did political science at the University in Nsukka, I will be working at the Senator's office."

"So you are the ones that will be stealing our money soon," he said, finally eliciting a faint smile from her.

"I was going to do business administration, but something happened that changed my mind," she said with a faraway look.

"I wanted to be born David but I had no say in the matter," he returned and she emitted a light laugh that quickly floated away over the heavy air. Then he continued in his eager way, "He is my favourite biblical character. Yes Daniel was brave, sitting in the lion's den but David killed a lion, then a bear, then a giant, then thousands of men. That is the legacy I want," he finished.

She found him amusing, so they became friends and met often for lunch.

She always showed up with a frown on her brow and left with a laugh. "My boss is a sexist, tribalist, religious bigot who thinks little of women," she said the first day.

"So he is a real man," Daniel joked, "Chai, you should see my class, some of those boys are old enough to be my father and they are still in secondary school."

"Are there any girls?" she asked, "The ones in my office are quiet and they are not given any responsibility. It is better in some other departments but my boss, with his golden tooth, just laughs when you ask him for work as if it is a big joke. The annoying part is that he always walks around with a Koran as if that justifies everything, but I know that is not true because my mother is a Muslim," she finished.

"The plot thickens," he said with mock exaggeration, "Let me guess, your father was a Buddhist."

"Actually not too far from the truth," she said with a cautious laugh, but lunch was over and they parted.

Over the weeks at unfamiliar lunches of tuwo shinkafa with miyan taushe washed down with fura denunu and kunu drinks that slowly won them over to the Northern culture, they shared her story. Initially, in his eager way, he was anxious to tell her his stories, but he quickly realised he much preferred her strangely accented voice telling tales from her unique childhood. However, she was often reluctant to begin talking and the same story sat on the tip of his tongue anxious to be told.

"It was not the first time I had seen a burnt body," he was going to say. "When I was a child, I lived on the outskirts of Lagos. Electricity was a rarity and water came from wells. The police were woefully undertrained, unprepared, understaffed and unequipped. Robbery was the profession of choice for young graduates. Then during the military regime the Governor decided to tackle crime. They pushed the robbers out of Lagos and towards the area where we lived. There were so many thieves. Finally, the neighbourhood got tired. At night, the men came together. They made a fire and told tales of better times. Their crude weapons — rusty machetes and ancient guns — sat at their sides. Anyone caught stealing was lynched — jungle justice. One day, the men retired to their homes at dawn, the usual time. Then the bread seller caught a robber. She woke up as her husband stumbled in to snatch a couple of hours of sleep before the creaking assembly line of Nigerian Breweries demanded his fatigued attention. There was a tinkering at the back door. She yanked the door open suddenly and smashed the man's face with the heavy pestle she used to pound yam. She sent her ten-year-old son to go and wake up the neighbours. They came with sticks and belts. A couple of hours later, I was on my way to buy eggs for breakfast. I was even younger than her son. I saw it, in front of her store, he pleaded from a mouth disfigured from hours of abuse. I got there in time for the finale. A petrol filled tyre was thrown over him and set ablaze. Years of suffering, sleepless nights, hours of fruitless toil made the now passive crowd immune to his screams. Eventually people started to drift away — to prepare for work, to conclude their interrupted sleep. I stood transfixed until my aunt came searching for me. As we walked into the house, it began to drizzle. I wondered if God always sent the rain to douse his burnt children. Here's a question: do you go straight to hell if you are burnt to death?"

The incident began to replay often in his mind, the flames reignited by the tragic scenery of his bus trip. But never did the cannibalistic fires invade his dreams. He thought to tell her this but he imagined it would induce nightmares.

THREE

Nneka was unsettled by the passive nature of the man in front of her. He seemed very agreeable, yet he sent a silent chill down her spine. He was here to see Alhaji, he had said in a calm voice that was eerily disturbing. It was only after Alhaji had surprisingly agreed to see him without an appointment and he had walked into the office that she realised what the problem was. His features were too normal – the only parts of him she remembered were his brown skin, his brown eyes and his quiet voice. The delicate melody of Hausa gently flowed out before they shut the door. He came out soon afterwards, politely and quietly, she did not get a chance for a second look.

His first mission was accomplished. Alhaji had been too easy to convince, he felt a slight contempt for the ease with which Alhaji accepted the proposal to keep himself in power. He resented the way Alhaji's hand strayed too often towards the Koran by his side as he was sure Alhaji did not understand it, otherwise he would not have agreed so easily. He hurried to the mosque to get there before the prayers. He slipped into the Cleric's office, silently studying the room in a cool dark corner. It took the Cleric a few minutes to notice the shadow, but he was untroubled by the brooding presence. He sat at his desk like he was alone.

"The Alhaji will summon you tonight, but I have made provisions. A man will come in tomorrow during the five o'clock prayers, he will be the answer to our prayers," he paused wondering if he should add more. He liked the Cleric; he did not ask too many questions, he understood the way things went.

Muktar walked into the mosque with a solemn, crackling grace. His white danshiki glowed with an ethereal aura and his unusual honey eyes were cryptic. He took his place quietly in a corner yet everyone noticed him. His presence shouted across the mosque as his lips quietly mouthed the prayers. The Cleric noticed him as well and realised he was the answer.

Afterwards, as he wore his sandals, unperturbed by the swarming bodies around him, a little boy tugged at his tunic. He looked down with his matchless grace, his still gaze causing the sweat soaked boy to stammer incoherently. But Muktar was patient and the boy finally stuttered out that the Cleric would like to see him. He smiled gently and gave the boy a new five-naira note. The smiling boy skipped away and Muktar reentered the mosque. With brisk crisp strides, he crossed the prayer room and knocked gently on the door. He entered without waiting for an answer.

The Cleric was just seeing someone out of the back entrance and as soon as he turned around, Muktar thrust his hand forward with the confidence of a man accustomed to being the most important person in a room. And what a handshake. It was not particularly firm, neither could it be described as lax. It simply was a perfect handshake. It seems trivial, almost, but shaking his hand made you understand why businessmen and politicians practiced that everyday transaction so assiduously. It did not matter how large or small your hands were, his hands would perfectly envelope yours and for the brief seconds it lasted you felt your poise melt through his fingers. He seemed to literally hold the balance of [your] life in his hands. He accompanied this with a steady gaze. It was a look of melted honey for women and hardened lava for men. It made women blush behind their burqas and caused men to heat up beneath their collars.

The Cleric managed a weak smile through browned teeth, placed a lobe of kola nut in his mouth and asked him to sit. There was a large barred window to the left of the door letting in a few strands of sunlight to bath the Cleric's capped head. He folded and unfolded his hands trying to regain his composure. He was surprised and pleased at the effect of the tall man opposite him. Yes, he was perfect for the job at hand. The Cleric had his own strengths. He could persuade a pencil to do a headstand. In his gentle voice like a placid wave un-anchoring a titanic ship, he could get a multitude to do what he wanted. He disliked talking to large crowds except to lead them in prayer, which was why the man in front of him was so useful.

The Cleric was never assertive. He had a few people around him whom he convinced to do his wishes. Except when praying, he seemed permanently nervous. Then a strange serenity would descend like a holy mist on his eyes and the microphone would amplify his soothing voice to the mass of believers. Afterwards, his hands would begin to rub incessantly against each other and his shoulders would hunch to shield him from the world.

Muktar settled casually in the print covered foam seat held by entwined rafter. He crossed his long legs and rested his slender fingers peacefully on his flat stomach. He always kept his hands in close proximity to his being as if to protect the magic of their contact. He also smiled; warm, reserved, disarming.

"Mallam …" the Cleric began.

"Muktar," the gentleman finished.

"Mallam Muktar, welcome to Jos," he said, not noticing Muktar's jaw tense slightly. "Inevitably you noticed the cemetery of saints and habitation of infidels. I am of course referring to the indigenes, the filthy Christians who have killed our dear brothers, may their souls rest in peace. They have turned our homes to cemeteries and have harassed our children. We must retaliate. We must have two souls for every one they have taken." The Cleric spoke in a tranquil manner, not a hint of the anger that bubbled beneath spilled through his lips. He spoke in concise verses not lengthy poems. Muktar remained still. The Cleric continued.

"I have noticed your charm, we want you. Will you do the bidding of Allah?"

His heart did a quick jump. His plan had worked flawlessly. He had made himself alluring, inaccessible, he had made sure his plan and name had been kept from the wrong ears. His brother was still predictable, he thought with a wry smile. He stroked his neatly kept black beard with its flakes of white like snow on a dark night. He patted an imaginary lump in his matching hair and settled again to his restive pose. Then he let his deep voice rumble forth like a steam train suddenly warmed to life. "Of course," he said simply and decisively.

The Cleric looked at his wrist-watch, he was five minutes behind schedule. He got it for his last job — his benefactor revealing a golden tooth as he smiled with the gift in one hand and the Koran in the other. Even on Saturdays when he spent his days drinking, Alhaji was punctual to the second. The gift had not been gratuitous. The Cleric hastened to the part of town with the noble trees and serene houses.

As always, Alhaji's compound was not quiet. There was the necessary array of goodwill seekers, sycophants, beggars, well-wishers and general mish mash of the jobless waiting for the daily meal Alhaji kindly distributed in his infinite benevolence. Unlike some of his colleagues, Alhaji had not been plucked out of obsequious obscurity, which meant he owed no allegiance to anyone. More than most, he enjoyed being the epicentre of owed favours. He promoted blatantly inept fellows who hung on to their jobs by Alhaji's munificence. They rampantly looted the coffers of the state because they never knew when they would be forced to vacate their unmerited seats. Alhaji's sole older brother had followed his father to the grave ten years earlier, making him the family patriarch. He gave out his sisters as first wives and daughters as second and third and was an in-law to everybody in the north that really mattered.

He studied Finance and Management at a university in the United Kingdom and sneered with undisguised contempt at the ignorance of the Nigerian-trained literature majors who wrote in the newspapers about corruption in the arms of government. Yes, unmerited oil blocks were handed out, undue contracts were awarded, exorbitant conferences were planned and meaningless government sponsored trips were held. But, in return, large amounts were deposited in Alhaji's account and that was sound business in his view. When he was told that the assets belonged to the state and, therefore, its people, he countered rightly that he demanded no taxes. With his wide smile and his twinkling tooth, he would point to his expansive yard and the hopeless masses sprawled beneath kind trees in the harsh sun that swarmed there for the scraps he was always glad to hand out.

But no one was really interested in this crowd, least of all Alhaji; it was the one in the air-conditioned room with the gold floor that really mattered. They sat there wearing their exquisite European watches that lasted several generations, Swiss made materials spun in the latest Nigerian design, custom made Italian shoes of quiet patterns and fat wallets hidden in folds of expensive fabric. The furniture was soft, the floor was polished wood shined to perfection, the glasses were out of the best designer shops, the conversation was expensive. Not a trace of sweat, the room smelled like a masculine orchid, the smiles were wide and the laughs were long. They talked in the quiet tones of the rich; they talked of amounts so large they barely crawled out of their fat mouths. They were all friends and their wives were all sisters.

It was through that crowd and this room that the Cleric would hurry through in a few minutes. They would all pay their respects to the man of God and he would bless them and expressly go in to see Alhaji.

Alhaji Ahmed had a false smile. A genuinely false smile. He had acquired many titles but he liked Alhaji the most. Perhaps because, unlike the others, it was not purchased. He also liked when he was called 'Honourable'. Honourable Senator Abdul Rahman Ahmed Abubakar. That was it in full and he relished the sound of it. "A name should be protected at all costs," he reasoned with his wife. Especially if it only cost the lives of a few infidels.

Alhaji was necessarily handsome, as one gets from continuous generations of the richest men marrying the most beautiful women. His wife was a small ambitious woman whose sole joy was to outdo her prominent sisters. They were born wealthy and married well but now they had to keep up appearances. He had three wives but only Miriam was officially acknowledged. She made sure of that and he did not mind. He had married the others because he was supposed to. And because Miriam bore only girls. He loved his girls, they were his princesses, but he wanted a son. Miriam knew the other wives were no threat so she treated them like little sisters. She was more concerned about his friends' wives.

"That Cleric is never on time," she said disdainfully. Just then, the bell rang and she disappeared to the family rooms.

The Cleric entered in his usual servile manner. His head was slightly bowed as if about to receive a blessing. He rubbed his hands together. He smiled too widely, nodding his head before anything was said. He sat on the cream coloured couch, tastefully done with an ornately carved frame of imported mahogany. A man came in with a saucer of groundnuts, a beer for Alhaji and a glass of ginger juice for the Cleric who had never tasted alcohol. The rug was of indigo decorated cowhide. It gave off a faint smell of manure that melted into the thousand other odours that was the room. The sun was fearsome outside but only fell softly into the room through tall, barred windows. A glass pyramid stood at the centre of the living room's roof and white light fell through it and scattered from the suspended chandelier in a hallowed dance.

"They retaliated as predicted," the Cleric said, a hasty spark in his endlessly black eyes as he extracted a lobe of kola nut from a pocket in his danshiki and placed it in his mouth. Alhaji was a shrewd politician. Although they disliked each other, he knew to be a successful politician in the North, one had to be a good Muslim, so he became a knowledgeable one.

The Cleric had heard all this before, but Alhaji explained again carefully. "Unless we take care of these infidels, we would never have real power," he spoke in a slow deliberate voice. Everything he said was always carefully weighed and calculated. First in his mind, then with his wife and then he refined it again. His words always came out smooth and sweet – very intoxicating. It was why he was the only Muslim representative for his state. He wanted that to change, as did the Cleric, so they helped each other.

"This time you must send out a strong message, burn down the churches, kill everyone inside, let the whole nation, the whole world know of this injustice," Alhaji emphasised.

"I know just the man. He is a prophet of fire. He can rally a crowd to destructive frenzy in a matter of minutes. His name is Muktar Abubakar," the Cleric concluded.

"Do you know him?" the Cleric asked noticing a faint cloud cross over Alhaji's placid brow. Alhaji shook his head unable to speak. "Perhaps one of these days you will meet him," the Cleric said, "I have to leave for prayers."

"Assalamu alaikum," Alhaji said.

"Assalamu alaikum wa rahmatullahi wa barakatuh," the Cleric returned as he rose.

FOUR

"So tell me about this Buddhist father. Did he meditate?" Daniel asked a few minutes into the next lunch.

"No, he used to protest. That's why they carried him away," she said with the sad, proud air that was reserved for unheralded personal heroes. "He was taken so long ago," she mused. "Then we still lived in this strange house that was far away from everywhere. It really was such a strange house, but I still remember it. We had our own little farm, some animals; there was my parent's room and mine, which was also the living room. I thought people only existed on television for a long time, we just hung out together and they taught me everything in the first years."

"Home schooled? You're joking!" Daniel interrupted, staring at her like she must be some sort of alien. "And nobody just hangs out with their parents," he finished.

She laughed loudly, as if it had been bottled up with withheld memories that had finally escaped. "You're looking at me the way people used to when I first started going to school, so I stopped telling them about my past, should I stop telling you?" she teased.

He laughed and she suddenly assumed a serious air as she continued. "Of course, my father had been taken by then and we had moved back ... among people I mean. It's strange, I only remember he had a limp, he used to go to the town and return with sweets. He smelled like mints. My mother gave me all my features, but I guess with the way she always talks about him, he's preserved as well." The last sentence came out like she wished he were still preserved better in her memories.

"When did he die?" Daniel asked

She looked at him sharply and he wished he had not asked so carelessly. "I don't know," she finally said in a voice that was too measured. "One day he went to town and never returned."

Luckily, lunch was again over and it helped assuage the stifling air that had descended like the black shawls hanging on the women that walked outside the window. They talked about everything but their history for the rest of that week. She constantly amazed him with the amount of knowledge she harboured but he only could guess the source and was far too afraid to confirm lest she shut him out.

The chill of the harmattan had been setting in and they both wore snug sweaters. Daniel arrived late at their usual spot with a letter in his hand. She watched him cross the street, avoiding one of the okadas that women were banned from using and waved to the toothless mallam who sold numerous knick-knacks in a shack with the giveaway red and white of Coca-Cola. He said a few words in what she assumed was faulty Hausa and realised with a melancholic smile that she would miss this place. He placed a scrunched up note in the bowls of one of the Almajiri and watched the bright smile shine from the grateful face. The necessary benevolence of Muslims meant the young boys should never go hungry, but it still upset her to see children as young as six roaming the streets begging. She fled from her musings to the face that sat opposite her.

"Love letters from your numerous fans?" she asked teasingly in a tone that betrayed too much interest.

"No," he said too hastily, "It's from my mum."

"Oh and how is Lagos? Actually you've never told me about your family," she continued without giving him a chance to respond.

"Well, there is my mum and my sister, my twin sister, our father is dead – he had a heart attack about three years ago."

"I'm sorry," she said

"Don't be, he was a nice enough man when he was alive, but when he died we realised he was a bastard."

Nneka shifted uncomfortably in her seat, unsure of how to react to the comment.

"Well, I guess he was at least a bit decent about it," Daniel said pensively. "We never knew the whole time, but at his funeral, we were all around the casket. I was trying to comfort my mother and sister when this young woman, probably our age now, came in sobbing too loudly. By the end of the day, we had three more like that. Two had children that were the spitting image of my father. He was one of those men whose children were unmistakably his." Daniel said it all with an air bordering on disbelief; the way you told a story that you wished was someone else's. "How was your day at the office?" he asked eager to change the subject.

"You won't believe it," she said, quickly grasping at the chance to ease the discomfort. "My boss relocated me to the desk outside his office."

"I thought you said he was sexist and tribalist?"

"Exactly, it is strange, he always seemed to be so proud of his perfect English accent, now he speaks only Hausa behind closed doors. I think he put me there because I cannot understand. I don't trust that man, I think he is planning something bad," she finished in a quiet voice.

FIVE

Emeka wished it were not so. The voice of the girl in Alhaji's office had yanked him forcefully to a past long relegated to the back corners of his memory's safe. For the first time since he assumed his role behind the corridors of power, his conscience pricked him. He thought about Muktar's daughters and remembered his Nneka had been that age the last time he had seen her. The span of time, her state of origin, everything added up and with a little digging he was assured that the Nneka before him was the same with whom an earlier reunion had been abortive. He decided to break his rule and give advice.

By their next meeting, Muktar's voice was already recognisable to most of the youth of the city. It was obvious he was enjoying his return to his home state; he liked the reverence that was paid him in the streets. Emeka knew he was blinded by the euphoria of his prominence and this would be the best time to manipulate his bulging ego.

Emeka sat in a car in the quiet dusk patiently awaiting Muktar's return. The flashy Mercedes pulled up to the gate and on seeing his car, Muktar got out and sat in the passenger seat of Emeka's Toyota Camry.

"You have done well," Muktar said, "but I am not to pay you the rest until next week."

Emeka let out a hidden smile. "I am not here for that. I don't trust your brother."

Muktar was startled. How do you know? He was about to ask, but stopped and smiled instead, "I see you're very thorough."

Emeka knew that would draw him into his confidence. "You should meet him," he said. Seeing the brief flash of anger that crossed his eyes, he continued, "it is for your insurance. You must tape him."

At this, he saw Muktar lean forward a little and it was obvious he had been waiting for an opportunity to revenge.

"You will record your conversation with him and then you will threaten to blackmail him later in the future. He runs his campaign on tolerance, so if you have a recording linking him to these events, you're insured," Emeka said it easily. It was not the real point of the conversation; he was out to protect another.

Emeka saw Muktar smile. He knew what he was thinking. He was going to record Alhaji then force him to resign. Muktar was then going to use his new popularity to run for the exact same office. It was a perfect retribution and it was exactly how Emeka knew Muktar would think. Muktar could barely contain his excitement when he tried to suppress a smile and said, "And on what pretext will I meet him."

"Oh tell him you wanted to bury the hatchet, placate him even though he was wrong. There is an Igbo, Christian girl in his office, tell him you wanted to advice him. Tell him to make sure she is safe, so he can claim tolerance and innocence at the end of all this." He said the last part as casually as possible, hoping Muktar would not suspect anything. But he need not have worried; Muktar's mind was already planning the overthrow of Alhaji Ahmed, his brother.

III
Fight to Finish (Central Northern Nigeria, 2001 – 2002)

ONE

In the Riyom Local Council of Plateau State stands the state's police headquarters. An army truck roars to an impatient stop in front of it, spurring chickens into uncoordinated flight. A cloud of red dust billows out in welcome and shiny black boots grind it back to the ground. There is a skeptical smile on the face of the police sergeant, they are not friends and they are rarely allies. The soldiers parade themselves with alert eyes that see nothing; many hold cameras instead of guns. They take pictures and film themselves by the mosque that will later be pulled down in front of disinterested policemen. One of them sits on a window frame of decayed wood from which a tailor will later escape while his older brother is hacked to death. They take pictures by the gutter in which fifty children will be laid, doused in kerosene and set ablaze. But none of that is happening now, so their cameras snap disinterested pictures and their trucks keep rolling from village to village documenting the fallacy of their protective presence.

The hot afternoon fades into a quiet evening with still air. The insects do not bother to flap their wings; they float lazily on heavy currents. The birds are too tired to sing in the sweating trees. The drowsy pigs lie in the mud, they cannot waddle. The panting dogs crouch in fatigued shades. Only one animal is restless and his state is contagious. It is an evening for vengeance.

As dusk approaches, here comes Muktar, the one who can set the mind ablaze in minutes with his silver tongue. Muktar, the prophet of fire who can rally a crowd to destructive frenzy in a matter of minutes. Muktar, who has a bone to pick with a woman that follows the other religion. There he goes, leading them towards a church, hate in his heart, revenge on his mind, machete in his hand. The mob surges forward led on through deception, their ignorance fuelled by poverty, like a destructive wave on the fragile shore.

TWO

Daniel greatly enjoyed attending service. He liked the solemn sermons, the enchanted worship sessions and the fellowship of other congregation members. He was an usher so he knew much of the congregation. Standing by the door, he always had a broad smile and a firm handshake for everyone. There was a woman with twin daughters who initially grasped his hand indifferently and barely returned his smile. But when she heard he was a Corper, she brought him food unfailingly. He always looked forward to that. Jollof rice with fried plantain, mounds of meat in palm oil fried stew. Sometimes she made him zobo or kunu drinks.

She took to enquiring about his family and during the first church picnic, when the weather turned warm again and the harmattan winds stopped blowing invasive sand, she had made him sit with her daughters and her under one of the countless acacia trees.

"Thank you, ma," he had said and she had waved it away with the demure grace northern women possessed.

"Why did you come up north?" she asked casually.

"It's a wonderful place, Hajia," he said.

She had smiled, "I'm sure you didn't think so before you were sent. It is a wonderful place but it can be a harsh place. It is like a woman. It is very forgiving of many things, but some things ..." she trailed off into a sad smile. "I have crossed one of their boundaries, I feel bad for the girls sometimes, they don't have friends outside the church, but I can't move them anymore ... Besides, I love it here too much, we are used to each other." The smile that somehow seemed to curve downwards returned.

He did not know what to say, he was about to say his meaningless 'I'm sorry, ma', when she said, "Nowadays, it seems your mere presence might be classified as unforgivable." He knew it was an abstract sentence but he felt a slight chill, as he was Igbo and he was Christian, people with only one of those flaws were being killed.

Tensions had been brewing in the city like dark ominous clouds. It hung thick and heavy covering the inhabitants in a shroud of suspicion. Over the six months he had been there, there had been small attacks, but something big was about to happen and everyone knew it. The Cleric now had a voice. The voice was a charismatic man with hooked brows and fiery eyes who found it easy to sway the minds of impecunious youth. Their minds fogged up by chemicals sniffed from decomposing gutters were like putty in his hands.

That day, his lunch with Nneka had not been filled with the usual teasing banter. It had been getting more serious over the past month and there had been talk of the Corpers being sent home.

It had started when Nneka had nervously said, "Alhaji moved me into one of the quarters of his house, he says it is for my own good."

"He probably wants to make you his fourth wife," Daniel had tried to say lightheartedly, but he was nervous. The city was nervous. "Living the good life now," he added too casually.

"His place has this ridiculous glass pyramid at the top, he thinks he is an Egyptian," she said and they laughed. "But I live in the back in these quarters that are practically cells, sometimes I think I am completely expendable to him and it is also the way he looks at me, it's like I am there to help him prove something, but he would rather he did not need me," she added thoughtfully.

They spent the rest of the evening talking about home as if by merely doing so, it would ensure they made it back there.

The rain had fallen earlier that evening. It made everything beautiful. The ground was washed clean and the sky looked like fresh laundry. An aroma of flowers hung sweetly in the air. The crickets and frogs complemented the sounds that softly escaped from the church windows. On his way home from teaching, he had seen trucks of soldiers walking around with cameras, ostentatiously taking pictures of themselves next to landmarks. As he made his way to the evening service, they were gone.

Distant sounds floated softly over the buoyant air. But the sounds were hard and harsh – the words were screams and their meanings were hate. The sounds approached gently, gradually swelling like a black cloud before an angry storm. Daniel stood by the last row of chairs wrapped in holy worship as a warm blanket on the chilly night. He felt a tap on his shoulder and turned to eyes wide with fear and apprehension.

Something happened to Daniel. He knew at once what the matter was. Somehow, the serenity of the worship still flowed through him. It was the chance to change his name. He instructed the fearful eyes to lock and bolt the door and marched swiftly but confidently to the front of the church. He picked up the red microphone that was usually reserved for the preacher and signaled the choir to wind down the song. Then he gave his own speech. One that echoed that of Muktar and made the men imagine they had sanctified fires ablaze in their bellies. Ever since he saw his first burning human at the age of eight, Daniel had had many dreams. This was one of them. He ordered the women and children to stand in the centre of the church singing and praying. Then the fiery words flowed from his mouth and when the rioters got to the doors, everything was in place.

He had all the doors locked and stacked tables and chairs to reinforce them. He had the speakers suspended from the ceiling with the thick microphone wires. He positioned this by the slender side doors and piled tables on the side to form a narrow passage. He was surprised at the alacrity at which he exercised his authority and the speed his commands were obeyed. Lambs without a shepherd, he mused. Today I am David.

First came the yells and shouts hitting the building like the impatient drizzle that forebodes a storm. Then the doors began to rattle and shake. The invaders soon found the side door purposely left unlocked and heavy swinging speakers met the first two that burst in, machete in hand. The first drops of blood fell on the hallowed ground. Broken faces, filled with hate, surprised by the sudden turn, the sharp blades of death were rendered powerless in those brief muted seconds by the door. Then a wave of the messengers of hate poured in, sweeping down the narrow passage and trampling their fallen comrades to death. The speakers kept busy, swinging and smashing. Chairs, tables, microphone stands, potted plants; all were utilised to dam the murderous tide. It was obvious the raiders had expected no opposition and the feeble defense surprisingly held – initially. After the first euphoric minutes, Daniel began to realise quickly that the frail fort would not hold for long. He was pulsing with hungry blood and angry adrenaline. He grabbed one of the fallen machetes and began hacking away. The floor was soon slick and sticky from layers of trampled blood. The church was on fire. Daniel was cut and bleeding. His hands were tired from slashing, yet they continued to swing mechanically. The resistance at the church was the spark for the volatile ethnic and religious pressures. Reinforcement gushed in for both sides and the community drowned in its own blood. Daniel realised he would never see Lagos again. His family, his dreams, his hopes were … because he was to be … no more. He imagined himself an avenging angel and he fought for the army of the Lord.

He cut, he fought, he sliced, he brawled, he bled, he screamed; he lived. He realised he had cut his way to the small field behind the church. He had sliced his way out of the battle. He decided to rest a while. He was covered in blood but was too full of adrenaline to know to whom it belonged. He felt faint; perhaps it was his. He was drifting into a fatigued repose when he heard the high voice of a woman in distress. He forced himself to move and slowly made his way towards the sound. He rounded the cluster of tall trees that shielded the pleading desolate voice. It was the woman with warm meals and cold handshakes. A large man was dragging her by her hair, while Muktar held firmly unto the hands of his two daughters who whimpered and pleaded.

Daniel was suddenly pulsating again with energy as he yelled loudly. In the brief moment of distraction, Halima wriggled free of her father's grasp and ran away. The large man threw Muktar's wife to the ground and chased after Halima. As Daniel approached, Muktar pulled out a gun and said, "I do not want to kill, but I would rather not be the one to die." He pulled the trigger as his wife lunged at him. Muktar was filled with horror; he let go of the gun and his daughter. Daniel stood frozen as Muktar's loud wail chilled the hot sticky night. When Muktar looked up, he was a man possessed. He looked around for his gun and snatched up the first thing he found. He grabbed a discarded machete and ran at Daniel. Bitter laughter bubbled to his lips as he raised his hand, which was cut by a flash from Daniel's weapon. He screamed with the pain and swung around with blind rage. There were two screams – one rumbling, one piercing. Then a flash of pain, another subdued scream and a head bounced with a silent thud to the darkened mud. Muktar – the voice of hate, was dead.

Daniel set off in the direction the girls had run. He rounded a corner and sunk to his knees. Halima was dead. The large man was dead. Aisha was sobbing on her sister's corpse. He picked her up. He gently pried away the cutlass embedded in her right foot. He was done fighting. He was done living. There was only one thing to do now. He hurried across the blood soaked landscapes, past hastily cut down lives bleeding to death, moaning and forgetting to say final prayers. He darted furtively behind sombre trees and treacherous bushes. The bundle in his hand was crimson. The night was blood, screams and fire. And the heavy clouds shed sad tears on the wanton destruction and desecrated land.

Daniel could barely move as his life expired in large red drops on the newly soggy earth. But still he trudged on with his bundle. There was only one place to go – he had to find Nneka. She lived in the quarters of her boss's house, in a part of town that instigated the madness but was exempted from it. Daniel was soon past the charred houses and fresh corpses. He made his way carefully through shadows and finally found the house with the glass pyramid on its roof. He was at a loss as to what to do now that he had made it this far and for once he felt the weight of his bundle, the fatigue of his soul and the exhaustion of his tired limbs. He slumped against the uncaring wall pondering his next move. There was a scratching noise to his left beyond the wall. He tried to hide but he was exhausted and the best he could do was stash the girl behind a nearby bush. He sat exposed in the lonely yellow light of the street lamp. There was a scramble at the top of the fence and just as Daniel was ready to be caught, the lights went out. NEPA (The National Electric Power Authority) had for once done the right thing and Daniel was now cocooned in comforting darkness. There was a thud as something landed in the soft sand to his left and he heard someone treading softly. The figure had a bag over its left shoulder and was creeping silently past him. Suddenly a short cough pierced the thick darkness and the roar of a diesel generator shattered the rest of it. Daniel remained in the darkness but a bright white light erupted from a lamp on the gate and caught the creeping figure of Nneka.

She froze, betraying her hope to flee unnoticed. Nothing more happened for an eternal few seconds and then she heard her name float towards her with a ghost like tremor. It took a few more harsh whispers for her to notice the bloody body splayed in the shadows.

"Oh my God!" she cried rushing to his side

"Why are you being dramatic?" he let out slowly, "it's only a scratch," he attempted a futile smile.

"What happened? Are you okay?" Her words tumbled out incoherently.

"I'm going to die in the next five minutes so listen carefully," there was a sudden silence as they both realised the gravity of his words.

"There is a girl in the bushes over there, I want you take her to this address," he gave her his wallet and pointed tiredly at the information slip which he had dutifully filled in.

"Anything," she said, still wondering how to save his life.

"You have to go now," he said interrupting her, "The city has gone mad, be careful."

"What about you, what are you going to do?" she was asking.

"Don't worry, I'll be home when you get there," he said it with an almost serene air and she knew he meant a different home. She wished she had the same beliefs he did.

"Please go," he said, "and Nneka ... thank you."

"Daniel, you can still try to come with us, if you made it this far ..." she stopped, realising she was talking to vacant eyes.

His death was sudden like he did not want her to share in it. She picked up the girl, who had fainted, observing the world through a curtain of tears.

Tomorrow, he will be swallowed by the loneliness of a mass grave and she will weep properly for him. Right now, she had to make her way out of town. She tied the girl to her back and wrapped her head in a dark shawl. They trudged on for what seemed an eternity, Nneka was lost in despair, she could not imagine how to make it to the train station. A car pulled over quietly next to them. The man spoke Igbo, but the initial comfort she felt at hearing it was drowned by unease at the familiarity of the voice. But she could not place it and had no choice, so she got in. The man drove quickly and silently to the station. The minty smell of the tomtom sweet filled the car, transporting her to forgotten parts of her childhood and making her nervous.

"Good luck," he said, "Allah go with you," he added in English. As she jostled for space on the train, the voice finally settled in her head and she remembered where she had heard it. It was the same man from Alhaji's office.

The train was a metal box of chaos, crying mothers clung to dead children and the recently crippled hobbled around in bloody rags grateful for their lives, even the men were weeping. It was sorrow, tears and blood. Although she had never been, Nneka headed for Lagos to deliver her bundle. The carriages were bursting; people lay on the roof and clung to the sides. The air was stale and putrid, the sounds a mixture of wails and silence. A man stood on one leg and held the other in his hand whispering gently to it. Many fainted, many died. Nneka wet herself and no one noticed, not even she.

The weary train happily disgorged its contents. She stood as in a trance at the chaotic Lagos station having no clue where to turn. An old man in a dilapidated Volkswagen had made it his mission to ferry people to the hospital. She gratefully accepted his offer but told him where she needed to go instead. The ride was silent, the man had heard too many chilling tales from previous passengers and Nneka was unwilling to talk. He dropped her at the innocuous gates and an eager gateman promptly opened the door. It was evident the occupants were expecting someone – the lights in the house were still being fed by a silent generator and the dogs remained chained. A rotund woman rushed out of the house with a girl that looked exactly like Daniel. The woman grabbed Nneka by the shoulders and looked at her with eyes that formerly used to smile often but bore signs of many recent sorrows.

"Where is he, how is he, what happened, what is happening?" the endless questions tumbled out of her mouth because she was afraid to get the answer she already knew.

"I'm sorry ma, I'm sorry ma," was all Nneka kept repeating. She did not know when she was ushered into the house, when the doctor came and attended to them, when she fell asleep next to Aisha.

She had been given a sedative so she woke grudgingly, as if her brain were conscious that the real world had become a nightmare and it was hesitant to partake of it. For a few seconds, her body refused to respond to her alert mind and lay in an immobile panic. She finally gained control of her limbs and turned her head to see Aisha's restive features. A wave of emotional fatigue doused her afresh and she cried silently. The room had obviously been Daniel's; his large smile remained immortalised in a tacky frame in which he embraced his sister. She made her way to the thick curtains that draped the glass doors. There was a spacious balcony behind them and she was grateful for the chance to get some air before confronting his family again.

It was a remarkable sky. The sun was setting and the sky was bronze. The moon had come out too early, enchanted by the spectacle. A wisp of golden clouds lazily floated across the firmament like a necklace until they finally found their target. They sat around the moon – a pale pearl on an endless neck.

"It will be cloudy tomorrow," Daniel's mother said in a voice that made it obvious it was the last thing on her mind. "God giveth and God taketh," she continued to mumble in a subdued voice holding Aisha a bit too tightly. Daniel's sister had listened to Nneka's story and retired to her room in tears. His mother was mostly silent; she had exhausted her tears the day before.

"So you're going home tomorrow?" she said the 'you' pointedly to confirm that Aisha was not leaving. There was a combined hope and desperation in the way she clung to her, like an amputee with a fake limb.

"Yes, ma," Nneka said, glad her narrative was over. She had broken down many times and in a strange irony, Daniel's mother had had to comfort her. She was exhausted physically and mentally.

They all stared off at the sky again. Each one lost in a personal moment of their shared horror and indescribable grief.

Daniel's mother got up suddenly. "Goodnight, my daughters," she said. "I will see you tomorrow before you travel," she said to Nneka. "Omo mi (my child)," she said turning to Aisha, "kabo, welcome."

IV
Teacher Don't Teach Me Nonsense
(Central Northern Nigeria, 2002)

ONE

It took a full month after he dropped her off at the train station but he found her. First in the files of a dusty office, then in a modest house with the woman he had once called his wife two towns away from where they had earlier spent many blissful years.

That bloody night, he had driven around aimlessly afterwards, spending many hours combing through a tangled cobweb of memories, until he had fallen into a calm dream. It was a large room of endless clocks; the hour was two, yet they were silent. He awoke with a shattered soul under a sparse palm tree. He lost himself in the searching of his being, drifting in and out of consciousness, forgetting his body in the unforgiving sun of the Sahara. A truck on its way to the mass graves mercifully picked him up with the numerous other victims of the city's madness. His body was the first to fall out, making the driver realise he had not backed up sufficiently to neatly empty his load into the waiting hole. The driver reversed until he was a whisker's length from running over Emeka's face and the corpses that were lying over each other tumbled lifelessly over his head. The driver grabbed him by the feet and dragged him from beneath the truck. As he hoisted him up to toss him into the ditch, he felt the unmistakable warmth of a heartbeat – albeit faint. In his alarm, he dropped him in the grave and ran a few metres away. He was going to leave him there but his conscience forbade him and he climbed back into the grave – put his ear to his chest and there it was again – the universal music that is a double note. He slapped him hard, more to assuage his fright than to resuscitate the dying man. He laboriously pulled him out and gave him some fresh milk, as that was all he had. As he drove back to town hurriedly, he saw one of the little boys that sold water in little plastic sachets and promptly called one of them over. He bought two and splashed them over the haggard face of the Lazarus as signs of life began to seep slowly into the dry features. He was about to shout to everyone to come see the miracle when Emeka silenced him with a faint grip on his forearm.

"Please," it was all he could say, but the driver understood the despair in his voice. He let him sit there, slowly gathering his strength, furnishing him with plastic packs of water. The day had gradually faded into a silent evening, the sun had turned an orange so hot it seemed red in places and then it had worn a golden evening gown. Emeka had remained in a pensive silence that infected his host who was still not sure if he were ferrying about a ghost. At that time when the sun makes too hasty an exit and the vain moon still ponders if the sky deserves its presence – the hour when most of Africa is shamefully shrouded in darkness, Emeka finally saw his light. It shone forth from his being and for brief seconds he possessed a physical glow. The enchanted driver obeyed his instructions with the servitude accorded a prophet. They drove to a part of town he had never been before. They got to a modest but beautiful house; Emeka pulled out a bunch of keys and opened the doors. He turned around and placed the keys in the hands of the startled driver.

"Thank you," Emeka said quietly, "when, you return tomorrow, everything within will be yours," he said and before the man could utter a word, he had vanished behind the shut gate.

In that city, it was not unusual for a beggar to become a millionaire in a day – but it was usually called politics.

Emeka packed a duffel bag, six suitcases and a small satchel with many tape recordings. There was no one else in the house. He did not hire a maid, driver, or guard because he did not want one – he did not need one. The suitcases were stuffed with money; Emeka had had an extremely profitable last few years. He had been excellent at what he did and the simple explanation of what he did was that he had embraced a system that had sought to destroy him. There was no particular point during his incarceration when he felt his soul decay. He had been freed to realise his life was no more. He adopted the first alternative that was offered to him. He had a command of languages and he possessed a head that forgot nothing. He adapted easily and had a rare quality that made corrupt people trust him completely. He smiled a sad smile. It was over.

He made one phone call. The voice on the other end was familiar. "How do we know we have done this long enough," he asked.

The voice had its habitual familiar laugh, "The world gives us signs," O.C replied.

"And if we can't read them?"

"Then it must show us, it must force us to see," O.C returned.

"Do you see the type of devastation we are causing? O.C we are killing our own people, destroying our land ... our future."

O.C was silent for a few seconds and Emeka could imagine his jaw clench. "Who cares?" he finally murmured. "Emeka, are you sure you don't want to wait a couple of years."

"You mean until after the next elections?" Emeka asked realising with a jolt that he had been just as soulless and callous a few hours ago. He suddenly became frightened of the man he had been and the person O.C still was.

O.C forced out a chuckle in response.

"I'm just reading the signs," Emeka returned, hanging up without bothering with a farewell.

TWO

As always, there were flies and dust everywhere. He hated them both enough that after seeing them for twenty-seven years, he still noticed them. And he was still irritated by them. It was why he became a driver, so he could sit in air-conditioned cars all day with the windows up and pretend the air hummed instead of buzzed. Pretend it was twenty-three degrees instead of thirty-three and laugh at the dust as it swirled around the large black body of the car unable to penetrate inside. It was the reason he kept the car clean and parked under leafy trees and why his boss thought him to be a good employee.

Mr Sukonmi was his boss. He was not a good person, but he was a good employee. He was the chief of staff to the state Governor and he knew how to get the wrong things done right. He knew whose palm to grease and by how much, whose praises to sing and for how long. He knew all the things needed to keep his job without having a clue about how to do the actual job. He was only thirty but had a potbelly; a block of fifteen flats worth twenty million naira each; a wife and a girlfriend. He knew how to enjoy life, how to collect kickbacks and how to help others enjoy life. He was the quintessential errand boy for the vilest of beasts and aspired only to one day graduate to the similar status of typical politician whose cauldron is the city's helpless poor; his counsel served only himself and his kind.

An election was around the corner. Tarfa sat in the shade of a tree whose name he did not know. A newspaper was open in his lap. He did not mix with the other drivers as they sat in the dust gossiping about everything, hoping for a life they refused to work or plan for. Tarfa rarely spoke; it was why Mr Sukonmi liked him so much. It was why he discussed secret government issues so freely and groped his girlfriends so nonchalantly in the car. Tarfa

140

watched the tired 504 station wagon pull up to the venue. It was late but the Governor was even later so it did not matter. No one was ever on time, except his boss. It would have been a redeeming quality but he used the time to make side deals and pocket quick hefty bribes. The man got out of the car, he looked exhausted but optimistic, his shoulders were sagging but not drooping: like he carried a heavy load whose burden he could finally bear. Tarfa watched the two of them avoid each other, his boss and the man. It was only proper that the first person the Resident Electoral Commissioner paid his respect to be the Governor himself. The man was nervous and fidgety like he was practising a speech made in someone else's head for another's mouth.

Sirens pierced the air; the Governor had arrived in his usual way, anticipated but unexpected. Tarfa watched everyone scuttle around like it was the first time this had happened. It always amused him how unprepared they were for his arrival at every location, he was always greeted by chaos, but he seemed to enjoy it. A police officer jumped out of the third car in the convoy, it was the middle car. He saluted with exaggerated competence and opened the door of the right rear seat. Expensive shoes were followed by an expansive man who was also irritated by the flies and dust. Mr Sukonmi hurried to his side and whispered hurriedly in his ear. He told him who was there and why he was there and with his wide smile and wider gestures, it was all Governor John O.C Abari needed to know. He often said only a poor politician wrote a speech before hand. It had taken him barely six years since he had been released from prison to make the right amount of money and right a number of connections. More importantly, he had the last name Abari and it meant a lot in the corridors of power. He strode forward confidently – the stride of a man who deserved to be where he was and was convinced that all his actions were justified. He swallowed the space in his slightly parted lips, everything turned to him as a default. Even the breeze made the trees bow slightly in his direction. He got to the stage and shook hands with the Resident Electoral Commissioner and the Chief of Police. He walked to where he belonged, at the centre of the stage with all the cameras trained on him. He looked into them confidently. "My dear citizens of Nigeria and in particular the privileged indigenes of Bayelsa State …"

Tarfa got out of the car as if on cue. The Governor never spent more than five minutes in front of a camera and it was common sense not to give a speech longer than that. Tarfa removed the gift basket from the boot of the car and strode to a discreet corner of the proceedings, a clean portion with a shade. The Resident Electoral Commissioner was speaking nervously now, the microphone in his hand jumping towards his side and back to his mouth as he struggled with what to do with his sweaty hands. "Your Excellency, it is my duty as a proud Nigerian to conduct free and fair elections with your esteemed assistance and properly serve the people of the proud state of Bayelsa …"

Tarfa slapped away an intrusive fly that was creeping towards the tantalising basket in his hand. The hasty speech was done and he moved quickly, unnoticed, to the side of Mr Sukonmi, the Chief of Staff, as he arrived beside the Governor.

"My Commissioner," the Governor was saying with an oily smile, obviously tickled by the entire farce, O.C enjoyed these aspects of politics most. The dirty aspects performed in front of a watching crowd who pretended to be ignorant so they could preserve their fragile hopes. He grasped the commissioner's hand in a tight clasp, letting him give the real speech he had been practising because it was part of the protocol.

"My Governor, Your Excellency," he said hesitantly, his nervousness oozing through every pore in his skin and pooling in wet patches beneath his armpits. From what he heard the Chief of Staff was usually not there, but the Governor made no signs of dismissing him so he continued. "Since I arrived, sir, I have had no accommodation and that is my vehicle over there," he said nodding towards the dilapidated station wagon. The man was twice his age so O.C decided to cut short his agony.

"That is unfair how Abuja treats you. Don't worry, my Commissioner, we will take care of you." His habitual laugh seeped out in comforting waves. "My people will take care of you," he said looking pointedly at Mr Sukonmi, who also wore a large smile that made him look idiotic. "They will help you settle down quickly." He finished giving the commissioner an earnest look that evoked a relieved smile.

"Governor, I must speak to you about something," Mr Sukonmi said. "Let me settle him first, I will be in your car shortly." In ten minutes, the Governor and his Chief of Staff were rushing towards another engagement in a cacophony of noise and Tarfa was observing the nervous movements of the commissioner in the rearview mirror. He watched the heavy lips mouth thanksgiving and the happy faraway stare of a man who had arrived at paradise too early. The gift basket sat clutched tightly in his arm.

The next morning, there was a quiet knock on the door of the presidential suite at the Wazobia Hotel. The commissioner opened the door with a look of contentment; the same greasy smile was reflected on both sides of the doorframe.

"My Commissioner, I hope you had a wonderful night. I'm sorry there was no entertainment last night, but we imagined you would want to rest first."

"Ah Chief, your hospitality has been wonderful already. I'm sure there is still time for entertainment." And they shared a boisterous laugh, which told Tarfa he should bring another gift basket of varied liquors and probably one or two of Madam's choice girls.

"I hope you are not in a hurry to go anywhere," Mr Sukonmi continued after their laugh, "but we cannot allow a whole Commissioner to be driving that car. Not in this state, this our beloved state," he said with obvious implications.

"Not today. Today I think I will rest some more and then enjoy the evening," he said, barely containing his delight.

"Commissioner, my Commissioner," Mr Sukonmi said, the laughter was now bubbling uncontrolled out of both their lips like a recently uncorked bottle of champagne. It was a celebration for the foregone conclusion of a future event. "The Governor sends his regards, he will be here tomorrow to check on you. Anyway, I must go now, but my men will bring over some fun tonight and a couple of cars tomorrow for you and your support." The last word carried dark and hideous meanings but they laughed again at its cleverness, not minding whether public purpose and private pleasures were mutually destructive.

O.C was having a reception at his Governor's mansion for his goddaughter's wedding. All the previous Governors had decorated the mansion to their personal tastes but none more so than O.C. He had bought out the entire street to expand the grounds, sometimes calling his old friend Emeka to help negotiate with some reluctant tenants. The thought made him shake his head briefly, he wished Emeka were still around. He had made everything so smooth and easy. The mansion had thirty-five bedrooms in case any member of his extended family decided to stay over for the night in privacy. There was a garage for sixty cars and a landing pad for two helicopters. He ensured there was enough space for a runway if it became necessary. The three living rooms on the first floor were tiled in gold and the entire house was a tribute to ostentation. But his proudest addition was the golf course – the only one in the state. O.C did not understand the tranquility of a bird's song or the serenity of a flower's scent and it was the only vegetated part of the endless property.

He had a satisfied smile on his face. He was adorned in his favourite expensive lace agbada, which he was so famous for, sellers all over the country asked if you wanted to buy the regular lace or the O.C lace. He made his grand entrance with his equally vain wife by his side. The drummers had already been singing his praises for half an hour and the newlyweds had practically been forgotten in the commotion of his arrival. O.C was having a grand time. His wide smile was permanently plastered on and he was happy to see many of his eminent colleagues in attendance. He saw the commissioner approaching, but could barely recognise him from the amount of weight he had put on. They had not seen each other in many weeks, since O.C had checked in on him to confirm that the Chief of Staff had indeed delivered both Land Cruiser SUVs.

"I am sorry I am late," the commissioner said, "but none of the roads are paved and traffic was heavy with all the cars."

"Oh!" O.C interjected, "you should have telephoned me and I would have sent the spare helicopter."

"Ah, ah, my Governor, you spoil me too much," the commissioner said with delight, rubbing his newly protruding belly.

And they both laughed at O.C's protestations of 'not enough, not enough!'

"Governor, my Governor," the commissioner began, "I need to start preparing for the elections. I must begin recruiting Presiding Officers. I will need about five thousand names of competent, trusted men," he said, adding emphasis to the 'trusted'.

"My Chief of Staff will see you," the Governor said, releasing a wide smile. "I hope you find everything else satisfactory," O.C finished, motioning Mr Sukonmi to join them.

"Well, your Excellency," the commissioner said almost reluctantly, "we will need to train the men and headquarters has been slow in releasing funds."

"How much will this be?" O.C asked casually, like he was purchasing a pair of shoes and not the gubernatorial elections.

"Well, it is about twenty-five million for each batch and there could be up to three batches."

"No problem," O.C said, his wide smile back in place. He turned to Mr Sukonmi, "Please see to it that our Commissioner receives thirty million before he leaves, another in two weeks and then a final bunch in a month."

"In what way should we prepare it, sir?" Mr Sukonmi asked.

"Put it under security vote," O.C said, sauntering off to greet another Governor.

Mr Sukonmi immediately called Tarfa over. It meant they would have to hand it over as cash. They headed for the basement and took out thirty stashes from the expansive freezer, throwing them casually in the chequered Ghana-must-go bags.

"The man that came up with this idea was a genius," Mr Sukonmi was saying freely to Tarfa. "It's a pity he disappeared eighteen months ago."

Outside, the commissioner was telling his electoral officers how generous the Governor was and the Governor was instructing his party chairman to round up five thousand loyal men.

As Tarfa drove away from the Wazobia Hotel, his car thirty million Naira lighter and his pocket twenty thousand Naira heavier, his phone buzzed. The text read, "All faithful members of the National Action People's Party should report for an urgent party meeting tomorrow morning at eleven." He smiled slyly; once again, the seat of power would remain with the NAPP. He quickly called his cousin to remember to attend the meeting. Serving as an election officer was the easiest way to make a hundred thousand naira.

Two weeks later, Tarfa sat with his cousin over a plate of pounded yam that swam in a soup full of delicacies. They were four calabashes of palm wine into the meal. Their laughter polluted the air.

"My brother, you know say na five thousand voters suppose come to my poll booth. Na only one thousand people show up come vote."

"Ah ah!" Tarfa responded, "I'm sure your hand was tired."

"My brother, you no understand, I voted about two hundred times, one of my boys, we call am Machine, he just dey dip his thumb in the ink go dey go through the stacks, I swear he fi vote one thousand times on his own."

"Ah, ah!" Tarfa exclaimed again and they both laughed.

"Well, I suppose go, I get class teach tomorrow. They don call off the strike after fourteen months. You know say I make more with this one day job than the entire salary they wan give me for the last year," he said with incredulity.

"We suppose dey do election every year."

They erupted in laughter and his cousin staggered out leaving behind a thick brown envelope to show his gratitude.

PART 4

NUMBER 33, OYELARAN SOYINKA STREET

I
Unknown Soldier (South Western Nigeria, 1967 – 1993)

ONE

He had a house of soft wood and prominent outlines. Thick curtains shielded plush carpets from inquisitive rays. As dusk approached, the tall windows cast intricate shadows that danced to exorbitant trumpets of Afro-Beat. A long winding staircase, which would have proudly adorned a Western gothic mansion, was not amiss in his hall. At the top fifteen bulbs filtered through a thousand glass pieces and scattered enchanted light on the green marble floor. His garden, carefully maintained by old Rufus, abounded with leafy fruit trees. He insisted on well-tended rose bushes that he never saw and a fragrant queen of the night he never smelt. But it was the right way to maintain a house and he remained eternally a servant de rigueur.

He was often home but remained a mere phantom until it was time for dinner and the seven o'clock news. He was formal in all his ways except television dinners. He could not take out the time to both eat and watch the news.

Then the house suddenly jumped to life. The stereo was turned off and Fela's husky voice was replaced by Dolapo Odukoya's booming laugh. It started deep in his belly, causing shakes and spasms and just when you thought he would explode, it burst from his mouth, joyously bouncing around the room and infecting everything in its path with unrestrained elation. Suddenly, he was teasing Mrs Folayo, his faithful maid who had spent a lifetime with him and worked through many hardships. Erudite and upright; he spent all day reading and working and she spent hers working and praying. They convened at night. She insisted she had to pray so much because Mr Odukoya refused to do so.

The fiery cauldron of crooked courtrooms was gradually replaced by the sovereign isolation of his library from whence he denounced, mostly to futility, the atrocities of successive military leaders and sham democracies – ruled by despots, passed on like monarchies. The library was a melee of wood and paper – a cluster of dead trees. It had rows and columns of out-of-print books, which were dusted by Mrs Folayo every Sunday evening, the only time she went through the thick oak door with the stories of local deities carved in small-segmented panels.

Dolapo was a prominent civil-rights lawyer and activist, which was how he met Akpokio. They attended the University of Ibadan together. They spent many stifling afternoons debating under almond trees and quiet evenings battling with pawns and rooks on chequered boards. When Dolapo Odukoya's cousin came to visit in their final year, it was simply a matter of time. She was shy, intelligent and small. Small manicured nails, small pouty lips, small intense eyes, small, small, small. And Akpokio was huge. She walked into the room one Sunday afternoon, undaunted by the black giant that sat in a wooden chair reading the autobiography of Gandhi.

"Is my cousin around?" Ranti asked abruptly.

"Who are you?" Akpokio returned, although it was obvious as she had the same high, smooth forehead as Dolapo, who spoke of her often.

"I'm Ranti, Dolapo's cousin," she shot back.

"Oh, the one that attends Queen's College. Welcome, indeed," he said switching to a ludicrous imitation of a British accent.

"Where is he?" Ranti said, giving a small smile that revealed tiny teeth, projecting a shy demeanour to counter her bold entry.

"He's in the shower, he should be back shortly," Akpokio said, but he did not return to his book. Instead, they talked about many relevant things in a few minutes; in the easy way only those who had caught Cupid's attention could do on a first meeting.

It was the first of many conversations held under the guise of a shared love for Dolapo, until it was obvious that Dolapo's presence was a hindrance to their covert flirtations. One day, during a quiet stroll through the campus under the pretext of according Dolapo space to study, he asked about her plans for the future.

"After school, I want to leave the bustle of the city and return to rural serenity."

"So you prefer being a village girl?" he said mockingly and they both laughed.

"Well, perhaps a little bit," she said, "I grew up in what I thought was affluence, then I came to the city and it helped me put things in perspective. There are people who really need help."

"Interesting choice," he said quietly. "Won't you rather start a hospital over in Lagos and become a big time doctor? Isn't it everyone's dream to become a doctor or a lawyer in Lagos?"

"Yeah, but it is not for me. I saw too many little children die from preventable causes. I feel I have a responsibility to go back."

Although Akpokio did not know it then, Ranti, his roommate's cousin, already occupied a tender place in his heart. Six weeks later, she returned with a basketful of food. Akpokio took one bite and exclaimed loudly. "Dolapo abeg thank your mother for me," he said happily shoving large spoonfuls of fried rice into his mouth.

"It's Ranti's cooking. It's her hobby," Dolapo returned distractedly.

And Akpokio was forever smitten. Because the phrase 'the way to a man's heart is through his stomach' was an often-overused cliche that was apt for Akpokio who was an only child and refused to eat food that had been refrigerated. He also knew the city was not where his destiny lay and now he had found the perfect companion with whom to pursue his real ambitions. Akpokio and Dolapo joined the same law firm when they graduated, remaining as housemates. Initially, Ranti had just been Dolapo's cousin and Akpokio was simply Dolapo's roommate. But her affections grew from respect to love and his ripened from fondness to something deeper. The year she finally graduated from the university, they were married and promptly moved back to the small town in the Niger-Delta where Akpokio had spent a happy childhood.

TWO

In Uncle's study was a wooden clock with a swinging pendulum and a little bird that popped out of a hole to announce the hour. Beneath it lay a love seat that was too comfortable and conspired with the hypnotic pendulum to lure its user into unplanned slumber until the bird jolted them awake in time to catch a book that was slipping to the exotic Persian rug. Next to these was a pair of thick wooden doors leading to a patio on the outside with two rocking chairs and a [silent] murmuring fountain [until Seun joined the household]. On hot days, it was a cool pensive spot with a shade from the balcony of Uncle's room. Like clumsy troops in fatigued formation, a regiment of orange trees completed the canopy, enticing the few insects and birds not seduced by their sweeter comrades. As the years progressed, the threat of global warming forewarned by Ojo – when quizzed by Dolapo about 'the no longer whistling' rainmaker's diminishing powers of controlling the clouds as his hair turned greyer – pushed average yearly temperatures from twenty-five degrees to thirty. Even Uncle was finally enticed to enjoy the many unplanned meetings and jovial conversations held in this family seclusion.

There was a large painting of Uncle's wife opposite the study's entrance, sitting solitarily on the wall above his chair. It was the most conspicuous thing in the room yet Seun barely remembered her mousy demeanor. She had a non-existent aura but Uncle would more than make up for it, as his booming laugh never stopped resonating in her presence. Uncle had nothing in common with his wife; when he indulged company, he was boisterous and exuberant. Surprisingly, she had an affinity for loud clothes and garish makeup; in fact, she had a generally tawdry taste.

Seun's mother – Ranti – had told him it was because Temitope had grown up poor and then her parents had suddenly come upon money. She had the telltale characteristic of this class of people – a grave reluctance to throw things away. Her father was a shoe peddler and when the military decreed that a Nigerian should supply the army's shoes, he won the contract. From then on, he rapidly developed the lucrative 'brown envelope' skill that won him many more. Temitope had been the middle among seven children because that had been the only way for her parents to amuse themselves in the stifling boredom of abject poverty. Her mother, constantly pregnant, or weaning a child, birthed two girls, a boy her, a boy and two girls; and everyone else paired up, leaving her the forgotten child. Quietly, she read books on her own and developed a fearsome intellect that made Uncle fall in love with her. She was generous to a fault, finding it mostly impossible to say no. She had one of those tempers that simmered quietly for a long time, forgiving wrongs but not forgetting them, until suddenly all was remembered and erupted like a vicious volcano out of the pit of her belly of seemingly endless patience.

It had been that way many years ago, when Dolapo had shown up a month before their wedding and said calmly, "I'm going to fight in the war." She had offered no response until the time he was to leave, twenty-nine hours before their wedding. She had broken down in tears for only the second time in her adult life.

"Dolapo," Temitope had said, "realise this, if you don't return, you have confined me to the state of widowhood at the age of twenty-three. Remember I did not ask for your love, but I accepted your affections. You have a responsibility."

Their meeting had been a result of the conjoining of her even temper and the irrepressible power of Uncle's youthful pen.

When he enrolled in the university, Dolapo had the confidence borne out of a superlative quality of life that breeds self-assurance in the typical middle class offspring. At the village, he had been the most important person in his age group as the Oba's nephew. At the Federal Government College, he had been the most intelligent. And once again, the hand of fate was heavy on his life, his star shone unlike others of his ilk who faded into the obscurity of partial significance. His life, it seems to all, was a predetermined ordination of a comet bound to perpetual upward mobility.

In his second year, he and his roommate began writing a column under the poetically enigmatic pseudonym: Anon. Their topics spanned everything from the cold war to the garish clothes of pretentious freshman girls who 'acted' pious and studious. Their usually provocative language garnered them a large readership and curiosity borne of shrouded notoriety. Even though it was widely suspected that they were the writers, they vehemently denied it, but after each issue, they always had the most number of dance partners at the local clubs. The quiet reserved demeanour that Dolapo wore like a mask at the university only aided his mysterious attraction. The relative affluence he enjoyed in the village was largely insufficient in the city, depriving him of the funds to purchase the latest clothes. Yet, he behaved as if it was planned and due to his self-assured stride and sharp wit, he remained fashionable and alluring. The only new trends he indulged in were the gangling Afros and platform shoes to shield his deficient height. Initially, save for his tall dark roommate and accomplice and a few select individuals, all anyone else knew of Dolapo was his loud booming laughter that seemed capable of raising the dead into joyous revelry. However, two years of fame and constant unsolicited attention from attractive females soon brought out a more outgoing side to him. He came into his own and quickly mastered his environment ... and himself. He still maintained his studious habits but to his irreproachable bounce was added an air of self-fulfillment.

As is expected, one day they published an article that went too far. The tendency in those days was for the affluent and middle class to purchase Harley Davidson motorcycles and whizz between the tripod of the great universities in Western Nigeria – Ife, Ibadan and Lagos. On the decrepit dual carriageway that connected Ife to Ibadan, with the mysterious long tapestry of virgin forest that stretched for miles as the only witness, a distracted rider crashed his bike and had his head crushed by a truck. In a fit of misplaced anger and grief, they wrote an article criticising the drunk driving and helmetless riding that was in vogue. Although it was necessary to be said, it was so ill timed it became their most read article and almost their last. The only positive gain from this piece was that a quiet, attractive second year student who had previously suffered under their scathing pen took particular offence and marched into their room to give them a tongue-lashing.

Her little frame, carried with a determined and angry purpose, was seen that damp evening striding through the grey cloudy light, over fallen leaves that lined the long walk to the men's dormitory. The path was mostly brick bordered by overgrown grass and drooping fruit trees. The buildings were the drab constructions of the early 1900's that never looked good with paint and they all wore a yellow coat. The paint was peeling but this meant nothing to the rotund security guard who felt it was ridiculous that a man of his advanced age was protecting five hundred men at the prime of their strength – but this job was his livelihood. She walked purposefully through the rusty gates that swung loosely on squeaky hinges and for the first time felt intimidated by her task. She climbed nervously up the four flights of stairs, past towelled men with bulging muscles and plastic buckets. The smell of burnt rice hung accusingly around the second floor distracting her from the careless litter that lay about. She went past the lower floors that had two bunks and four tables where the melancholic sighs of young men in love drowned the buzz of mosquitoes. She got to the fifth floor that was usually reserved for seniors but where Dolapo and his roommate a year early had a room for two. She was striding down the corridor when she completely lost her courage and had to grab the railings to steady herself. She looked down into the quadrangle that was crisscrossed by clotheslines and trampled grass. The noise of a hundred intimate moments, careless laughter, loud farts, unrestrained belches, chair on floor, fork on plate, were temporarily silenced as she stood outside their door frozen by the sounds of their aggressive chatter.

"But he is wrong!" Dolapo was saying, "Yes, communism is inevitable, that is right; yes it will be fuelled by the destructive but necessary greed of capitalism, but from then on, his theory is faulty."

"What are you talking about?" his roommate returned with equal vehemence. "You misunderstand the man."

"Let me finish, let me finish," Dolapo cut in again. "What I am saying is, he thinks communism will come because the markets will get too volatile to support themselves and there will be an uprising of the pitiless masses against the excesses of the privileged few, but he forgets a fundamental aspect of group psychology. The masses will not arouse themselves, because by the time it gets to that point, the masses will be too accustomed to a life of subjugation ..."

"But ..."

"And and, the market will always right itself. If anyone is swinging in a direction too outrageous, he will be checked by competition."

"Haha, so you think competition is always the answer?" the roommate asked, forgetting that just the day before, this had been his argument. For they often had the same debates, unwittingly switching sides because they were more interested in the most correct conclusion of an argument than in the substance of their mangled and confusing theoretical positions.

"No, but since the masses cannot rally sufficiently when the markets punish them, as they often constitute the most vulnerable and deprived among us, they will look to a strong group of individuals such as governments or trade unions to champion their cause and steady the volatility."

"But ..."

"But, that is not the only reason why we need governments," Dolapo interrupted again, about to play his trump card. "Resources are always finite, the need for government will be in ensuring that a new path is taken in time before the scarcity of a good drives the markets into unsustainable paths." It was a new aspect to the argument and it kept his roommate silent for a few seconds as he pondered it, giving him time to add. "For example, right now petroleum is currently being drilled in large measures, but there comes a time when this resource will be exhausted, at that point, it will be up to the government to ensure that an alternative source of energy is developed before oil companies ..." he was saying when the door burst open.

155

She decided to barge in before she could change her mind, ignoring to knock and paying no attention to the peace sign stuck on the green door that was then famous in America.

She spoke in whispers all the time, even when she was shouting, which only happened on the rare occasion when she was extremely furious and she let out a string of loud almost audible words that were more sensual than threatening. Dolapo was in a shabby towel and his mouth remained open from his unfinished statement, the approaching storm gave the air an electric feel. The combination of anger and nervousness induced from her a torrent of invectives for five minutes, of which none was heard, with her voice having the solitary effect of getting Dolapo aroused. The boys remained speechless understanding that she was angry and guessing what provoked the angst. She uttered a few emotional sentences, broke into frustrated tears and left as hurriedly as she had come in, the fire in her eyes dulled to embarrassed embers.

Dolapo chased after her, forgetting he was in his towel and only succeeded in making her more uncomfortable. She was unreachable for the first three flights of stairs but by the last, he had caught up with her.

"Who are you?" were the first words out of his mouth and the look she gave in return made him immediately regret them.

"I mean, umhh," he tried again unsuccessfully.

"I'm just a girl who wears garish clothes and pretends to be studious. But at least I have the heart not to be callous about the death of fellow students. Who do you think you are?" she returned, gaining some composure.

It took him a few seconds to realise that she was the freshman they had picked at random to write about the previous year and although long forgotten, she had carried an enduring anger and contempt for far longer than they could possibly imagine. She had invested more time than anyone in uncovering their identity, had acted on her hunch and followed them around for the past month when she had the time.

"I'm, I'm just a guy who doesn't always know the best way to express himself," he said with eyes full of self-reproach. She realised with embarrassment that the reserved eyes she had observed for

156

the past month had an appealing sheen to them, the contemptuous mouth had an inviting smile and his skinny body had its attraction.

Dolapo had never been made to apologise for anything his whole life and this was the closest thing to an apology he could muster. And as tends to happen, he became curious as to whom the audacious beauty with the sensuous voice was that stirred up unfamiliar sentiments in him.

So, he found excuses to apologise to her and make up for it numerous ways by buying her lunch, then dinner, then taking her to the movies. Each time, not realising her cool external cage harboured a heart pounding like a trapped rabbit, Dolapo found his performance always unsatisfactory and left her dejected. Before they were to meet, an obnoxious pimple would develop on his nose, or he would produce nervous sweat patches, or forgetfully have a meal choked full of garlic. He always met her feeling inadequate and his eroded confidence cost him his usual charm. But it was this vulnerability that attracted her to him, because to the rest of the campus, he was an enigmatic loner with everything in place and she being long starved of attention was pleased to have a piece of him that was personally hers. During his sixth apology and third movie invitation, she asked coyly, "Why do you keep showing up?" and she loved the way he stuttered to find an answer.

"Do you not want me to?" he finally managed.

"One apology is enough, thank you very much," she replied haughtily, but to his sagging shoulders she added, "but you can still take me to a movie if you want." And she loved the smile of relief that broke on his face even more.

In the conservative world of the Nigerian university campuses of the late sixties, a budding romance had the overt luxury of being obvious. And in his confident way that had made him a contended recluse, he began planning their wedding without bothering with a proposal.

Dolapo returned from the war more himself than he had ever been. He was unchanged – almost. At times when he was quiet, he seemed more pensive; when he laughed, he seemed overly exuberant; when he showed loved, he seemed extravagantly caring. They were married exactly two years after the initial planned date.

Temitope's parents, doubtful that their bookish introverted child could be the first of their daughters to entice a man's attention talk less of affection, were hesitant to facilitate the wedding. It was the first time Dolapo spent any of Emeka's money.

Mrs Temitope Odukoya was to have been one of those women whose legacy was preserved only on an exquisitely framed canvas and in the mind of her husband, the sole audience to the vast extent of her brilliance. They had no children, so even the security of that requisite legacy was denied. But in the explosive year of 1993, fate conspired to ensure her immortality and transport her from the quiet confines of the only heart and mind that she cherished to the transient permanence of a national heroine. The day was June 12, when the nation held its collective breath for the announcement that never came. The day the desired new dawn was arrested. At dawn, the lines of fate with its untold consequences emerged and snaked patiently, unbowed by the warm rains and unrelenting sun, ignoring the military officers and their dancing whips, unfazed by the hired thugs. The presidential ballots were cast and the votes were counted and declared on the spot. The Muslim, politician, philanthropist from the West with the gift of a thousand proverbs and a penchant for singing church choruses had almost two thirds of the vote and celebrations began early. All that was missing was a presidential announcement that would never be made. For the first time since independence, Nigerians united under a shared banner. It was a rude awakening to the collective stupor to which the people had indulged in, the sharp retort to the endless transition designed to keep the masses guessing as to the next move of Babaginda – the evil political genius.

When the elections were annulled eleven days later, workers stopped working, drivers stopped driving, the people went rampaging; a nation in revolt – the birth of the rowdy infant that precedes revolution. The mob took to the streets in righteous fury and on the Lagos mainland, the streets were a carnival of chaos. Upturned cars sat next to their charred comrades. The streets of Lagos had never known a silence like this or an unquiet as was. Cars ventured no further than front yards and businesses were prohibited from opening. Cupboards slowly emptied, but the winds of change carried away unheeded the growls of hollow stomachs. Mrs Odukoya's sister was due to have a baby but the streets did not care. A mother's travail in childbirth is a ritual much expected since conception and the baby born a blessing – in times of peace – but an inconvenient interlude of the daily routine in times of war. Downed and overloaded phone lines sabotaged contact. Major, the Odukoyas' gateman heard a tired knock on the seventh day, a man named Sule wanted to speak to Madam. Mrs Odukoya was overjoyed; it was her sister's houseboy. He was exhausted and needed two glasses of water to persuade his tongue to sustained conversation.

"Madam, the streets don craze, mah," he said, the harrowing day still swimming in his mind, "Nah miracles I take get here."

"Is my sister alright?" Mrs Odukoya asked as soon as she saw he could finally speak.

"Yes, mah, but you no fi use car get on that road madam, the only one I see nah the ones dey don burn well well, madam I for die today sef."

"What? Are you alright? What happened?"

"Mhhh, madam dis people don kolo, dey don craze. I walk today madam, my leg wan commot. Madam I trek trek I get from Surulere to Mushin. My own madam don give me money say if I fin taxi make I take and I hide am well well for jeans, because dis people with dem craze jus dey waka about dey shout." He stopped and took another generous gulp of water.

He was pleased to have the whole household listening so attentively to his tale. Even Mr Odukoya had come out of his study and was seated at the edge of his seat. Mrs Folayo kept dutifully refilling his glass and he was determined to prolong his time in the limelight.

"Madam, na so I don dey tink sey after all that waka I go have to turn around wen I see this peegot, in no get stripes and in no yellow like regular taxi but in sey he fi take me come here but I must pay upfront. Madam, criminal charges e won collect all my moni so I tell am say I go pay am half now small more wen we enter Ikeja and I go top am as we land dis place." At this point, Mr Odukoya cleaned his glasses and Sule used the time to gulp down another glass of water not wanting him to miss any part of his story.

"Madam, mhhh, dis no be small business oh, we hire three guys make dem dey hang out the window dey shout SDP, dey wave plant. Na so we dey waka oh madam, we dey waka, we dey waka dey shout."

"Get on with it," Mr Odukoya interrupted impatiently.

"Ah sir, madam, jus as we dey tink sey we go safe, we don dey approach Ikeja side, I dey look how I go give the driver the moni make these thugs no turn me upside down carry the rest. All this time we dey pass burning tyres, dey pass burning cars, madam dey just dey burn everything. No car dey for road madam but you no fi speed. Dis man just enter the front of the car say make we all commot, come down." He saw the way everyone leaned forward in their chairs, so he decided to take another gulp of water.

"Madam, mhhh, they say commot, come down, lie flat! At this point I don dey say my prayers dey beg Baba God. I lie for ground dey kiss am. Suddenly madam, pah pah. My back dey burn, den flog us like say we no get mama. Den he ask us say, nah who tell us say make we dey jump around for road or we no respect democracy. Madam im eye dey red, he don shack, he carry im gun he wan shoot us. He say make we dey sing 'demonstration of craze', as we say craze he dey wipe us with koboko, madam I can barely sit now," he said, remembering they had only given them three strokes and moved in his seat like he had received a hundred.

"Madam, na so im pull out gun wan blow our brains away, but Baba God hear me. I dey tell am my madam dey pregnant abeg sir, finally him say make we get up make we dey do frog jump dey sing 'jump everyone jump, jump everyone jump, all of our troubles will vanish like bubbles, jump everyone jump'. Madam I jump tire, I sing tire. Finally he say make we go, nah so I dey waka come here," he finally finished.

Mr Odukoya looked pensive, "This is barbaric, but this is necessary. We need to show Babaginda we are serious, no more of his Maradona tactics. He cannot keep manipulating the people to perpetuate himself in power. We demand democracy not a military leadership."

Mrs Odukoya was worried, "What will we do, my sister oh," she said with uncharacteristic hysteria, holding her head.

Sule moved uncomfortably in his seat noting the magnified effect of his slight embellishments, "Your sister is no ready bon the pikin yet madam," he said, "and our neighbour, she be nurse, she say she go come help if hospital no open."

"I must go to her," Mrs Odukoya said.

"Absolutely not!" Mr Odukoya interjected, barely letting the words escape her mouth.

"Darling, I don't have a choice. My sister is giving birth in her own living room, hey!"

"Honey, but you must wait. They say the situation will become calmer in three days, so people can buy foodstuffs, you can go then," Mr Odukoya said gently but firmly. "How about you, Sule, will you wait until Madam is returning?"

"Ah, no sir, I go rise for dawn go make my way sir, I no fi leave my master with pregnant madam for so long," he said, knowing they would give him a generous amount to make his way back. He intended to walk to Mushin and join one of the numerous street parties, then visit that girl with the big chest and go home the morning after. He had structured the narrative of his ordeal in the first half of the journey, so no one would question him too much on how and when he got back.

"I will give you some extra money so you can stop by my driver's house and tell him to report on Wednesday," Mrs Odukoya said.

"Yes, ma," Sule said, trying to hide a smile. Now he had a perfect alibi.

The occasional cars that dared to venture out had green leaves stuck to their windshields to show solidarity with the fight against injustice. The only people who were busy were the youth who had been unemployed for too long – the streets were entirely theirs. Mrs Odukoya's driver was enjoying the holiday. For nine days, he crawled through Allen Avenue in Ikeja, a bottle permanently stuck to his face. Finally, his wife, absolutely indignant and contemptuous of her husband's irresponsible behaviour, found and dragged him out of the bar and slapped him so hard he dropped the bottle that had become his perpetual companion during the quotidian bedlam. He blinked rapidly, in his usual nervous way at the sound of the shattering Guinness bottle hitting the pavement, almost jarring him to his senses.

"Useless man!" she spat with vehement contempt. "Your boss wants you to report tomorrow," she said with derogatory scorn. She looked at him, blinking and muttering to himself, hissed and walked away.

He came the following morning, late and nervous. If he did not always look for ways to avoid work, perhaps Mrs Odukoya would have been a bit more willing to indulge his whims that day. Unfortunately, he was the man who always cried wolf and would excuse an absence from work with 'inclement weather, madam'. Despite his permanent state of undisguised anxiety, he still remembered to stick some leaves to the windscreen and was the only person Mrs Odukoya trusted to chauffeur her through the pandemonium that was the streets of Lagos. Unsure, hesitant, he drove the car like he ferried a crate of eggs and other drivers decidedly avoided his ponderous manoeuvrings. Perhaps if she had been in a better mood, she would have heeded the premonitions that urged her to stay home. Turning out of the street, they were besieged by a flood of danfos reversing in uncoordinated flight, yielding the first scratch on Mrs Odukoya's Mazda 626. An ongoing robbery along the main road had intensified the chaos on the road. A gang of thieves who had been cornered at the Union Bank across the street had barely escaped with their lives as a mob demanding instant justice surged towards them. The bandits, startled by the agitated mass, contrived a chaotic getaway. The hot nozzle of a sophisticated rifle nosed determinedly out of the passenger window of the Peugot 505 station wagon ferrying the bandits and instantly and ferociously spat out rounds of bullets that started a stampede of vehicles. Engulfed in the retreating melee, Mrs Odukoya's driver suddenly came to life reversing the car with uncharacteristic alacrity. Hidden behind a duplex building, wedged between a bus that proclaimed, 'God's time is the best' and another adorned with the red jerseys of Arsenal Football Club heroes, the car shuddered to a stop. Like the car, unaccustomed to such exertions, the driver trembled in his seat, further exacerbating Mrs Odukoya's anger as she was doing likewise. Despite the incident, she decided to forge ahead because of the way he said, "Madam, it must be an omen that we return home."

Initially, it seemed the day would have an early crescendo as nothing of significance happened for the next hour of their cautious journey; occasionally, they were slowed by drunken rioters who cheered when they saw the leaves on the windshield. Armpits that had not been washed in days were raised in shows of solidarity and mouths that had not been cleaned shouted the familiar refrain of: "On June 12 we stand." They were alternatively singing the praises of the election winner and deriding the loser as much as they did the military rulers.

"On a Christmas day, on a Christmas day, looking for a ram to eat, on a Christmas day, Tofa oh, is our ram oh."

"On election day, on election day, looking for a man to win, on election day, M.K.O., is our man oh."

At the roadside markets, the sellers came out with sparse commodities at exorbitant prices and were crowded by desperate women in green and white wrappers. All along the roadside were similarly coloured stickers that said 'Hope '93' with the SDP stallion rearing in its victorious glory. Next to it was the smiling face of the man known as M.K.O. Abiola in his characteristic flowing robes. Remnants of bonfires had been hastily pushed to the sides of the road. The road was almost exclusively left to the yellow mini buses, which were packed as only a few of their members had resumed their duties. They made the turn onto Allen Avenue and the driver hid a secret smile as he remembered the eventful past week. He looked with irritation as the vehicles in front of him halted. He honked impatiently until the buses began disgorging their contents rapidly, only then did he lower the windows as he heard the confident chatter of guns in the hands of men who wielded their weapons with impunity. The army had finally been called in.

It is ironic that a man who spent his life in permanent trepidation will die for his sole act of bravery. He immediately bolted out of the car at the sight of the gun-toting soldiers but realised Mrs Odukoya still sat frozen in her seat, a mask of disbelief barely visible through the tinted windows. He ran back to her hastily tapping on the window with his unkempt and broken fingernails; but frozen by shock, Mrs Odukoya's door remained shut. He finally got her out of the car and just as they were about to dock between some buildings, he felt a sharp sting in his back that halted him in surprise. Another bite and then another, he realised he was staring into the already dead eyes of Mrs Odukoya, a line of red thick liquid trickled gently out of a crimson hole in the centre of her head. In his deep pain and disbelief, he saw the slow rivulets that oozed between her staring eyes and parted down either side of her broad nose framing her lips and pooling on her jutting chin before dropping slowly as he stared mesmerised by a fate too confusing to be apprehended by his suddenly foggy brain. He realised that although she had been a nice woman he had never liked her, he realised he did not really like anyone, he realised he even hated his own wife. They both slumped slowly to the ground and his face rested by the shards of a brown beer bottle. He thought again of the last week and a jagged smile formed on his bloody lips.

THREE

On August 27, Uncle sat starring at the television screen as the haggard face that mirrored his announced that he was stepping down from power with immediate effect. He cursed the sombre looking face of Babangida and finally broke down in silent tears as the last couple of months finally crashed down on him.

It had been surreal; he sat uneasily, unsure of what to do when his wife did not return. He tried the phones but all he got was a busy signal, he paced back and forth and Mrs Folayo tried to calm him down. He tried to sit at his desk to write for that was the only thing that usually relaxed him unfailingly, but not this time. He did not know how long he sat staring into space, but he did not notice the darkness slowly envelope the room like a mourning shroud.

He heard the crowd approaching from down the street, but his mind did not register the noise – even when it seemed to stop at his gate, pounding softly like a violent wave with sorrowful tidings. He did not hear the gate open or Major's brisk steps as he walked to the kitchen to inform Mrs Folayo. But he heard her wails and he knew. He sat frozen to his chair because he was afraid to look into the eyes of his wife that would never see him again. The door to his study burst open.

"They've done it! They've done it!" Mrs Folayo was hysterical and on seeing Mr Odukoya, she fell to the floor and began to roll around. He hastened to pick her, numb and in shock.

"Where is she?" he asked in a calm voice that shocked him and briefly halted Mrs Folayo's thrashing.

"By the gate, oga."

"By the gate?" he asked in a childlike voice that betrayed his calm as a flimsy charade. "Why not bring her in?"

Mrs Folayo suddenly seemed to register that was the right thing to do and hurriedly got up, but Mr Odukoya was already striding out of the door. The cacophony of voices outside was overwhelming. Someone had recognised Mrs Odukoya as the wife of the great civil rights lawyer and in the two-hour trek that it had taken to get her body to his house, an entourage had formed. Mr Odukoya looked at the vast mass that filled his street and kept spilling into the invisible darkness. They were mourning his tragedy, yet he found his tears unable to fall. He gave a speech which he would never remember and which no one that heard it would ever forget. He did not remember when the corpse was brought in or the innumerable masses that congregated at the burial. He did not remember standing next to the Governor as they renamed the street where she fell after her.

He only remembered when he had asked frantically, "How … how did this happen?" No one had said anything and then a timid voice had volunteered.

"It was a stray bullet, sir. An unknown soldier."

II
Jjd (Southern Nigeria, 1985 – 2001)

ONE

Seun Odukoya stood like an iroko tree on a cloudy night – tall, dark and pensive. It was an unusual stature for my Yoruba name and I was often told so. My reaction to this fact, as always, is sadness, but I often force a smile.

I was born Akpokio Ehurere, like all the men in my lineage. It was one of those solitary lines in which only one male child was born each generation – just enough to preserve the Ehurere name. I was not tall or particularly dark then, so maybe you could say we were almost two different people. I lived in the land of a hundred streams and it was impossible to play in any of them. The surfaces of the water wore shimmery silver shawls and dirty dainty rainbows. My father told me tales of how he used to go fishing and swimming as a boy and promised me that one day, I would be able to do so, too. This was why father went to the nightly meetings. He usually wore a dirty kaftan and carried a stick to look like one of the watchmen that stumbled around. One day, curious, I stayed up all night awaiting his return. I lay as a log in my bed feigning sleep when father's large head peeped into my room as it did nightly. The sharp smell of Robb ointment, which father swore was a panacea for everything, overwhelmed my nostrils and I sat up with a sharp sneeze. Akpokio, my father, seemed relieved by my innocent companionship and took me outside where the moon was a full, bright, silver ball. To our left, the black waters snaked like a scourging whip with many heads. He told me a story.

"Once upon a time, there was a small village by a river. The men caught fish, the women farmed and everyone was happy. They had a chief; he was wise and kind and had two sons. He settled disputes among the people but he could not unite his own family. One day his younger son seized power. He killed his father and brother – forever cursing the land. It was said that as he killed his father, his brother unsuccessfully ran to his defence and where their noble bloods met became an indelible black stain. His brother with his dying breath vowed to revenge."

Father paused briefly as the moon disappeared behind a cloud. He resumed his tale, his voice ominous in the darkness.

"A few years ago, some people came to us; they said they had found liquid black gold – oil, that it would make everyone's life better. Your grandfather fought against it, he told them it was the same black blood that had grown and it was cursed, but no one listened. Now the people die younger, the streams are sterile, the ground is barren and the children have nowhere to play ... The children have nowhere to play," he repeated. We were silent after that. Father stared into the full moon like its puckered surface held mysterious answers. When I woke up, I was in bed and father was already out again.

Akpokio, husband to Ranti, was a quiet man with a serious demeanour. He was tall, very tall and very dark. I once read a book, which had described such a man – they called him a Nubian giant and I always thought of father as one. Although they had nothing in common besides size, as the dark goliath from the book was a truculent man who exploited people. Father's life was dedicated to the service of others. Sometimes I wished he would bash in some heads with his massive fists; instead, daily after his work, he would stay at the courthouse arguing case after case for people who could not afford his fees. He had a deep, quiet voice, like the low rumble the motorboats made when they sped across the rivers. I often wondered if like them, his words were on a special errand that made them particularly important.

In the evenings, Father sat in a chair on the verandah that had intricate hand carvings and rocked gently. I sat at his feet and mostly people would come to ask his advice. Those were my favourite times. In nine years, I never heard father raise his voice.

It was the holidays after I completed my primary education, while I waited to begin secondary school. I was merely nine years old, young for my class, but old for my years: I was often told so. I got into the secondary school in the next town as well as the famed Federal Government College in Lagos. Although I was more excited about going to Lagos, I did not tell my parents to spare mother the disappointment.

Then one day, father burst through the door, bellowing like a wounded bear. I was frightened and when mother started to cry, I wanted to do the same. "They are going to do it! They are going to hang Ken Saro-Wiwa!"

"But he has made a global name for himself," mother interjected through her tears. "Surely there will be repercussions, the international community will not stand for such an atrocity. He is the face and voice of the Niger Delta."

"The military government of Abacha does not care about sanctions; the country has too much oil," father said dejectedly, "This is a spit in the face of the global community."

The newspapers proclaimed loudly, 'There will be riots', 'The people will not stand for it', violent speeches that troubled Ranti's motherly instincts. It was decided that I would school in Lagos and live with Dolapo, her cousin. I was pleased with the decision and although mother imagined I could not understand her concession to let me school in Lagos, I had spent enough hours at the foot of father's rocking chair to almost grasp the sensitive nature of the political climate.

TWO

Mother knew I was excited and feeling slightly betrayed, she tried woefully to be supportive. She never really knew how to hide her emotions, they pooled in her eyes like the ready tears that announced her joy or sadness. I liked the tales by moonlight, but they paled in comparison to the bright lights of the big city. Warri, Sapela, Benin all went by in an exhilarating blur.

I did not know my uncle very much. We saw him rarely when he came every other year to visit. There was always much excitement. Father and mother always smiled for a week before his visit and for the same amount of time after. His big shiny Mercedes would cause all the village children to run along it, staining it with their muddy fingers. He was very generous. As far as I could remember, he came alone, but mum insists I met his wife a couple of times.

"I don't know her," I said.

"Of course, you do," mother said getting inexplicably upset very quickly, "She is the one that bought you those pyjamas that you wore every day for a year."

"I remember those pyjamas," I exclaimed with a smile, "but I don't remember her."

I don't know why but mother was really upset and she became silent for a long time. I was falling asleep to the hypnotic rattle of the engine when suddenly mother perked up in a seemingly better mood. She chuckled gently to herself and said, "I remember when your uncle became a man, he was just about your age."

You see, this your skinny neck, your uncle's neck is just like that, it should have been beautiful like mine. She told me a tale from her childhood. It was the first time she had ever spoken of that period. I was amused and curious to know more, but I imagined there was a reason it had taken a decade to hear my first story from that time.

Mother finished the tale and had a big smile on her face. "You see, your uncle and I are very close. How can you say you don't know him well?" she enquired in a happy, past-inspired glow.

I did not bother to respond, I was glad we had taps at our home. I could not imagine fetching water from the diseased streams of the Delta. "So why is the tortoise bald?" I asked, remembering she never said in her story.

"What?" mother asked, surprised. "Oh, I'll tell you later. Go to sleep," she finished, realising what I was asking.

We drove by miles and miles of misused land and untapped potential as the driver raced from Bayelsa to Lagos. Ijebu and Sagamu were mere lanterns in netted windows and just when I began to imagine the journey would never end, we arrived. It was late in the afternoon and mother was to spend the week.

The sturdy black gates swung open as Mr Odukoya was informed that his cousin had arrived. At once, his eyes lit up and his chuckle reverberated to the tall ceilings, warming the cold white walls. He stood at the door with his polo, khakis and well-worn leather sandals. He glanced down at the cracked leather and remembered with a wry smile how he got them as a gift for defending an arid little village in northern Sokoto from a pharmaceutical company that had tested a drug on little children, destroying their livers instead of curing their typhoid. They had initially refused to pay the compensation, claiming the villagers had come forth willingly for testing. It had been a particularly difficult case as the jury had remained impassive to the many pictures of children cut short in their prime. He had finally won it on a technicality and it left him wondering if a rich man could truly empathise with an impoverished stranger.

Our old Volkswagen made its way to the shade of one of the large trees, which stood majestically with dozens of fruit in varying shades of green and yellow. Mr Odukoya believed fruits should be allowed to decide when they were eaten and unless they fell, no fruit was plucked. The driver was the first out of the door. There was a diagonal strip of sweat across his back, as he did not understand how a seatbelt should be worn. Mother and I came out and were engulfed by the sweet sickly smell of ripe guavas. A smell that made young boys fall in love with a new place and I was no exception. A wide smile lit my lips, jumped over my dimples and rested in my big brown eyes. My mother wore a matching look and dried her cheeks.

It was an occasion of contrasting emotions, of big laughs and a shy smile, wide hugs and a small bow, copious kisses and hidden tears. Mr Odukoya was so excited he even remembered to point out his flowers and old Rufus was secretly pleased behind a grave almond tree. There was no TV dinner that night and Mrs Folayo laid an array of aromatic dishes on the large oak table. There was the usual excited conversation of many years crammed into a few moments.

"So, how is your village and your health centre?" Uncle asked with a chuckle in his voice and a twinkle in his eye. A twinkle that had disappeared with the death of his wife and only appeared when he saw his favoured cousin. A twinkle that made mother sad because its meaning was that she was the only person not allowed to mention Temitope's name.

"Dolapo fi mi si le, it is not a village," mother responded with equal joy and then continued in a graver tone. "Things are tough at the centre, the oil spills are making so many people sick. But it is well," she concluded, managing a tight smile.

"And my roommate?" he asked, not wishing to spoil the mood so early and seeing she was not yet ready to discuss it.

"Don't mind that your friend, he is still crusading," she said with quiet pride. "Although things are a bit tense with the whole Saro-Wiwa case," mother finished, casting a hasty glance at me that Uncle somehow understood. I wondered at the silent language of adults that was conveyed with looks and touches.

Uncle promptly turned to me and asked too loudly in a voice obviously meant to change the topic of conversation, "So, how is school going? I hope you are still reading books."

"Yes, Uncle," I replied, hastily gulping down some of my Ribena.

After that, the conversation continued in gayer colours until I was shown my room after dinner. I put down my bags: they were the plaid patterned bags popularly and aptly named 'Ghana-must-go' that got their title after a past head of state in a populist move kicked out Ghanaian immigrants in a bid to create more jobs. The Ghanaians had had such little time to pack that the raffia woven bags were the quickest thing they could secure for their belongings. They sank silently into the plush carpet next to my feet. My father was not poor. Our walls had been made of cement and when the rains fell, they sounded like muted applause for the lone house with a slate roof on the street. It was louder but it never leaked like our neighbours' thatched versions. Yet, I was struck by the luxuriousness of my room. My bed was larger than my parents' had been and had more pillows than had been on display at our entire house. Everything was larger and softer.

A book lay carefully on the stool by my bed, it was a very dirty copy of *Things Fall Apart* by Chinua Achebe and as I read the first lines, I could still hear loving laughter bubbling up the stairs, bouncing around the walls and resting on the static curtains.

THREE

I woke to a new day in a room of white, wood and burgundy. It was a comfortable room that projected none of its luxury to my soul, the atmosphere was nothing but melancholic. I awoke to the floating feeling of unexplained detachment. I could not hear my sister's squeals or my mother's laugh, no motorboat sounds floated in through the netted windows and the sun did not hit the wall above my bed. Instead, there was just profound silence and intense darkness. I lay on a surface too yielding and the air around me was too pure. I jumped out of the bed in fright and landed on an unfamiliar softness. Despair was enveloping me and I grabbed at the walls, but my fingers seemed to sink into them. I yanked my hand away and the thick curtain tore open to reveal blinding light. Slowly, I realised where I was and opened the sturdy windows. The room was immediately flooded with birdcalls and fruit scents – all the familiar smells that make a young boy feel at ease and I heard a dog bark in the neighbour's house.

There was a bathroom of marble and mirrors and I made my way there, unsteady with excitement. Lavish toiletry: Crest toothbrush, Close-Up toothpaste and a towel of real Egyptian cotton, rendered my collection inadequate. Happily, I stashed my shabbier possessions at the bottom of my bag and stepped into a bathtub for the first time. I picked up the pale caramel soap, which had a little crest in the middle that read Imperial Leather. Puzzled, I wondered at the blue and red knobs that were connected to a large white cylindrical sphere at the top corner of the room by some hoses. I shook the pipes and finally traced their end to a small metal spigot that once had a blue coat. The entire bathroom had once been adorned in blue. They were for the five boys Mrs Odukoya had desired, who had all been birthed, but suffocated by the oppressive stench of their future society, decided not to stay. They had all been given the fortunate gift of foresight, but tragically, this gift was bestowed prematurely. For glimpsing life, overwhelmed by the task ahead and unaware of the special talent bestowed on all Nigerians to adapt to every situation no matter how dire, they decided to abort the journey. And what was it that these children saw that induced an abdication of life, causing repeated heartache to the Odukoyas, (Uncle, Mr Dolapo Odukoya suffered much for his country). They saw two pictures of Nigeria, one at the birth of their father, a time in the past and one at his death, in the future. They realised the fate that awaited them at birth would neither be different from the penury and peonage into which their father was born nor the paradoxical sorrow attending his later life though lived in affluence. And realising the country was stillborn; they came out similarly.

I burnt myself turning the red knob and finally settled for a cold shower. I wore my clothes and pointedly ignored the slippers laid out for me. The floor was tender carpet, cold marble or warm wood and I liked the way they felt.

As I made my way down the stairs, ornate masks and woodcarvings jumped at me from the silent walls and I was caught in fantasies of romantic adventures. Suddenly, a loud chime echoed through the house, almost toppling me down the stairs. The grandfather clock chuckled to itself and settled with a satisfied sigh. I wandered through the mysterious house, musing and amused. The soft Afro beat music made it mysterious, the thick curtains made it mysterious, the large spaces and afternoon shadows, the strange smells and carved objects made it mysterious. It was a house built with care and made to be enjoyed and I had never before had the pleasure to tour such a home.

I heard soft voices conversing in serious tones and followed the sounds that faded with my appearance.

"Your nephew wanted to come to Lagos and the whole Saro-Wiwa issue basically forced our hands. I did not believe Abacha would go through with it. No one thought they would actually hang them," mother said.

"Well, it's what you get when we have a commodity the world needs, in fact a commodity the advanced economies cannot do without and on the other hand, irresponsible leaders who prefer easy rent to riches of the commonwealth; you have an explosive mix of rebellion and poverty," Uncle returned sadly.

They heard my footsteps and fell silent as I walked in. I came upon a room that made all the others seem mundane, a room so spectacular I forgot all about my seated Uncle and mother. I stood in awe as my eyes took in layers and layers of books. Transported by wonder, frozen in astonishment, I was rendered mute by the abundance of words before me. Uncle had given me two books every year since I could read and my collection of fourteen was the largest of any other child I knew. That such a number of books existed in a room to which I now had access was beyond my imagination; I stood there mouth agape. My mother's angry voice quickly dragged me down to earth.

"Seun! Where are your manners? And what are you thinking sleeping past nine? It is already after one in the afternoon!" Mother usually called me by my Yoruba middle name when she was with her cousin. In this instance, it was both a rebuke and atonement for my imperfect manners. Yorubas demand absolute respect for elders and greeting and the neglect of felicitation is something akin to a cardinal sin.

"I'm sorry, ma. I do not know what happened," I stuttered.

"Oya! Apologise to your uncle and greet him!" she continued.

I did so promptly but could see that Uncle was secretly pleased, as all book connoisseurs are with the induction of a novice book lover. I had stayed up later than ever the night before reading the book by my bed and had already gotten to where Ikemefuna joined Okonkwo's household.

Mother was suddenly tender, as mothers tend to be after a good scolding. "My dear, have you eaten?" she asked in a softer voice touching my shoulder gently.

"Oho, now you remember the poor boy's stomach after yelling at him," Uncle said in his carefully constructed tone with a hint of mirth.

And on cue, Mrs Folayo appeared to announce that lunch was ready.

The week passed by in a strange blur of excitement and intrigue. Each day I found a new room to read the endless supply of books. There was the dining room with a largely unused table where I spread myself on the cool surface, the living room with the large Sony television, the other living room where imposing masks grinned joylessly from the walls, but my favourite spot in the whole house was the kitchen where Mrs Folayo always had something cooking. Uncle and mother conversed in quiet tones during the day and with raucous laughter in the evenings. We had meals together and Mrs Folayo floated in and out. A child is the best witness in the home and the worst in the courtroom, because they have the uncanny knack of brutally betraying the truth. That first week, I did not climb trees or admire flowers. I did not meet old Rufus or Major. I did not know of the rabid dog that lived down the road. The entwined tale of mother and Uncle's childhood was still untold. I did not love Aisha or adore Emeka. I did not ache to know their story or inscribe it. That week, I was completely consumed by the house on 33 Oyelaran Soyinka Road, Ikeja, with its infinite mysteries and unexplored secrets.

Lagos had been a blur of crowded streets; in my mind, there were no sounds or smells, simply rapidly fading tall buildings; Uncle's house was the summation of the city. Mother's imminent return to our home in the Niger Delta necessitated a shopping trip that finally introduced me to the bustle of the city I had often heard about.

I dressed carefully, like a debutant, wanting Lagos to have a good impression of me. I wore a black T-shirt that said 'I heart New York', a black face cap with NY on it, a pair of baggy black jeans and a black pair of Nike trainers. I even added my black belt with the big iron buckle that had 'Calvin Klein' inscribed on it, which I got for my eighth birthday. I proudly descended the winding stairs and Mrs Folayo loudly exclaimed, "God forbid!" drawing her right hand over her head and snapping her fingers.

"All black? What? Ko ni sele, it cannot happen!" Mrs Folayo was an old woman with ancient superstitions. When she saw the frightened look on my face, she softened and said, "You are not in mourning. You must change something," and then went to the kitchen to fetch me a glass of chilled Ribena.

Uncle, as that was how Mr Odukoya told me to address him, had two cars. It was the early nineties and everyone who could afford one drove a Mercedes and every office had the Peugeot 504 as its official car. Uncle had a 'baby Benz' (the Mercedez 190 was so-called affectionately); it was the first Mercedes with a tapered front. I sat in the front 'passenger seat' and mother sat at the back 'owner's corner'. The man behind the wheel seemed like he could barely reach the pedals and see over the wheel at the same time.

"Ma ma mama ma, my name is mo mo monmon Monday," he said, starting the car and reversing dangerously out of the driveway. Mr Monday was extremely angry at the world and with his insufficient height and stuttering speech: he perhaps had reason to be. He did not bother with pleasantries or say another word as he darted through the congested roads of Lagos, cutting through the stifling heat and navigating potholes, okadas and danfos. The streets were commotion and Mr Monday smoothly thrived in it. His hand would shoot to the horn as he cut off a driver and avoided a jaywalker. His grip on the wheel was intense but his face was a mask of composure. An accident threatened to occur every minute, yet the frenzied performance played on at a permanent crescendo with no causalities. He was at once a part of the bedlam, one of the orchestra directors of the organised chaos; he seemed entirely unaffected as they all were. Lagos becomes you and you her. I was sure as with many Lagosians he would immediately fall into severe depression if denied, by some magical transfer to a more organised clime.

I was fascinated as all the props were precariously set and everyone played their part to perfection. The danfo drivers cursed and screamed stopping their vehicles and jerking them back to life at the most inappropriate moments. The okada drivers swerved dangerously in and out of traffic, piteous beggars carried desiccated bowls in decimated hands, tall buildings stood at rigid attention in the melting heat, petty traders ran with tray-laden heads to the rolled down windows at every opportune moment and the ice cream man weaved tiredly through all this on his bicycle. Yet, I, captivated, was the sole audience to this absurd normalcy.

But all this was serenity compared to the market. A Lagos market in the nineties is the pinnacle of organised chaos and non-stop excitement that gives the uninitiated nightmares. An unlocked door or open window was a faux pas of which the ignorant were promptly remedied: a few minutes earlier, a woman had her bag picked off her lap through a door left ajar. And right before that, a lady had driven off bleeding as her earrings had been snatched off her ears for having the impunity to display them through the open windows of her car. We found a muddy lot guarded by touts with brown teeth and minds distorted by marijuana and ogogoro. They were burnt black from the sun and bathed in foul sweat. They had bulging muscles, alcoholic breaths and all promised to take proper care of the car. Mother and I descended and Mr Monday remained at his wheel with a defiant scowl.

Mother's face was adorned with only a determined pout and her bag was securely fastened through her arm, above her elbow and beneath her armpit. The last time she had been here, a seemingly mad man had poked her in the chest, twisted her ears and muttered about her being disrespectful. When she got over her surprise and reached up to assuage her throbbing ear, her earrings were gone and the mad man had disappeared. The market was no place for careless people, for delicately bred 'aje butters' as they were called. The strong and the determined make their living here and the violent take what does not belong to them. Yet day in day out, night and day, dead of night, trade abounds; it overflows with human traffic, the market, all the length and breadth of it: here dreams are made and hopes die.

My left hand in mother's unyielding grip, my inauguration was fast paced. We approached the first stall with a rickety wooden table laden with assorted materials. A rotund woman in the next stall was already beckoning mother over to 'sample her wares instead'.

Mother looked the short fair man in the face as he wiped his hands on his soiled vest and adjusted his jeans.

"Madam, wetin you wan buy, I go give you correct price," he said.

"He will be going to The Federal Government College here in Lagos," mother said proudly. "He will need some red, chequered material."

"Ah, nna fine boy, you're a big man oh," he said in a slightly nasal tone, his hands rapidly fingering fabrics. He pulled out two identical pieces and quoted two different prices.

"Chai, you wan kill me!" mother exclaimed. "Na how you go dey give price like that?"

"Haba madam, I see say that you sef know quality, you know am well well. Madam as you see dis one so, dis one na correct material, na from China madam. You fi wash am fifty times, e go dey still dey shine like ruby, I no fi lie madam."

Already, the other piece was forgotten and they squared up like boxers in a tight ring, jabbing and squaring, haggling and bantering. Finally, mother bought the material at half the initial price and twice the price of the ignored fabric. Both of them had the satisfied smile of a hot, loud quarter of an hour well spent. Mother and I made our way tortuously through the market; bargaining, walking away in disgust, being pleaded with to return, grabbed at the hand, poking at materials, swearing at sellers, being sworn at, laughing, sweating, walking, haggling ... Mallams swore and 'Wallahied', Yoruba traders greeted *'Eku asun mummy'*, Ibo men said, 'Nna make we talk,' and female sellers begged, 'My sister patronise us now.' Traders bought us chilled cokes from men who walked by with buckets full of ice and bottles and mother told the sellers to keep the change for their children. Through all this, my tired hand, attached to mother's firm grasp, dragged along my tired mind on my exhausted feet. The initial excitement was short-lived and my stygian garments stimulated more misery.

By the denouement, my mind was buzzing from too many drinks, yet I could hardly move my legs and my mouth was cemented shut from fatigue. Laden with bulging bags, we marched tiredly towards the car. Mr Monday saw us approaching and with brisk steps of his tiny legs, he was soon gathering all the bags in his short, stocky arms. He sneered at the dirty pale children that hounded tired shoppers. A young, skinny boy with large honey eyes and light caramel skin covered in grime approached the woman to our left. There was a bloody gash above his left brow attended by a contingent of dancing flies. She was moved to compassion and made the mistake of giving him ten naira. In a matter of seconds, like a swarm of locusts, a dozen impoverished children, clinging to her arms and clothes, seized her. Her act of charity was not going unpunished; slowly her dignity was unwound with her loose wrapper. The more she tried to placate them with her goodness, the tighter they clung, until she was crying in agony and distress. Suddenly, one of them was sent sprawling to the floor by a blow to his head. One by one, they were torn off her with vicious blows and kicks. She wanted to stop the muscular dark man from hitting the sensitive looking children, but could not. Her eyes were streaming with tears as she hurriedly got into her car and handed the man some money as gratitude for extricating her from the discomfort.

As Mr Monday drove out of the market with his stern features, an armless man nodded at the car and cried for mercy. He was from Maiduguri. He had had his arm amputated for stealing a goat to feed his hungry children and then put on a train heading south to Lagos. He had one large red eye and another that was tightly shut – a legacy of a water-borne disease that almost took his life when he was six years old and pale skin covered in old wounds. And if you looked close enough, you saw in the weary eyes reflections of a future that once was, a hope that died, a dream unrealised; all that was left was the body of an emaciated boy. He was begging for money enough to get through the day, although many Lagosians believe these denizens are mere pawns in the hands of powerful men.

And always, at all this, the sun pounds ferociously on person and place alike, its harsh stinging sentence, ignored by the dwellers of this city, is meted to all.

The ride home was mostly in silence. Mr Monday guarded his stammer while mother and I were thoroughly spent. The road had lost both its magic and mythical menace. A looming police roadblock barely roused our interest until we were pulled over.

"Licence and registration?" the officer asked with affected efficiency. Mr Monday silently handed these to him.

"Madam, please step out of the car," he said with exaggerated pretence to competence. Mr Monday wordlessly stepped out as well. The officer kept up his interrogation with a barrage of customary questions. "How many of this and what, where of that." Mother was so fatigued that when he finally decided in his benevolence to let us go despite the major offence of Madam ignoring section 57 of the long forgotten and completely disregarded 1954 law to wear seatbelts at the back, she was only too glad to give him a few hundred naira for his efforts. His corrupted fingers had not stashed the money in his grateful pockets before Mr Monday suddenly became animated and snatched the money back from his surprised grasp and returned it to mother.

"Ma mama mad mad mad madam, don't do do do do that," he finally forced out. "Ple ple please get in th th th the car," he continued. He gave the policeman a look that froze him in his sullied stance, got in the car and drove off. The car was cocooned in stunned silence and it remained so until we were once more parked under the expansive guava tree in Uncle's compound. Providence smiled on us to keep the policeman dumb for that moment. Police checkpoints have been witnesses to 'accidental' bullet discharges.

FOUR

After mother's departure, I took no time to quickly settle into Uncle's house. I spent most of my time enjoying the feast of literature, settling occasionally in one of the numerous quiet corners of the massive house until Mrs Folayo appeared with a plate of goodies and a cool drink. Initially, I stayed at the boarding school but both Uncle and Mrs Folayo immediately missed the clatter of bare feet on the wooden floors and after just one term, I began daily trips from the house straight to the classroom. And though it was never mentioned, it was obvious I provided new distractions for their old sorrows.

Five years into this arrangement, curled on a plush green couch, I turned the last page of Enid Blyton's *Children of the Faraway Tree*. Uncle had been particularly busy holed up in his study for the past few days, so I relocated a pile of books to my room. I ascended the stairs with the slow purposefulness of ownership and walked into the room I had tamed to my preferences. I set down the books and deliberated on which one among the three before me I should next savour; I could not decide between *The Secret Seven*, *The Famous Five* and *The Three Golliwogs*. As my mind luxuriously contemplated its choices, a flicker of orange caught my eye through the window. I made my way slowly to the netted opening, my curiosity not completely aroused. It took me a second to locate the source of the pale glow and when I did, adrenaline was suddenly shooting through my body and out of my mouth as I excitedly screamed, "Fire! Fire!"

I ran down the stairs, the chant becoming a frightened scream spilling from my lips. By the time I got to the last step, a worried Mrs

Folayo and a disgruntled Uncle stood in panic at the bottom. Mrs Folayo was making loud benedictions that was adding to the racket until Uncle interrupted with a firm and necessary, "Where?"

"At the neighbours house," I said excitedly already heading for the door before Mrs Folayo could force me to remain indoors. When we got out, the fire was more obvious and most of the street was outside the yellow wall with its barbed wires. No one called for the fire department, as it would have been futile. Instead, the mallams had sprung into a concerted, if amateurish, coordinated action, forming a chain that carried buckets of water mixed with 'Omo' detergent and dumping them on the fire that was rapidly spreading towards the house. I was excited by the commotion and tried unsuccessfully to help until Mrs Folayo finally restrained me. I stood sulkily next to her until I spied a young girl roughly my age standing alone a little way off. I wrested my hand from Mrs Folayo's grasp and made my way over to her.

"Hello," I said with a bright smile that was amiss in the cacophony around us. She kept staring at the fire silently, ignoring me, much to my annoyance.

"I said hello," I repeated more forcefully. Slowly, her gaze turned to me.

"I'm Seun. What's your name?"

"That's my house," I said pointing, ignoring her reticence. "I've lived there for five years." I was beginning to get irritated by her refusal to respond.

"You're very black," I said suddenly, "Do you even speak English?"

"Yes," she said abruptly and before anything else could be added, she turned and ran into the house on the other side of ours that had a similar white coat.

Major, Uncle's watchman, was one of the heroes of the fire. He suggested the human chain to speed up the bucket delivery and when the fire began to spread, he came up with the idea to use wet sand to impede its progress. He was tall, thin and dark – very dark. So dark that he seemed to glow and when the moon gave only a faint light he floated luminous like a gloomy apparition. He was one of the many night watchmen who had once been cattle herders in the north before interminable droughts drove them south. The adults swore they were the best because as the folk story has it, their ferocious eyes did not close at night and the children loved them because during the day they manned stalls laden with sweets and other knick-knacks where children indulge their fancy. Animals were always comfortable around him and he often said that he would have made the best robber. And he was right. He threaded silently and was deceptively strong. His voice came forth in forceful whispers that seized the ears of those it was intended for and remained inaudible to everyone else. He often forgot to smile but sometimes a white line would leak across his face like a brief bolt of lightning on a black stormy night. He breathed without a sound and heard everything. He was excellent at what he did and loved people that did likewise. He loved Mr Odukoya.

I had a blue BMX bicycle, which I got for my fourteenth birthday. Often, I asked Mrs Folayo if she needed something from up the road so I could see how quickly I could pedal there and back. After the fire at the neighbours' house, I biked around with a small notebook and pen, 'making observations to safeguard the residents of the street' to the amusement of the mallams who hid discreetly behind the tall gates. A stray dog would occasionally prowl around our road and it was my duty to frighten it away by ringing my bell incessantly when I saw it. I was on my usual tour of the neighbourhood when I saw the girl from the night of the fire buying some chewing gum from the mallam across the street from our house. I rode up with the smugness of a child ready to make her explain why she behaved so immaturely and perhaps, show off my bicycle.

"Hey, why did you run away the other day?" The question I had been dying to ask for those three months.

"None of your business," she returned surly.

With that question out of the way and her dour response, I did not know what to say next. "Hey, do you want to ride my bike?"

"No."

"Why? It is great."

"Leave me alone."

"Do you not know how to ride?"

Although it was not her reason for not wanting to ride, it was true and immediately made her defensive.

"Of course, I do."

"It's okay if you don't. I just taught myself recently. Look," I said pointing to a formidable gash on my knees to show the cost of my prowess. I saw her hesitate and knew I almost had her. There were not many children on the street and in Bayelsa I had been accustomed to always having other children about. "I can teach you some other time but for now you can ride on the back."

"Okay," she said. She got on and I extended my hand for a stick of gum.

"Bicycle ride ticket payment," I said. "What's your name?"

"Aisha," she said handing it over and settling down properly. "And I'll give you because your mouth smells."

I knew my mouth did not smell, but could not think of an adequate retort; I was still stinging from her clever remark when we got to the top of the street. The dog was there and as always, it barked at us. I felt Aisha stiffen in the back seat and still feeling the burn from her earlier comment wanted to regain the upper hand. I rode at the dog and braked suddenly ringing my bell loudly. The dog backed away. I laughed. Aisha screamed and I did it again. The third time the dog began snarling and instead began advancing. I became as terrified as Aisha and soon we were pedalling down the road at full speed with the dog hot on our heels. Aisha was screaming at the top her lungs and I was doing all that I could to prevent myself from doing likewise. I went by my house in a whizz looking for the first open gate and finally realised the snarling noise behind us was gone. I dared to look and seeing the dog sitting calmly by Major, I spontaneously hit the brakes. Aisha fell off the back and I flew over the handlebars, badly bruising my other knee. I came up with a grin on my face to counter the look of horror on Aisha's.

We hurried back to the house after Major sent the dog off in the other direction. Major saw us coming and smiled: his job for the day was done, but he took the bike as we hurried towards the kitchen and Mrs Folayo.

"Ah, ah! This boy, until you break all your bones you will not stop with that bicycle," Mrs Folayo grumbled good-humouredly. "And who is your friend?" She asked, spying Aisha hanging back shyly. "Poor child. Come here, I see he has tried to kill you as well," she continued without waiting for an answer.

"Her name is Aisha," I volunteered. "She lives next door."

Mrs Folayo cleaned Aisha up and gave us both Ribena and puff puff. Aisha left quietly while I was still being cleaned up. But the next day there was a knock on my door.

"There is someone here to check on you," Mrs Folayo said with a smile.

And on an eventful bicycle ride, just like that, an everlasting bond was formed.

III
Zombie (Southern Nigeria, 2003)

ONE

Mrs Ranti Ehurere's unrestrained wails were the despondent soundtrack to Sagamu's rapidly fading lush scenery. Prescient tears streamed from ignorant eyes. This is the eternally enshrined image I have of my mother. She was wearing her favourite bubu, its yellow and black streaks sat elegantly on her slender shoulders. She wore no jewellery on her neck – it was a work of art in itself. Her proud chin quivered as she talked incessantly. Her svelte fingers gripped mine tightly but I looked away, embarrassed by her large penetrating charcoal stare.

I had already been in Lagos for over five years and each time I returned, mother cried like it was the first time. But this time was different, I had come home for the long holiday before the final senior secondary school examinations and mother had gotten used to my presence. She realised my childhood was ending and she had missed a significant part of it. Once more, she was returning with me and this time she did not attempt to camouflage her sorrow. Our arrival was like a déjà vu of the first, except I now walked with the assured steps of someone who had arrived at home. Mother noticed this and it saddened her because each time I came to visit in the Niger Delta, I walked with the cautious gait of an intruder and opened drawers with the timidity of a guest. I promptly went upstairs to take a shower and although I had bathed with a bucket and bowl until five years earlier, I felt I needed the stinging sprays on my body to wash away the products of three months of improper hygiene.

Mother and Uncle barely exchanged pleasantries before politics hijacked their discussions. It consumed every home in Nigeria and was present at every meal. After banging his head against the tyranny of military governance all his life, the last and worst of the dictators had died unexpectedly. The corpse was long buried, but juicy details still emerged casting a surreal light on the death and prompting renewed rounds of dinner table discussions.

"I hear he was killed by prostitutes," mother said in disbelief.

"I am sure the CIA was involved," Uncle returned in a quiet voice, as though someone was listening. "I mean how could both Abacha and Abiola, the dictator and the president-elect die mysteriously within the same month?"

"Let's just hope this Obasanjo knows what he is doing," mother replied. "He was once a military man."

"He is still one!" Uncle retorted, "The other day he told a Senator to shut up. In my opinion, we are still under military governance, especially if this party stays in power."

"Only God will help us," mother said tiredly.

Uncle smiled at this. He was tired of people sitting back, with arms folded as the country fell apart, waiting on divine intervention. But he knew mother and father did what they could so he let the statement pass.

"But how is your side?" Uncle asked suddenly with obvious concern. "The place must be in a shambles again. I thought you were approaching some calm finally after the Saro-Wiwa disaster, but these militants have turned the place upside down once more."

"I know you people fought Abacha from here, but you should have seen the area after they hanged Ken and the other Ogoni leaders. I could only thank God that at least Seun was in school here."

"My dear, I know," Uncle said, "remember I visited. So, what is happening now with these militants? I am unsure if they are fighting against the state as the government claims or for the people as they say. I never trust armed uprisings."

"And it is the government you trust?" Mother retorted.

"Well, I also do not trust military rulers that return as civilians. So, which is the frying pan and which is the fire?" Uncle asked.

"We will wait and see, o jare. I am tired of these people and their wahala, all of them," she said throwing her hand up in exasperation.

"So the militants are causing more trouble?" Uncle asked as though he already knew the answer.

"Some of them started nobly, but as usual the politicians have gotten their fingers into the water and muddied it."

"You mean the politicians are involved?" Uncle asked with disbelief.

"Of course, nothing can be proven, but suddenly these boys went from disgruntled men protesting oil spills to young boys carrying machine guns siphoning oil and kidnapping as they wish. I'm sure you heard of the twelve murdered policemen."

"So who is involved?"

"That is what we don't know. But I am worried, because even if the federal government is profiting, they will not turn a blind eye and there will be retaliation soon. Obasanjo has been rather truculent about his plans to handle the issue."

"You see, Seun is having a good time here. In fact, tell that your stubborn husband that he should take a break and you should all come up here for a while," Uncle said, trying to change the mood.

Mother chuckled, "See you, you want us to completely take over your house. You have already been very gracious with Seun. He seems to be enjoying himself. And who is this Aisha girl he keeps talking about?"

"I think your boy has a crush. She is this Hausa girl next door. If you stayed longer, you would have met her," Uncle ventured in a last bid to extend her stay.

"You know your friend. That last time I was here and he did not see his wife for one week, you'd have thought the world was about to end," she said it with the happy sigh of a woman who believed a wife's place was by her husband's side. "Seun better not fall in love with a Hausa girl oh," mother was saying when Uncle's laugh cut her short.

"And look who is talking. Where is your husband from? The man does not even understand ekaro?" And they both laughed.

The purity of the untainted blue sky made Mrs Ranti Ehurere happy. Everything else was polluted – the water, the trees, the pleasures. The roads were mud, the houses were bare cement and people cooked with crude firewood contraptions. She kept her eyes to the sky, trying to forget that just one week earlier she had left Seun behind in Lagos under a sky that leaked continuously like her eyes. The riots were unrelenting, Akpokio was convinced the government and multinationals would be forced to acquiesce to their demands. He refused to listen when he was told to stay home during the melees and Ranti was worried. When they reasoned with him that as one of the organisers he should be safe, he simply laughed and carried on in his quiet stubbornness. "The government will come to negotiate soon," he would say. "I must be there to welcome them."

A few kilometres away, a silver frog was serenading in burps from a black lake. Another drowned in a tar pond attended by large dragonflies with too many wings. Ranti decided to do the laundry to distract her mind and carried a pale green bucket outside. She called repeatedly for her daughter to bring some detergent and realised her voice was too loud. She stopped yelling and listened, it was much too quiet and she looked around slightly disoriented.

Suddenly a loud boom was heard and the air exploded in a thousand lights, arousing the few animals left in the dying forests into coordinated cacophony. The bucket dropped from her hand and Ranti ran towards the main road, unthinking, heading towards the sound. She had a feeling her daughter was there, she knew her husband was. She burst onto the road and was overwhelmed by the chaos: stones and bottles were being hurled at soldiers and in return, they sent bullets and bombs. Mrs Ranti Ehurere died quickly and painlessly five minutes after she heard the first boom and it was best.

It was best because she did not see her eight-year-old daughter pinned down by a sneering soldier as he slapped her roughly and raped her maliciously. She did not see the second soldier do the same and then shatter her skull with the butt of his gun. She did not see Mr Akpokio Ehurere's giant frame expire slowly as the hasty bullets of an automatic gutted his stomach, leaking acid on his large fingers as they tried to save his slowly expiring soul.

She did not see the crying old women as they rolled around on the floor repeatedly hitting their heads against the bloody mud. She did not see her neighbour curled in the foetal position in the pool of blood of her dead baby that she still clutched to her breast. The indiscriminate boots that trampled down doors and the impartial bullets that met whatever was behind them. She did not see her house in flames or the blackened remnants when the merciful acid rains finally came. She was not there when I heard the news and she did not sit by my bed for six months. She did not see the sad makeshift tents of nylon and old sack that housed the survivors. She did not see our entire town burned to the ground. It was best that she did not hear the sad excuses the government gave for the massacre at Odi in Bayelsa State. The finding of the military tribunals was always the same: the mayhem was committed by 'unknown soldiers'.

In the background, the stream of oil continued spurting out the black gold, but the dollars flowed not into the Central Bank but into the politicians' pockets as the gas flares blazed at the top of long poles apexing the flags of the oil multinationals. The militant camps flooded with disenchanted youth anxious for the drugs that made them numb and the guns that gave false strength. In the capital, Governor O.C Abari congratulated himself for getting his first hole-in-one on his personal golf course.

I was playing ludo with Aisha when Mrs Folayo walked in. I had just rolled the die and was moving my marker when a sombre face followed the quiet knock. It was immediately apparent something was amiss.

"Aisha, I think it is best if you go home," she said gently, "Seun, Uncle wants you in his room."

"It was not me. It was already cracked," I was already protesting, sure Mrs Folayo had found the mug I had broken and stashed at the back of the cupboard. Uncle rarely summoned me to his room and I was thinking of the best way to avoid a scolding. Uncle's red eyes and gentle voice surprised me when I walked into the room whose heavy curtains were mostly drawn.

"Seun," Uncle started quietly, his usually steady voice wavering slightly, "there was a military attack in Odi." The name of my hometown did not initially trigger anything in me and I continued to stare blankly at Uncle.

"Many people died," Uncle continued, his voice cracking completely and tears pooling in his eyes.

"Is mummy okay?" I cut in in a panicked voice. Uncle's silence confirmed what his mouth could not.

"How about my sister and father?"

"Seun, everyone in your family ..." Uncle was saying with unrestrained tears when I suddenly slumped to the ground.

TWO

For six months, I drifted in and out of a coma, Mrs Folayo, Uncle and Aisha kept constant vigils by my side. My weight disappeared and I grew exceptionally tall and dark. On one dull day, all days seemed the same in that season of anomie; with soggy clouds, my eyes fluttered open. Not much was made of it; I had apparently done so many times in the preceding months only to collapse again into fitful nightmares. But I kept staring into Aisha's frightened eyes and finally said, "Hey."

"He's awake!" she yelled in delight, giving me a tight hug until the nurse tried to eject her from the room. After checking to make sure everything was okay, the prim nurse disappeared down the hall to telephone Uncle with the news. By the time Uncle and Mrs Folayo arrived, with tight smiles of relief across their faces, Aisha and I were caught in a deep argument that placed larger smiles on ours.

I returned home from the hospital different, I was tall, dark and brooding. Uncle had formally adopted me, changing my name from Akpokio Seun Ehurere to Seun Akpokio Odukoya. I missed my final examinations and spent six months recuperating in the company of long gone masters of fiction, for my life was nothing but a surreal existence of the unimaginable. But my interest had shifted from storybooks to literature, substituting Enid Blyton with Charles Dickens. When I was well enough, I spent another six months studying, until I took my final examinations a year later than planned. I had the best secondary school graduation result for the previous five years and when the constant riots crippled the Nigerian university system, Uncle did not argue when I said I wanted to school abroad. During that year before I left for England, my world was school, books, Aisha, Uncle and Mrs Folayo.

There are few things to compare with the Nigerian aunty and Mrs Folayo typified this rare breed. They cared like a mother, listened like a friend and were excessively generous, scolded only when necessary, encouraged all good ideas irrespective of how outrageous, because they were proud of you the way a father would be without the weighted responsibility of the consequence of failure. So, when I lost my family, Mrs Folayo stepped in aptly. When she had heard of Aisha's tragedy, she had pulled her into her fold as well.

Mrs Folayo once had a family of her own, a nervous husband who was a police officer and a little girl with a lively mind, but an irredeemable asthmatic with a frail frame. Mr Folayo was not an alcoholic, but he enjoyed the bottle, particularly the local brews. He drank palm wine in the mornings, buruqutu in the afternoon and ogogoro at night. He attributed this to his noble patriotism but it was simply because they were cheaper. He kept a moustache, which was the only tidy aspect of his appearance. He had all the necessary features of a corrupt officer – the rotund paunch that sat on a heavy belt, the stern face that quickly broke into a servile smile, the greasy fingers that were quick to stop innocent drivers and pocket hasty bribes. He loved his daughter and that was the only thing commendable about his character.

He was never charming but could be agreeable when he tried because he knew many stories and told them well. When he was in the right mood, his face was a contortion of well-rehearsed features that were intended to be endearing but were rather aggravating. Mrs Folayo had been lonely, her mother made her cry and he made her laugh. They had a joyous wedding but an unhappy marriage. When the child came two years later, it was a welcome distraction from each other. Mrs Folayo was fervent about religion and he was avid about disregarding it. This caused many problems. She nagged him for taking bribes and he railed at her for disturbing his sleep to pray at night. The accusations were often baseless and unfortunately endless. Perhaps she could have done better as Mr Folayo had never been a desirable husband but he had once been suitable. Mrs Folayo had lovely cheekbones that complemented her angular jaw but the rest of her face seemed like it had been squashed together, giving her a look of sorrowful penitence that suited her character and made people wonder which came first.

Mrs Folayo usually dropped off their daughter at school on the way to work and her husband picked her up in the afternoons, leaving her to play in their scanty apartment with the other children from the neighborhood while he had his afternoon drinks. Mr Folayo worked the night shift because that was when his wife was home and he preferred to never see her. One day, he had his heavy head in his worthless hands on a drunken table rather than in the helmet of his shabby motorcycle with his daughter in tow. Her school was by the busy Mile Twelve bus stop and after three endless hours of waiting, the little girl was certain she could retrace the bus route her mother took her through in the mornings.

It was a hot, dry day and the large buses were kicking up thick clouds of smoke and dust, inflaming her lungs and making her head light. She made her way to the shade of the few trees that hung back from the chaos of the stop. She took rapid puffs of her inhaler and began to feel better. Her mother's boss had given her a gold chain for her birthday and her mother had attached a cross to it. She was gladly fingering this and failed to notice that some of the leaves on the ground seemed suspended mid air like a puppet show. Then she disappeared down a hole, taking the miserable girl out of her misery.

Mr Folayo was driven to despair trying to find her and was continuously frustrated by the indifference of his fellow officers. He took this out on Mrs Folayo, who felt the best remedy for their missing daughter was fervent prayer. One day, he walked out of the house and never returned.

Her tragedy was an enduring twelve-year-old pain and even though the scar remained fresh, she bore it with grace. And she remained the anchor to the orphans of the state that inhabited number 33, Oyelaran Soyinka Street.

PART 5

QUESTION JAM ANSWER

I
Fefe Me Efe (Southern Nigeria, 2003 – 2004)

ONE

He weaved around the questions deftly, easily, like a featherweight dancing around the ring. The audience was mesmerised, even the reporters that were to scrutinise him. As a practice tennis match, they lobbed the questions at him, high and easy and he smashed them back, eloquently asserting his innocence. He intended to ignore the vexatious light-skinned reporter in the first row. He wearied of her tenacity. But today, even she, upright and persistent, could not taint his joy; fore procured, victory was assured next week. Even justice could be subtly persuaded with flashy new cars and unaddressed brown envelopes.

"What question do you have for us now, Nneka?" he asked with contempt. He intended to humiliate her. She would ask about the trial and his answer would be eloquent.

"Governor Abari," she began with a smile that silenced the room. Her honesty was widely respected but rarely replicated. "How did you make your first million?"

"What?" he asked.

"How did you make your first million?" she repeated with the same smile.

"Well, I ..." he sputtered. A frown came across his face, "I did some investments with, eh, eh ... you see, when my father died at the hands of that vicious regime, which also persecuted me, I inherited some money." He was shaken and upset at the unexpected question. His victory would be tainted; his life would be persistently hunted if that reporter stayed. He made some more general statements and cracked some more jokes, but his joy was diminished.

When they got into the car, he turned to his assistant and said, "We must get rid of her."

"Oga, are you sure? People will suspect …"

"I don't care!" he snapped. "Make it innocuous. Armed robbers, car accident, the roads are bad enough …" he chuckled, the thought of her demise brought back some of his mirth. "Do it in about a month, when the smoke has cleared around me. We can make it an anniversary of sorts."

TWO

He squinted at the paper, his rheumatic eyes slowly took in the words; his mind absorbed them even more arduously. He tortuously read the whole article and then did so again. He picked up the column from the earlier week titled, 'Ex-Governor shaken by millionth question'. He studied them both by the light of the flickering candle until dawn broke and slowly bathed the room with a faint yellow light. He picked up his stick and unhurriedly arose. He stretched his old limbs, pulled his coat a little tighter around his frail frame and stumbled out of his room. He set about washing the car, slowly and deliberately. For the past two years, he had done everything slowly and deliberately. He went back to his room and said his prayers. He always said the same prayers, which consisted of only a few lines:

"Forget my past transgressions as I forgive those of others. Protect my wife and my daughter. Give me the strength to begin what must be done and the grace to complete it."

He finished just as his boss was getting ready to leave. He approached the permanently harried man and said, "I am leaving and I won't be back."

There was nothing for the boss to say. He muttered a 'Thank you, God be with you' that was full of remorse. Except for the one room he lived in by the gate, he asked for only food and the old newspapers. He did his job thoroughly and collected a salary that was a fraction of what other guards earned. Of that, he gave twenty percent to the church, sixty to the poor in the neighborhood and kept the rest of it. Very rarely, he would dip into his savings to buy a candle or some cloth to wrap around his skinny, scarred body. He was the dream of every employer.

He nodded, turned around slowly and opened the gate. When the boss left, he wrapped all his belongings in a bit of cloth and tied them to a two-pronged stick he kept in the corner of his room. The stick was as tall as he was when he stooped, which he always did. In a few minutes, he was ready to go. He slung an old gun that was newly purchased over one shoulder and started off, leaning heavily on his stick.

Along the way, he stopped by the bread seller's stall. She liked him because he always gave her money and rarely took any bread. Today, he gave her money and took some bread, trudging laboriously down the road as quickly as he could.

He walked for a long time, but he did not mind it. He thought over his life. He was old, but not too old, yet he felt he had lived many lifetimes, he felt he was old enough. When he was younger, he dreamed of making huge contributions to society, but he was not sure he had. He was going to rectify that … finally.

The first month had been the most difficult. After he found his family, he had debated how to approach them. He lurked outside their home for many days quietly observing his wife and daughter. Then one day as he stood outside the gates loitering, a car had driven up and indicated towards the house opposite theirs. The windows had come down and a voice had asked if he was there for the gateman's job. He had initially been surprised, then looked down to realise he was dirty and unshaven and finally understood why his wife and daughter had gone past him numerous times without a second glance. Before he could think, he said yes. "Report tomorrow," the man said abruptly and drove in. He went back to the room he rented in the 'face-me-I-face-you' and decided that after the many atrocities he had committed in the north, this was the extent of happiness he deserved … but still he had no peace. He placed his large reserves of accumulated wealth in an old bank and shut out his former life. Over the years in the stifling solitude of his shed, with the knowledge that just across the road lived a family he could not approach he wrestled with his ambitions and his memories. He wrestled with his soul. Sometimes the fact that he was so close to them left him tortured, at other times, it was his relief. The only habit he could not kill was the daily perusal of the newspapers and because he understood what horrors the passive and nebulous headlines shielded he detested the man he had been. He despised the man who had made him that way and resented the role he played in making the man what he had now become. When he saw the headline, he knew what he was going to do before he thought about it. The name that was scrawled across the front pages had come to represent every part of himself and his past that he resented. He shuddered in disgust as he heard the insatiable laughter leak through the pages from the frozen, oily smile.

He knew the Governor's mind intimately and when he read the first article two weeks earlier, he was almost frightened. Nneka, the reporter – his daughter – had crossed the line with that question, it was one that birthed more revealing queries. The only thing the Governor detested more than a loss was a sullied victory. He knew time was short. He reckoned the Governor would wait a while but not too long; he had to act quickly. When the newspapers carried the story that the corruption cases against Ex-Governor Abari would be concluded in the next couple of days in Lagos, he finally felt some relief; he knew his mission.

He did not stop walking until he got to the bus stop. It was eight miles away, but he trudged on, only stopping to sit under the shade of a bombax tree when the sun reached its zenith at midday. He ate one of the loaves of bread, said his prayer and leafed through his tattered Bible. He had not stepped into a church in a long time, but he faithfully read his Bible, numerous times every day. He especially liked the story of Moses.

He got to the bus stop at sunset and bought the first ticket to Lagos; he had to get there by noon the following day.

He alighted from the bus, extended his tender limbs and rubbed his tired eyes. He set off again in his slow amble; he really had no time to waste so he hailed a taxi. The driver could tell the man just got to the city, the way he held on tightly to his sparse belongings. He was surprised though that his passenger paid no attention to all the buildings and wondrous bustle. He did not seem to notice the shabby upholstery or the bare innards – the metal that poked out of the door and wires from the dashboard. He seemed only concerned with time, his eyes constantly straying to a watch that belied his simple appearance.

The taxi driver grossly overcharged him. He, however, did not mind; he would have no use for money after today, he thought. He left the taxi driver with too much fare, a blessing and a fleeting feeling of guilt. He marched towards the rented crowd around the courthouse. They were singing the praises of someone who was not yet in sight. He heaved a sigh of relief that he had made it in time. The crowd was deafening in their obsequious jubilations, but he remained unperturbed. The ex-Governor's judgment on the corruption charges had not yet been read, but they already knew the outcome. The whole country knew the outcome and that was why the old man was there.

A few minutes later, the ex-Governor came out of the courthouse with his right hand held up high and his left waving at the crowd. He had a big smile on his fat face and his protruding belly bounced from side to side with each step. He stopped a few metres from the crowd and they fell silent. He said a few words and they burst into chants and applause. He held up both hands and silence reigned again. Before he put his hand down, the sound of an explosion reverberated through the air and a red stain started to spread across his rich, white muslin agbada. The oppressive silence that followed was punctuated by another explosion and bedlam ensued.

The crowd took to raucous uncoordinated flight. Many held their heads like it would flee without them. The banners and placards proclaiming the majesty of the recently slain were quickly abandoned on the hot asphalt. The police officers that had been hired to protect the ex-Governor instantly took to their heels as well. In less than five minutes, the only humans left under the baking sun in front of the courthouse, were the bleeding corpse of the ex-Governor splayed across the ground and the impassive old man sitting a few metres away from him. His gun lay on top of a discarded placard that read 'long live John O.C Abari'.

Emeka had imagined he would die in a hail of bullets, his only regret being the probable death of innocent bystanders. It was the least he expected from the notoriously trigger happy police. He had made his way to the front of the mob and aimed carefully through the throng of bodies hoping his first shot would hit his mark. Instead, he had had time to shoot off a second, watching both bury themselves in his victim's chest. He was surprised by the policemen cowering behind the courthouse with the rest of the crowd. He did not know what to do, so he sat down because he was tired.

His vision began to fade but his eyes remained open, staring blindly. He heard heavy boots approaching and felt a blow to his head. The darkness slowly seeped to the rest of his senses. It was not the first time he had shot a man and it was not the first time he had slept from the lullaby of soldiers' boots. The cell was more spacious this time; he was the only one in it. When he awoke, he did not know how long he had been there or how much longer he remained. Everywhere was darkness, his eyes refused to look at the world anymore because he saw much more within.

"They have come for you," the voice said, carelessly jumping through discoloured teeth and bouncing around the stained rough walls. Emeka did not even think to ask whom, he got up like he had been expecting someone. They went through a hall of stale lives, Emeka could not see them, but it was a stench familiar to him. He did not notice the dull flickering bulb give way to fluorescent tubes. But he felt the rough broken cement become overused linoleum beneath his feet; he noticed the air become fresher and more desperate. Then he confirmed something he had always suspected, that the much harsher masters of poverty and corruption chained the guards.

"It's been many years," the voice said and Emeka smiled because even though the booming laugh did not rattle the barred windows of the joyless room, he immediately knew to whom they belonged. He took Emeka's arm firmly and led him to the car. It was not until they were inside that Uncle finally said, "They granted bail because you did not run and because, well … you're old … Why him and why at your age?" Uncle asked.

"Not too long ago, you were saying I was too young," Emeka said with a soft chuckle that implied there was time for questions later, so Uncle did not ask about his sight.

The car ride was mostly silent. They sat at the back, side by side, with matching smiles – men who were conscious they were approaching the final act of their lives.

"Thanks again," Emeka said.

"Please, I'm sorry they even held you for up to forty-eight hours," Uncle returned.

"You know I mean the other thing. Why did you join?"

Uncle was quiet for a bit. "I had to," he said it quietly, like he was ashamed. "After you left that bundle in my hands and said to spend it if you did not return, I put it aside. But after a year of work, I knew something was missing. Your words echoed in my mind. But if you died in a war I did not partake in, I would have been unable to touch it. I walked into the barracks and said I wanted to fight. They were not recruiting but they eventually let me go as an officer's assistant. That man you shot in that room, he did reconnaissance after we cleared an area and I assisted him." Uncle paused briefly but Emeka's face registered no reaction. "I should thank you," Uncle said and still Emeka was silent. But it was a loud silence that conveyed words with too much importance to be voiced.

"I quit right after I saw you in that room ... I was convinced you would die and it made me sick. I went home and could not return to my old firm. Finally, I used your money to start my firm. I imagined you would agree." Emeka resumed his smile and placed his other hand over their entwined fingers.

They had gotten to the house and Uncle said with a short laugh, "And here is the second fruit of your labour. I built it as soon as we sorted out the office." There was the pride of many noble achievements in his voice.

THREE

Uncle had become a human's rights lawyer because he loved people intensely and believed strongly in the sanctity of each and every life. Once, he had happened upon the remnants of a children's illustrated book and had read the line, 'a person is a person no matter how small' and the words had stayed with him. Over the years, he had adapted the last word many times to fit a case, although more often than not he simply used, 'no matter how poor'. Despite his tender nature, save for five people whom he believed possessed the necessary robustness of character, he could not stand being left alone with another. He often said he was born with the wonderful misfortune of having too many interests (which he called his infinite curiosity), which meant he often found others boring. And in turn, they thought him rude, despite being initially fascinated by him. He distrusted small groups except of select people because he had a morbid fear of being stuck with the unattached bore. It was why he often kept to himself, turning down most invitations to socialise and was generally considered snobbish. And although he much preferred a few drinks in his home with the 'FoN (Future of Nigeria) group', he thrived in the midst of large crowds, darting between different groups with a large smile and leaving each discussion more fiery and intriguing than when he initially arrived.

He built his house like he constantly expected to entertain a vast company, with wide spaces for general dialogue and intimate corners for more sensitive topics. He had decorations that started conversations and there was the general feel of an expected mob – done on purpose to spur Uncle to finish the endless tasks he had scheduled before the looming interruption that never came. His living room was oppressive for one, intimidating for two but wholesome for six.

That Christmas, five and a half years after my departure, Uncle's house was alive. The trees bore more fruits than Old Rufus could pick off the floor and the birds came in large droves, the air filled with their melodious whistling. The flowers blossomed and the insects buzzed in their beautiful efficiency. Just a year after their reunion, Emeka's arrival had banished Uncle's reclusive nature to a quiet corner of his brain and invited brilliant but stubborn characters with unshakable ideals. It seemed Emeka was intent on making up for his many years in forced isolation and chosen solitude and coerced Uncle to be more accepting of company.

Uncle still woke up at seven and locked himself in his library until noon. Emeka woke an hour before him and unfailingly looked to the rising sun mouthing quiet prayers. He would go outside and sit silently next to Old Rufus, or Major and even occasionally Mr Monday. He never ate breakfast and barely spoke but when he did they never had a clue what he was talking about. But it was noticed that he was particularly pensive on the days he sat beneath the guava trees, especially when they were ripe. Emeka was blind for two months and then one day as he sat under the tree, contemplative and its fruit released its first scent of the season; it slowly came into a hazy focus. Emeka greeted his sight like one would an old friend who was never really missed because his loyalty was never in doubt.

And a few months later, when I returned, I would join him on the rare days I arose in time and Emeka would paste on his face a wry smile. He would put a wrinkled hand on my young shoulders as if passing currents of unseen knowledge. Then he would say something like, 'Do Muslims worship God?' Questions so initially banal they were rhetorical. He would then answer his own questions so illogically that I was never sure if I was convinced or amused. But the real discussions started just after lunch, around three, when a troupe in the august of their careers invaded the house for company, palm wine and the numerous delicacies Mrs Folayo conjured.

They jokingly called themselves the FoN group – Future of Naija and Oyinbo (white man) always came in first. He had a favourite chair he was afraid to lose even though everyone always sat in the exact same place. Oyinbo got his name because he was extremely fair, almost like an albino. His eyes were pale brown –

hazel, but he had no problems in the sun, his hair was white from age and wisdom and he avidly stayed indoors but only because he was sure a mosquito would get him if he was outside for longer than a few minutes. Many knew him by his other nickname, The Scribe, which he earned as a thrilling columnist when he wrote for *The Guardian*. Despite his unrivaled penmanship, he was mostly silent during discussions, only interjecting with inciting objections that often sparked a round of debate he rarely took part in. I wondered if he was ashamed that he was not as eloquent as his pen or if his disposition prohibited him from making an argument that was not completely thought through. He would always politely request his palm wine mixed with zobo in a bowl, as Uncle had no calabashes.

Mr Adedoja came next and planted himself in the armchair across Oyinbo. He sat forward in a truculent manner with his fingertips pressing into the cream patterns of the chair's arms. He had been uncle's partner at the law firm and happily argued every point with vehement skill even when they were contradictory. He was just a few years younger than Uncle, but his hair was all black and kept in stylish waves. He pulsed with a vibrancy that threatened to explode the big vein shaped like the Niger-Benue Rivers that throbbed at the centre of his forehead. He had been a permanent visitor in the house for many years. He had lived alone with his overbearing mother until he was well into his thirties and his initial shy nature had been forced out in a desire to be rebellious in his early teens. He had begun arguing with everyone but his mother by his late teens and had never dropped the habit. But he had the needy tendency of being completely indecisive, as his mother had always taken that aspect as her duty. So initially, he had come to Uncle's house to escape his mother and then to seek advice after her death. And now he came to escape his wife who was as domineering as his mother: but was the only type of woman he knew how to love and respect. He did everything with the forceful efficiency of a reluctant perfectionist.

"That makes absolutely no sense!" he would explode, his voice rising even before the palm wine had a chance to take effect. "You cannot remove the subsidy on petrol. Do you have any clue how expensive fuel will be!" All his remarks always seemed like they should be followed by exclamation marks and his arguments always centred on 'the average man'. "The average man can barely afford to feed his family, he probably already spends ten percent of his miserly income on transportation. Ten percent! It will be doubled! You might as well pull his children out of school!"

"I believe they are already out of school, the teachers are on strike once again and the government refuses to negotiate," that would be Prof's quiet voice. He was a worthy, gentle adversary for Mr Adedoja's rants but was often absent on missions for the United Nations. Prof was a brilliant man whose calm voice betrayed an active mind in overdrive. He seemed to understand everything in detail and was looked upon to ease irresolvable disputes often started by Mr Adedoja. He had the unique ability to seduce a room into agreement, with everyone feeling like their point had been understood and integrated into his conclusions.

"Well, the average man will definitely join the teachers in their riot if the government dares to touch the petrol subsidy, perhaps it is necessary for privatising the refineries, but not now and not by these people!" – his favourite way of referring to the government.

"They have, eh, privatised the eh celle – tele – phones," Oyinbo would barely manage to get out, "and that has been eh quite eh successful," he would finish and then sink back into his corner of the couch.

"Producing quite a number of jobs, not to mention an avenue for businesses to flourish," Prof would add, pushing his circular Awolowo like glasses up his oily nose.

"Come on, monkeys could have privatised that industry. There is no risk. That was simple common sense! I am saying, these people cannot touch anything of consequence, look at electricity. Where were we ten, twenty, fifty years ago? Where are we now?" Mr Adedoja would query, exploding in a fit of childlike giggles as he often did when he rounded off an argument with what he imagined was a demonstration of evident ineptitude from the government.

"Tufiakwa!" Mrs Ikechukwu would spit out, snapping her fingers and shaking her head, "Electricity, let's not go there, because that one just makes my blood boil. These their commissions and projects have simply been a sinkhole of public resources." Temporarily all the men would forget their advanced age and be caught up in her ageless beauty, following her perfect teeth as they carelessly spat out her words. Her husband a Mr Ikechukwu – was startlingly unattractive. To put it bluntly he was as ugly as baboon, yet he had the uncanny gift of having every woman he met fall in love with him. He had a heart as large as his father's, who had been an even greater eyesore. The older Mr Ikechukwu had loved so much that in the era of rampant polygamy, he had two wives that he kept ignorant of the other's existence so each would think she was special. When they found out, he promptly married a third because he reasoned two could gang up against him, but it was impossible to make allies of three competing females. The younger Mr Ikechukwu was equally romantic and had snared the then Miss Abia State despite his unfortunate looks and the fact that he had been penniless. But, he had become very successful in the shipping business and constantly fell in love with other women and they did likewise with him. And it was always with a funeral aura that he would tenderly take their hand and apologise for being married. But it was common knowledge that he loved his wife unconditionally and would never even consider adultery. So despite having men of all ages chase her with hanging tongues, she, unlike her husband refused to flirt back, but observed his episodes with pained detached humour, unable to leave him because she knew it would promptly kill him. However, she was one of the rare women of that Catholic school raised era who had a respectable non-philandering husband that also understood the needs of the female body in its entirety – especially one as intricate and voluptuous as a thorough Nigerian woman. Mr Ikechukwu rarely came to these gatherings but as soon as he saw Aisha and Seun together, he always asked after them and had an almost fanatical hope that they would live together forever.

Emeka, who loved comparisons, would then say, "Do you know South Africa, which is a third of our population, produces easily three times more watts than we do and still they are trying to produce more!"

"It is ludicrous! The average man will never get access! And those people going from Never Expect Power At All (his interpretation of the National Electric Power Authority commonly known by their acronym NEPA), to what's their new name, do they think they have deceived anyone?" he asked, following it up with his childlike giggles.

"Do you know the possibilities this country has? Two mighty rivers, an abundance of sunshine, surplus oil, coal, gas that is being flared. Do you know what we could do with all that gas?" Prof would chime in, adjusting his glasses and shaking his head in frustration.

"Well, it is obviously not a lack of resources, just a lack of ideas and integrity," Emeka would spit out in disgust. "I mean look at the Niger Delta, you cannot tell me the politicians are not behind the bunkering and gangs, it's practically America and Iraq all over again, except these soulless men do it in their own country. They hand weapons over to hooligans so they can profit at the expense of the country. To imagine these men are walking around scot free."

"Prof, why don't you run and save this our country, eh?" Mr Adedoja would ask suddenly.

"Eh," Mrs Ikechukwu would return immediately, "you want them to kill Prof. Tufiakwa!"

"Look at what eh happened, what eh they did to Bola Ige," Oyinbo would say sadly.

And Mrs Ikechukwu would add another tufiakwa for emphasis.

"If only these mercenaries will point their guns in the right direction!" Mr Adedoja would say forcefully.

At this point, the alcohol would have slowly made an impact and they would all feel jolly enough for someone to say, 'Toast to our avenging angel', raising his glass to Emeka and everyone would laugh and follow suit.

II
Parambulator (Southern Nigeria 2008)

ONE

I had not been home in almost six years and I did not know why. Perhaps I shied from the reality that life was not halted for the sorrows of one soul. I did not know, but Uncle did and obliged my wish to remain away, thinking it best as he launched a tireless but mostly ineffective campaign against the tyranny of the government. I had done two years of A-levels in London, but even there had been too close to home and I finally left for Washington, DC, instinctively to get as far away as possible, I think.

The plane ride was uneasy. I fled from the unease of the turbulence into fitful dreams, uncomfortable and discomforted. I often wanted to return home, to Nigeria, but always I imagined the banished ghosts that threatened to materialise even in the dead frost of the DC winter would surely rise like the mirages that animated the baked tarmac of the Lagos airport runway. The hostess said coffee or tea and distracted I said simply, yes. She gave me coffee. Gradually, the butterflies in my stomach began fluttering happily, not from agitation but from excitement. I began to smile as the plane made its descent, my eyes scanning the rapidly expanding land outside the window. I wonder what I sought, assurance perhaps. It certainly was not familiarity, for in Nigeria, I was terrified of the known.

I walked off the plane and the intense heat and nauseating smell of diesel were as a brick wall – solid and unyielding. In a matter of seconds, the brief romantic notions of homeland I harboured became as fragile as my unsettled stomach. But suddenly I was not afraid anymore. As I swayed almost dizzily from the force of the heat, I decided that one bad memory should not eliminate a hundred joyous ones. I walked through the rooms with alternating temperature of the Murtala Muhammed International Airport with the brisk steps of one long exiled from home – the way one walked into a familiar place and still harboured happy memories – one hoped were preserved. By the time I got to customs, I did not mind the long line because for once it was not under the banner that accusingly proclaimed 'Alien'.

"Welcome to the country, Mr Seun Odukoya," the bored voice said.

"Thank you," I replied with a huge smile. For a few minutes as the conveyor belt squeakily vomited my bags, I was lost again in cheerful revelries and then I stepped out of the airport and was again hit by the brutal force of Lagos' realities.

"Oga, come here, I go drive you sharp sharp! My car get correct AC."

"Oga, no min am, he's a bloody liar, him car no get fan sef. Come look my own, na correct peegot. You go sit down like Governor!"

Oga this, oga that! Incessant shouting. Darkened men in kaftans and white skullcaps with yellow patterns from sweat stains. It was an assault on the senses – unbearable heat, pungent smells, overwhelming noise and for a brief moment, I questioned my decision to return. A part of me shrank back intimidated, the other half looked around with a large smile and muttered to itself, 'The many faces of opportunity'. I looked past them until I saw the placid face of Mr Monday spotting an uncharacteristic smile.

The road was a jumble of disparate vehicles; lumbering lorries, ancient taxis, large buses crammed with exhausted humans standing nose to nose, smaller buses with children on adults' laps, audacious motorcycles, barely preserved Toyotas and hardly used Mercedes. To the sides, forests of cement and steel and a few sparse trees oversaw the chaos. Live wires dangled precariously over dilapidated buildings and tired people milled around always with a burden in their hands or on their backs.

The trickling traffic was finally dammed. A young lady emerged from the side of the road with a glass case of puff puffs on her head. The mounds beneath her T-shirt were perfect and the thin fabric, washed until it was almost see-through, was just loose enough to cause a gentle friction that kept her nipples permanently erect. She purposely forgot to wear a bra and was making good business as many men called her over just to see her chest bounce with her well practised run and bought the stale buns in the parched afternoon out of shame.

Over the bridge, hundreds of little dishes clung like pirate earrings to the faces of high-rise buildings. Single antennas protruded to the skies to get glimpses of a better world. Closer to the water, the sea of rust that were the roofs of decrepit houses shone like a large neglected coin in the uncaring sun. They spilled into the black murky waters, balancing delicately on thirsty stilts. Beneath the shacks, long-bowed canoes traipsed, with wiry young men at their helms and emaciated children in their bellies. A waste dump served as a bridge from water to home. Pigs and children fought gaily for whatever was salvageable.

I took my eyes from the terrible scene that was in plain sight of the bridge yet invisible. As my haunted eyes fled this tragedy, the sun mockingly hit the water and bathed it in gold as a solitary old fisherman cast his net in the water making it all beautiful.

Just then, the car braked suddenly as one of the numerous yellow taxis with their black speed stripes cut across our path. "Oloshi!" the driver yelled, jumping into the next lane without indicating. Mr Monday turned on the radio and a polished voice said, "Ray Power 100.5, the premier FM," and his voice was seamlessly interrupted by the pensive blast of Lagbaja's saxophone.

There is beauty inherent in life and there is life in the dumps. In the heart of the city, at the centre of its trash, a thousand people sleep and rise and call it home. They arm themselves with discarded sacks and metal crowbars and become alchemists. They sift through discarded waste and come up with gold. The smells are overpowering but they are immune. The place is homely and exotic and caters to all needs. There is a barber's shop, restaurants, bars with the best homemade moonshine, three cinemas and a place to touch your head to the mat and say your prayers. Allah in his infinite mercy provides for all.

A contended smile broke on a sooty face as the radio he had been tinkering with over the past week finally let through Lagbaja's saxophone in fuzzy blasts. He looked exultantly out of the window past the dozen men who were taking cleansing baths in the black waters. He was going to sell the radio and have enough money to buy some studio time; perhaps in a few months he would also be in a Mercedes driving over the bridge listening to his own song on the radio. Tomorrow, the natural gases that had been fermenting in the compost would start a fire and cleanse the land of unwanted waste, rid the state of the few illegal structures, relieve the country of a few unregistered aliens, unburden the earth of a few unwanted lives.

There is beauty inherent in life, but it sometimes has an ugly face.

The car pulled into Uncle's yard and parked under the ancient guava tree. I walked towards the house inhaling all the scents of my childhood that somehow smelled less fragrant. I was excited to be home but was disappointed by the realities. In my memory; the walk to the house still stretched for miles past proud flowers, the house still gleamed in its delicate white evening jacket, the rustic carvings on the big oak doors still held mysterious secrets and the grand stairs still stretched upwards forever. Many 'stills' were no more, for life is never still, even in the quiet of death.

It moves on, quietly, hectically, propelled by the innocuous baton named instead.

Instead, the kitchen was too small and the toilets too low. The flowers were sad and the trees, drooping and weeping, had lost their posture. Old Rufus was as crooked and bowed as his favourite pawpaw tree. Uncle's booming laugh now ended in a hacking cough and Mrs Folayo had shrunk to fit the house. The shadows still danced on the wall – the sole lasting memorial to the earlier days. I took it all in with a melancholic smile and went through all the right motions. But the question that eclipsed my thoughts like the white majestic African moon I was yet to experience was, 'Was she still there'?

She was, but was changed now. I awoke from my nap to the sound of contended merriment. I heard her laughter mingle with

215

Uncle's and another that was unfamiliar to me and bubble up the stairs. It seemed familiar with the spaces, embracing and caressing them, but uncontainable, sauntering away unfettered. It lingered in my ears. Spirited laughter, old and new, mingled in my nervous mind as she made her way up the winding staircase responding with mirth to Mrs Folayo's banter. But her knock was timorous.

"Come in," I barely managed, half muted by sleep and a newly acquired timidity. I was surprised by my feeble response, as she must have been by her knock. She had bounded through those doors innumerable times in the past. Upon entry, her unease was ephemeral, supplanted by the profundity of my shock.

"Hey," I stammered.

"Seun," she yelled, across the room and in my arms before I could get over my surprise. The scent of her coconut pomade was in my nose as her slender hands wrapped themselves around my frame. I took her in.

She was beautiful. Her body had filled out and her features conspired to dazzle. Her smile sat confidently between lofty cheeks. Her jaw ran undefined from ear to ear and tapered into a graceful neck. Her dark complexion finally suited her posture and complemented her thick hair. She had learned the finery of a lady and the wiles, too. Her eyebrows were sensual curves and her lips were highlighted by the right amount of sheen. She knew where the lights hit her best and which poses were just right. But most of all, her eyes ...

She finally understood them. The fears and nightmares that had kept them shrouded when she was younger were now glazed by a strange confidence. She stared out of their chocolate depths defiantly and they wore a permanent smirk. They asked a question that only she could properly articulate. The object of their attention induced into the limiting feeling of inadequacy. They were gentle and hard, alluring and aloof, questioning and content. They took you in and found you terribly wanting, always. I was captive to them.

And then I realised I had also changed, for together we swayed in an eternal embrace, dismayed we were emotionally separated by the corrosive division of time. We had not spoken in years and despite her assurance, she was betrayed by the insecurity of her conversation.

She hurried to tell me that she modelled now, that she studied law, that she had an ex-boyfriend. And this saddened me because I had forgotten to break up with the girl I was not sure I still loved. We hung out. As friends – like we had when we were children. Except the innocent grace was now replaced by restrained affections. Jerky movements, awkward shy smiles, disarming eye contact, the occasional uncomfortable spaces.

We sat in my room and listened to my music that was foreign to her. I constantly turned down the volume as the strange guitars and honeyed voices hung uncomfortably in the room and squeezed out the air. Yet, it was the only thing I could relate to in the unfamiliar space, so I let it play. A new eatery had opened up and we made unenthusiastic plans to go the following day. It was the only way we could think to halt the uncomfortable trajectory that was that first evening.

When she left, I looked out the window and saw the great guava tree in its brooding solitude. For a second I thought of all our shared losses and my composure almost failed me. The moon hid behind a flimsy grey quilt and I wondered if I was ready to return home. It was the sort of melancholic view that one was meant to fall in love to, but it seemed that there was no longer someone to fall in love with.

The beauty of home is that it embraces suddenly and all the old nostalgias reconnect forgotten familiarities. Jetlagged, I awoke long before Mrs Folayo's brisk knock and though she refrained from storming in and tearing apart the curtains, it still brought a happy smile to my cautious lips. I pried open the curtains myself and when I opened the windows, the glum of the previous night was quickly banished with a string of familiar smells and the song of the oderekoko, I remembered my mother's favourite phrase that 'Life starts afresh every morning.' And even the tepid faltering shower failed to sink my buoyant mood.

Determined to regain my self-assurance, I was adorned in all the eminent western fashions as I drove Uncle's Toyota Rav-4 out of the gate. Before I could honk at the gate next door, Aisha slipped out in an adire skirt, a mature white button down and an intricately tied headscarf that made my durag seem limp. My black Baltimore Ravens jersey sat uncomfortably in the stifling heat and my baggy jeans and basketball shoes suddenly took up too much space.

In Africa, the conspicuous chivalry that the American feminist movement had silently erased still existed so I opened the doors for her, bought her food, carried it to the table and pulled out her chair. I tried to impress her with my imported knowledge and eclectic ideas.

"Hemingway says," I said knowing fully well she had no clue who Hemingway was, "What is moral is what you feel good after and what is immoral is what you feel bad after." I imagined her best response would be, 'But doesn't that make morality subjective,' the same answer my girlfriend had given and I had polished a speech about individuality long after the conversation died, which I was eager to deliver.

Instead, she stared at me with her impenetrable gaze and simply said, "Some things take a long time to feel good about and some take a long time to feel bad about." I sat like a deflated balloon and drank my milkshake.

The conversation jerked on awkwardly like this for a few moments and finally she said, "I am being hard on you and I am sorry. I just imagined you have been away from home for so long, you will be curious as to things that have happened here!"

It was barely an apology but it was all that was needed. An easy smile diffused my discomfort and her eyes finally slit open and let me in. And as is for people with long histories and secret crushes, the conversation flowed easily after the laboured start.

On the ride back, I was relaxed enough to enquire about the sights that in my memory were home.

"Is Waterparks, still there?" I asked as we drove down the main street in Ikeja.

"Yes, but now little children just piss in it all the time and some area boys go there to shower," she answered.

I decided not to ask any more questions because the world of my past was rapidly shrinking. But I realised with a shake of my head who the traffic warden who danced every day unfailingly at the junction with his white gloves, white socks and short trousers was long gone, as was most things.

"I have to drop by Chemist," I said, referring to the corner store where a fair Ibo man sold everything from Peak milk to Panadol. Aisha laughed at this partly because it was our private joke to call him so and partly because she was relieved we were sharing old jokes again. I stopped the car by a huge open gutter that was filled with spirogyra and discarded nylon and we crossed on a rickety wooden plank that wobbled and creaked. The large ungainly building that stood next to his store was still uncompleted. The owner had been a corrupt civil servant who had been sacked during one of the coups d'etat and he had three houses in sulky grey cement overalls scattered throughout the city, lacking the funds to apply the final touches. The wall still read 'Post No Bill' and 'Beware of 419, this house is not for sale', but the 'Do Not Piss' had been changed to 'Please Urinate here, witchdoctor needs piss for medicine' and I realised with a chuckle that the acrid smell of urine that always hung about the place was finally gone. I almost yelled aloud in surprise as Chemist the skinny, jolly man had become Chemist the fat, jolly man. Aisha could not help herself and burst out laughing at my surprised face.

"Ah, where have you been?" Chemist asked at the same time as I exclaimed, "Chemist what happened to you?"

"My brother," Chemist said in his jolly way. "You know the Bible says he who finds a wife finds a good thing," he said with his small eyes disappearing behind his recently dimpled cheeks as he chuckled as well.

"E be like say Bible no dey lie oh," I said with an easy smile, speaking pidgin I thought I had long forgotten. "Maybe I go go find one, too."

"My brother, na wetin you dey do with this lepa wey dey stand for your side. If you no snatch am, me I dey look am dey think of second wife o," Chemist said making Aisha and I both slightly uncomfortable.

We hurried back into the car talking about Chemist's new look and she told me of the other changes in the area. We were again at ease with each other and when we got to the front of the house, there sat another personality from the past. She had been the wife of Madam's driver. He had been a nervous little man who blinked too often and it made him seem weak, which he was. About once every three months, he would show up with a bruise saying he ran into something, but we all knew his wife beat him. Ever since he died, she appeared about every other year with a new business venture that was bound to fail. She had been a tailor, a shoe trader, owned a petty stall, sold at the market and even tried being a cheap jeweller. She had the characteristics of a successful Nigerian businesswoman; she was calculating, bossy and plump. Unfortunately, she had been born with a face more beautiful than her position in life and she spent her days gazing at reflections to avoid her ugly surroundings. She sat in her vanity looking ostentatiously in faded mirrors even as she waited for handouts.

"Is that ..." I started.

"Yes oh!" Aisha exclaimed.

"And is she fairer?" I asked.

"Mhhh, yes oh," Aisha said and hissed, "You won't believe about three years ago she came with a baby and said she was going to set up a provisions store. She used half the money to bleach. Uncle was so angry he chased her away last time she was here. I wonder what has happened to the baby or its father."

"I always feel sorry for these people," I said.

"About what?"

"You know, they just don't know any better ... the leaders exploit them, the economy is hard, they are barely educated ... I guess they must take solace in little victories."

"A lack of education allows for some ignorance, but it does not make you stupid," Aisha retorted. Her eyes were bright and passionate and I could tell her mind was back in her violent childhood that had been too easily explained away as the ignorance of poor masses. I realised that look in her eye was what I had been feeling since I had come back home. The feeling of almost tangible disgust with a broken system – the way one felt when an old dog that should know better still peed on the carpet in the living room. It was a feeling no class or intellectual discussion could stir because it had nothing to do with your mind. It was the emotion you felt when someone invaded your home and you felt powerless.

When I turned off the car, I forgot myself in her smouldering eyes for a few seconds and only realised when they matched her lips in a rare smile. We shared an uneasy few seconds and alighted from the car.

"You should come in. I don't want to meet him alone," I said. "He was out when I arrived yesterday and in his room all morning."

"Alright," she said eagerly. "You'll love him. He fought in the war and knows everything!" she exclaimed.

She was right, he knew everything and I loved him.

TWO

Aisha bounded out of the car and towards the door with a familiarity I was yet to reacquire.

"How often do you come over?" I asked as we pushed through the oak doors.

"You mean how often can I get her to leave," Mrs Folayo interjected good humouredly, "she spends way too much time with us old people."

"Just enough to learn and be inspired, you oldies have the most interesting tales," Aisha said, as Mrs Folayo winced at the term.

We walked into Uncle's living room, which was crowded with laughter. Uncle's rose loudest above the rest but barely.

Mrs Ikechukwu was saying, "Is it not you Yoruba people, na so so book you go dey read, you no fi do nothing. Abi dey say power sharing. We wait sote, Obasanjo enter office, he dash all the jobs back to the North. His tenure is almost done and save for banking, telecommunications and a few ministers, there is nothing to show."

"Eh, you see, he had to be diplomatic," Prof's quiet voice calmly stated. "He was the first one in this their deal so he had to be balanced and he has also tackled corruption quite handily."

"That is the problem with our people," Mr Adedoja jumped in. "We respect institutions that these people don't care about and the average man does not understand and even their handling of corruption is doubtful!

"With all the professors and intellectuals in international organisations, you mean Obasanjo could not make decent choices? This is ridiculous! You think the Hausas will say they want equality and fill the positions with people from across the country if they are in power? They jus wan chop, my brother."

"It does seem like it is only Obasanjo that respected this unity nonsense, the Hausas won't and you people are hard," Oyinbo said nervously turning to Mrs Ikechukwu. "I went to this bank last week and asked for one of the employees. The gateman told me, 'He no fi work for this place.' I was mildly irritated and so I said what do you mean? You mean you know every single person that works here? He responded, 'Oga in name no be Igbo, he no fi dey here.' Imagine in Lagos here the gateman boldly telling me that only Igbos can work in that bank!"

"Yes, it is true," Mr Adedoja interjected amid loud laughter. "Look at our finance minister, she has surrounded herself with Igbo men!"

"Abeg we deserve am jare, the next position we need na president, we go change this country sharp sharp," she often spoke in pidgin perhaps to detract from her beauty, or to keep up with the men, or maybe just to handle the constant jibes of the men who still harboured slight unspoken bias against the Igbo.

"It can't happen," Emeka said sadly, matter-of-factly, "Look at America, after the civil war, it took a hundred years for a first president from the south. Biafra will haunt us as if we did the massacres."

I used the ensuing silence to introduce myself. It was strange; it was such an important part of Nigerian history, yet it was only the third time I had heard it mentioned.

The first time had been when I was at boarding school in the Federal Government College in Lagos. It had been a day of endless sun and no homework, one of the rare days electricity was constant and water flowed through all the taps. The type of day when little boys had no worries and gentle breezes encouraged them into mischievous activities – when the devil came out to play with idle hands. Adolphus, my roommate had a sly grin on his face and something hidden in his hand. Initially, I imagined he was going to tell one of his ridiculous stories that had everyone spellbound and the boys from the village believing in outrageous things. The day before, he had been telling them a story of when he visited London, he said the plane had gotten so hot, he had wound down the window and put pieces of cloud in his pocket for good measure. He had said it with such confidence that even when they all looked at Janded (the boy who got that nickname because he knew everything about everything foreign), there had been uncertainty in his voice when he challenged him.

I had acted disinterested in what Adolphus had to offer, as he had marched by me with the same impish smile, shouting, 'Where are my nna boys.' His father had given him a Biafran note, which he had forgotten among one of his textbooks and had just found. What had started as a little prank began to rapidly lose its purity. He began with viewings of his cultural treasure reserved only for the Igbo boys followed by a reserved 'Hail Biafra', but soon they started clustering in marauding groups whose initial innocuous raids quickly became harmful bullying. In a week, they were demanding their own room separate from everyone else and refusing to talk to non-Igbos. It only stopped when a prefect finally seized the note, but what I found most worrying was that before then, I had never even heard of Biafra – an issue that was obviously sensitive and inflammatory to my closest friends.

Perhaps I had heard the name whispered over time, but Uncle never spent time on the issue, except to denounce Ojukwu any time he was mentioned in the paper. It was never taught to me or an issue of conversation. I finally decided to read about it during my freshman year at Georgetown University, when one of my friends had joked that 'Eat your food, there are Biafrans going hungry,' and then said that was what his mum used to say to him as a child, in the whispered tone of a solemn shared secret that was best forgotten. I could not believe the things I read or how little it was spoken about. It was like the most significant thing in Nigerian history that never happened.

Our entrance was a timely interruption and Uncle seized the opportunity to introduce his beloved nephew. Mrs Ikechukwu said I was far more handsome than my Uncle and made me blush. Oyinbo nervously shook hands. Mr Adedoja yelled in his exclamatory manner, "Georgetown University! That is great! You must be looking to be a great lawyer like your uncle!"

Emeka said, "So you must be the young man I have heard so much about, it is a pleasure."

Prof said, "Welcome, we need more people like you at the top universities; I hope you will come back," pushing his glasses back up his nose. Uncle wore a proud smile and Aisha found herself embarrassingly doing likewise.

As we walked up the stairs, I asked Aisha, "Is it not strange that our history is so shrouded?"

"Do you mean all this nonsense they teach us about Mungo Park discovering a river that had been there for centuries?" she asked offhandedly.

"Well, that too, but I was referring to more recent stuff like Biafra and independence." I thought for a few seconds and then said, "Actually the whole thing dating as far back as whenever. Why were such differing people jumbled together, I mean it makes more sense for the Yoruba to have been joined with the southern parts of the Republic of Benin or Togo."

She looked at me admiringly, "Move back," she said, "we'll rewrite history together."

Long after she was gone, those words floated in my head in all its varying connotations.

I was enjoying the banter and lightness of home. I could hear Uncle and Emeka conversing in his library. Aisha's statement struck me and I tried to aggregate the combined experiences of everyone in the house.

"Seun, come and properly meet my oldest friend," Uncle said. I did not know those words would be the introduction for the greatest tale I have ever heard, one that would light a fire in my belly stronger than nostalgia and more consuming than ambition.

"Nice to meet you, sir," I said again somewhat shyly. He was an old man, but he had an aura of dignity and history. He seemed like he had importance bestowed upon him.

He smiled delicately and it was obvious he was once very handsome. In his lips was the same caution that tainted mine, Uncle's, Mrs Folayo's and Aisha's smiles and I knew he had also suffered the sort of loss from which one never fully recovers.

I was curious to hear his story and then I realised how little I knew of the past. Over the week, I asked about their childhoods.

I asked about how they met. I asked Uncle what my mother was like as a child.

The following morning, I again awoke early and decided to inspect the garden where I had spent many happy childhood moments. I made my way around the side of the house to the porch beneath Uncle's room. Emeka was there.

"Good morning, sir," I said.

"Hello, Seun," he said quietly. "Please sit down," he said indicating the chair next to his. I could briefly smell the sharp scent of TomTom, but it was soon lost in the beautiful morning aromas of the fruit trees. I was not discomforted by the silence, but I felt I should break it. Before I could, Uncle's cough cascaded from his window. It was harsh and sharp like I had not been aware of the day before and I realised he must have worked hard and suffered in silence so I would not notice.

The sound terrified me. I had enough of death. I asked the first question that came to my head to banish the diseased sounds that surrounded us. "What is your earliest memory, sir?"

He did not answer for a couple of minutes and I imagined that perhaps my words were improper. Uncle began to cough again and I desperately needed a distraction. I was going to ask another question when he said, "Well, this is not my earliest memory, but it is the beginning of my story, do you still want to hear it?"

"Yes, sir," I said enthusiastically.

"Well then, you will have to stop calling me sir," he said and we both chuckled. He told it passively, like he admired the story but wished it were not his. It was the story of his birth; it was the most beautiful tragedy I had ever heard. When he was done, I had forgotten about Uncle's coughs. Strangely, all I could think about was Aisha. I was suddenly extremely excited to see her.

TWO

It was a typical Lagosian weekend with innumerable celebrations – weddings, engagements, introductions, naming ceremonies, funerals, birthdays, graduations ... The sweet scent of women's perfumes gleefully mixed with sweat, jollof rice and fried meat. Car horns competed with live bands and imported music blaring from oversized speakers. Halls and houses were packed and spilled happily into jolly streets. Neighbours became family and families became friends. Revellers rapidly shuttled between events adorned in intricate headgear, saying quick congratulations before rushing off to other appointments. Aisha and I were on The Island at Tasty Fried Chicken as it was what young people did to amuse themselves. The day was beginning to retire and people were heading to their parties of preference, settling into corners with tall glasses and thick bottles. Suddenly, the air was rent with loud explosions and it seemed Lagos was under attack. 'Bush has come for oil', 'Bin Laden is in town', 'Ojukwu has reemerged', all sorts of theories were whispered fearfully as pandemonium halted happy parties with gloomy premonitions. Musicians and praise singers took to their heels, forgetting their instruments; geles tumbled off terrified heads and shoes got stuck in mud and were left behind.

In a matter of minutes, the third mainland bridge was choked with cars rooted in the chaos-induced traffic. I sat impatiently behind the wheel unsure of what all the bedlam was about. Cellular phones and the Internet had still been a limited luxury until that year and Aisha and I had not spoken much over the past few years. I was returning to The States in a week and could sense Aisha's pleasure at the enforced solitude. Despite the cacophony outside of the hooting cars and panicked populace, she seemed tranquil next to me because she knew then that even if I never returned to Nigeria and nothing became of our silent affections, I had loved her that summer. She looked at my impatient smile and was going to ask me to come back home after my graduation again when another loud explosion accompanied by bright flashes emanated from beyond the bridge. Cars emptied and their former occupants began to run around like beheaded chickens. A few climbed on their vehicles for a better view and soon word emerged that the Mobil petrol station was on fire. This caused a brief moment of almost calm but the continuous explosions implied a different explanation. Like wild fire, another theory swept the bridge that the Ikeja military cantonment was under attack and this caused a tidal wave of panic that swept back and forth between The Mainland and The Island dowsing the people on the bridge with crippling fear as we watched the explosive spectacle that raged for another hour and a half. On the mainland, windows and glass doors came down in spectacular shards and people stampeded into swamps. Stampeded to their deaths.

The traffic began to inch forward slowly towards the stationary tragedy. It was obvious at this point that whoever was behind the attack intended to first take out the military base, so Aisha and I decided to go to Uncle's sister-in-law's house, which was in Maryland, just off the bridge. As soon as the car turned into the street, we saw Sule running around in panic. I pulled the car over next to him. He had his hand on his head and was repeatedly muttering, *'Egba mi, Egba mi'* to himself.

"Sule!" I called out and it took him almost a second to recognise who had called his name.

"Good afternoon, sir. I don see trouble, sir," he replied.

"What is the matter?" Aisha exclaimed, worried and unused to Sule's exaggerations.

"I don lose pikin, ma," Sule said reluctantly.

"What? You lost Abiola? What do you mean you don lose pikin?" I asked sharply.

"Sir, na de confusion, sir. De glass dey fall everywhere, de window, de door, everyting jus dey come down gbam. Na so I grab Biola we run out of house, we tink sey na de end of de world. We commot de house, we see everyone dey enter bush dey shout bomb, so we join dem." He paused for a second and decided that telling them that he had let go of Biola's hand for a few minutes to talk to the girl that sold bread [because she had forgotten to button her shirt and he was thinking of grabbing them just once before he died] was not a good idea.

Instead he said, "I see say dis child don fall down, so I tell Biola make she stand still, I go pick am up, na so I get up, I no see her again. I don dey search for am for an hour. I come ask people if dey don see her."

"So you thought the neighbour's child was more important," I said without sympathy. "Oya, take us to where you lost the girl. Wait till your madam hears of this."

"Please sir, no tell her, sir," Sule was begging repeatedly as I drove past him and into the compound. I walked through the beach of broken glass to the sea of chaos that was the living room: the tremors from the explosions had knocked everything down. I picked up the phone and luckily, there was still a dial tone. After numerous tries, I finally got Mrs Folayo on the phone and told her that Aisha and I would be staying at my aunt's house. I did not tell her that the child was missing or that there was no glass on the windows or sliding doors, I simply said we were unharmed.

I hung up the phone and turned on Sule. "Where is uncle?" I asked.

"Eh sir, he don go join madam in de oversees. She suppose bon second pikin soon," Sule said.

"Oh yeah, they're in Ireland. Aunty is expecting another child," I said to Aisha. "Please let's go find my cousin."

Just as we stepped out of the house, she emerged from the gate across the street.

"Uncle Seun," she said running across, unaware of the anxiety that seeped from my face in large salty drops.

"Where were you?" I asked gently. Sule hoped she would not tell us that he had left her hand to hold the bread seller when she said she was afraid and give her an unnecessary reassuring hug.

Luckily, Abiola simply said, "I was with the neighbours. I saw them in the bush and we came home together." I was so relieved that I just hugged her and did not ask more questions. Sule swore to himself to walk her personally into her classroom from then on and only make dodo for dinner because it was her favourite food.

Later that night, Aisha walked into the room I was sleeping in, the vulnerability in her eyes creating an angelic halo about her. I was speechless as she walked over to the bed and pulled the sheets back.

I moved over silently and obeyed mutely when she said, 'Hold me' in a childlike voice. The scent of coconut in her hair, jasmine from her neck and mint from her mouth billowed out softly from her, tenderly caressing my face. I placed my hand gently around her waist and held her hand. I stayed immobile the whole night, my fingers entwined in hers, listening to the gently tunes of her breathing, too scared to even get an erection.

Dawn was creeping in and I was finally beginning to fall asleep. The whole night had been spent in excited trepidation as Aisha had snuggled closer and closer to me as the glassless windows had made the room increasingly chilly. I suddenly had the sensation one gets when one is being stared at and my eyelids fluttered open slowly, caressing some of her hair. A bird sang noisily outside the window and it made me unsure I could hear the message her eyes were telling me. Finally, she reached out and gently placed her delicate palm on my dark cheeks. "You will come back …" she said softly, in my mind, I imagined she added 'for me'. I was unsure if it was a request, a command or a premonition. I was tingling, my mind was racing and my heart was thumping so loudly in my chest, I was sure it would disturb her ethereal serenity. Suddenly she placed a gentle kiss on my lips and turned her back to me.

The next morning brought with it the dual emotion that follows an uncertain tragedy. Humour as people remembered how they barely escaped with their lives from nothing and remorse as many lost their lives for nothing. Sule had heard what had happened as he bought eggs that morning but he was hesitant to bring up events of the previous day given his grave error. He also did not know what to make of Aisha and I exiting from the same room so he maintained a polite distance. A hurried breakfast was followed by an even quicker departure; we only paused to give Abiola a couple of hasty hugs. Nothing was said about the night but the urge for a rapid exit was fuelled by a shared willingness to leave the scene of our aborted romance. For the rest of that week, Aisha would act with the alluring awkwardness of an attractive girl who knew she had the restrained attention of the guy she loved.

The traffic was light even though it was supposed to be the rush hour, as people were still afraid of leaving their homes. We drove towards the scene of the previous day's chaos, rounded the corner of a desolate street and turned on another of mayhem and gloom. People milled around with faces frozen in identical expressions of confusion and dismay that made them all seem familiar and similar. The bright light of the fierce sun suddenly seemed too dim and even though I had wound down the window and was sweating, I massaged my chest with a free hand. One of those women who wore their head tie like it was about to fall off their heads and loved to be the harbingers of bad news saw the fresh shock on our faces and approached the car as we pulled to the side of the road.

"Mhh, it is a tragedy," she said in the syrupy gossipy tone that made you want to stop her but were powerless to do so.

"Yay, like cattle oh, like cattle, they drowned like cattle," she yelled, spinning around with acute dramatisation.

"Tinubu wan kill us, Obasanjo wan make we die, but God no go let am, eyaaa!" she exclaimed, letting out another prolonged shriek. I was not sure if she was enjoying the gathering audience, but when a sufficient number of people had congregated round chiming in with wails and sorrowful head shakes, she finally calmed down and began telling the story.

"I was over there in my store, minding my business, when gbosa, na so we hear explosion," she said pausing often for effect and mixing English with Pidgin.

"What caused it?" Aisha asked with terror in her eyes, hoping desperately it was not some sort of internal turmoil again.

"My sister, we no know oh," the woman said, "I hear say, the government dey store weapons, all sorts of ammunitions in case of attack and that is what went off."

"That is ridiculous!" a man in a business suit and a British accent interjected. "Storing war ammunition next to residential buildings is just absolutely ludicrous!"

"Ma brother you dey mind dem? We no count as long as e no touch Governor's office, they go put bomb under your bed, they no go think twice!"

"But what is happening now?" I asked, the question that had been eating at me as I saw emergency services concentrated not around the smoldering cantonment but the swamps next to it.

"Mhhh, my brother, that is the real tragedy!" The woman said, then paused as if the weight of the event was too heavy for her mouth to tell.

"When the first explosion came, we all ran outside to see what was happening. But then when it started going off left and right like fireworks, everybody find their own way. Some of them run there, think dey fi swim the water, but the plants too much, it dey grab their legs but dey no fi turn back because the people behind dey push forward. So plenty plenty people drown oh, just like that my brother, hew!" she finished with an exclamation.

Aisha could not listen to any more and softly gripped my arm.

"Thank you, ma," I said and hastily drove off as she began spinning again and raining generational curses on the government.

THREE

Many children of the nineties only knew inconsistent phone lines, petrol queues and bad roads and subsequently embodied the phrase 'out of sight, out of mind'. There had been no use bothering about friends one could not communicate with: the subtle effects of economic conditions on social norms.

Save for Aisha, I had not spoken to any of my old friends. While away, I held no nostalgia for them, but now that I was back, curiosity more than anything made me enquire about their whereabouts. During my third year at high school, the summer after I had begun to seriously wonder about why women wore skirts and lace panties – after I had seen one hanging on a windowsill in Aisha's house and had got the first erection I was completely conscious of its genesis. I had fallen for a girl in the last class on the corridor. She had been there the whole time, but one day she walked by, her skin the colour of the sea on a moonless night. And the same warm feeling that had crept through my body, the strange excitement of a newly discovered wonder that I had felt when I had discreetly worn the panties for the five minutes Aisha was in the bathroom came upon me. Her smile was a sliver of the moon. She was not tall, but she walked like one who was – long strides and bent shoulders. She carried a book bag that was much too heavy for her delicate frame and when she took it off, her shoulders forgot to relax. Save for a truncated core, she had generally elongated features – a thin long nose, thin broad lips, eyes that reminded me of kung-fu movies, arms and legs that seemed like they could go round twice in a hug. With her extreme ebony complexion, it gave the impression of a sauntering smile. She sat opposite the door, by the wall towards the back of the class so that in the mornings the sun dissected the louvres and teased her smile. I knew every pearl in that mouth, I had watched them, longed for them, dreamt

233

about them. But even though the smile began to linger longer just for me, I never was introduced to it.

Sitting in the centre of her class was a boy gifted in the art of storytelling. The way he spoke, it was obvious his grandfather had at some point lived with him. He pronounced the syllables in every word and used words like 'wailing' in place of 'crying'. When he spoke, the world belonged to him and it was a world you wanted to be a part of. Perhaps it was because by the window sat the best view in the world, or it might have been Obinna's (that was his name) vivid eloquence, but I preferred to hear him narrate a movie than to actually watch it, because the cinemas failed to adequately capture the magic of those moments.

The dark skinned revelation was soon forgotten as the year wore on and a more approachable replacement emerged; however, Obinna's stories were irreplaceable. He always threw in the right amount of exaggeration to make the story believable no matter how improbable. Unexpectedly I had just received an email from him and so I decided to pay a visit. Aisha's statement, 'I just thought you'd be more interested in what was happening here', haunted me more than I cared to admit and I had began to wonder myself. I had been told to drive the car to the national stadium, as there would be nowhere to park near where Obinna lived. Although only a few people had mobile phones at this point, Obinna gave me two numbers to call. The traffic was light, the day was passive, it was a forgettable Friday for most. I approached the gates of the stadium where a man held a bottle of Star in his hand even though the sun had not yet set.

"Good evening. Please, where is the parking lot?" I asked in a nature out of touch with my surroundings.

"Jolly just drop!" the man returned rudely.

"Excuse me?"

"No min am," another one on an okada said. "Come I go show you, dey drive follow me."

We drove straight unto the pitch that now hosted everything save for the intended football matches. I parked the car away from the crowd in an innocuous looking corner with the tout promising

234

to be its angel for a little money. I stepped out to the stench of fresh piss and raw shit and realised why that section was largely ignored. The goal line was marked with food and drink sellers. I walked past the suya, pepper-soup and Chinese casserole stands. I stood around awkwardly not knowing if to return to the car or try to act casual, Obinna was supposed to be by shortly. I strolled the length of the pitch being solicited by hookers from all along the West African coast. As the darkness fell, the touts became more rowdy and the prostitutes more persistent. Just as I was about to give up on the failing night, an audacious BMW drove towards me. When the door opened, the touts shouted greetings of familiarity and two of the street girls walked confidently towards it.

"Not today," Obinna said with an impatient smile. His voice was his sole preserved attribute. He had grown perhaps a foot and half and was almost seventy-two inches tall. He had been small and skinny but now his stomach alone seemed capable of containing his old self. There were thick rolls of flesh around his neck and his thighs rubbed against each other – always. He marched over to the suya stand, picked the spicy roasted meat wrapped in newspaper and said simply 'take', dropping a large paw on the table and opulently leaving behind more money than was necessary.

"Obinna, is that you?" I asked cautiously although the voice was unmistakable.

"Oh boy, there you are," Obinna exclaimed like he was surprised I was there already as he caught me in a large hug. "Come, come," he said to me and then he turned to the band of rough men and smooth ladies and said, "I will see you people later." To which some of the men yelled oga wa! And it was obvious Obinna was thoroughly enjoying it.

"Those boys ehn," he said to me in his voice that had gotten only slightly rougher from beer and cigarettes. "My man, how you dey now?"

"I'm fine oh! I'm just managing."

"Managing, managing? My friend abeg commot, get out." He said like a heavy car on a gravel driveway. "See your fresh face from yankee, you're saying you're managing."

"What are you up to these days my guy?" I asked, an easy laugh escaping from my mouth.

"What am I up to? What am I up to? My brother you don't want to know, but I will show you," he said chuckling. Then as if he had forgotten about the conversation, he said, "So how about those oyinbo chicks now, you suppose find me wife for there oh, you know I'm an aje butter." Just then, he turned into a tight parking spot that a guy stood watch over smoking a bored joint. "Oga," he said to Obinna and nodded at me.

We walked past a busy street consumed by itself. Everyone gave a nod of acknowledgment when we walked by, but none seemed to actually notice our fleeting presence. Competing tunes floated out of windows to form a strange harmony. We walked through the narrow streets bordered by filthy drains that were almost as wide, full of black water and green spirogyra with old cans and used condoms floating around clouds of black and yellow striped nylon bags. A short gate was manned by a red-eyed, sour-breathed youth; his greeting was similar to the first guy. I was starting to wonder if my friend ran some sort of brothel when we walked into a room humming with ten computers and an air conditioning system. Ten heads looked up briefly, said, 'Oga' and went back to work. Obinna was beaming proudly. And it was then I noticed that my eyes had seen many small cars along the street with too much adornment, a large generator that chugged quietly by the gate and a towering mast that sat uncomfortably on the house in front of which we had parked the car.

Obinna watched my eyes as my mind slowly understood and said, "Yes oh! That's right, first thing na hummer, one million dollar," singing the catchy song that glorified the unscrupulous profession. His endless laugh rolled out of his proud mouth. "I used to be like them but then I pulled off two fantastic scams and got my own thing, come let me tell you," he said handing his workers the suya.

"You don't think it's wrong taking these people's money," I asked.

"Not at all!" He replied vehemently, "If they were not greedy or crooked, they will not fall into the trap. Take this guy for example ..."

We walked into a small room with too many electronics. A stereo system loud enough to entertain the whole street was turned down to a whisper. A muted flat screen flashed dumb images. Four or five people sat around the room in a couple of enchanted conversations. They barely let themselves be interrupted by the new entrants. Obinna nodded at a boy by a thick door towards the back of the room. Strands of the conversation unwound around my ears – all were talking about business. The boy who went into the back room returned with a tray laden with two bottles of Guinness, a lighter, a long joint and two glasses. He poured the drinks and I declined the smoke. Obinna's laugh came again as he lit it, exhaling fat plumes of smoke and coughing deeply. As if on cue, the rest of the room turned to us and it was obvious the workday was over. Obinna seemed to melt into his chair, passed the joint to his left, took a sip of his drink, let out a satisfied sigh and suddenly sat up in his chair animated.

"As I was saying," he said like there had not been a fifteen-minute interruption. "My first big coup was a classic and even you must admit that the person was just plain greedy! I used the Abacha line: I am his son, send me your bank details, blah blah ... the man should be arrested! He was conspiring to defraud our poor country and they say I am doing 419, no I am exposing criminals," he said it in an explosive rush like he needed to convince someone. The joint was back in his hand so he took a few long drags. I looked around the room, the formerly animated occupants lay in lethargic poses and bottles of beer had materialised everywhere.

"I don't feel guilty about anything I have done. Not at all, oh."

"Obinna, how did you start this thing?"

He chuckled, "My brother, forget that side, na story for another day. Let's just say if the government won't provide jobs, we'll employ ourselves."

"What was your next big job?"

"Ehen, after I cleaned out that guy's account, the guy was rich small. I still struggled with minor things sha. I asked people if I can send them cash so I can use their card, you know. Generally mumu people who fell for stupid things I came up with when not thinking clearly. My last post ehn, they just smoked all the time, we came up with minor ideas. Over here, these boys," he said pointing around the room. "If they don't initiate something solid, nobody goes home, unless we have a guest," he finished with a soft laugh and a happy glance in my direction.

"Thank you," I said with mock gratitude, starting to feel light headed from the smoke that swirled around the room.

"So, this one day," Obinna continued suddenly. "I met this guy," he said pointing to a guy in a tight T-shirt that said 'Arise oh Compatriots' who was slumped in the corner. "He is a genius, men, he said I should bring my money he would invest it."

"I'm sure you did not trust him."

"What? Of course not! I abused him. I told him, 'Do I look stupid?'"

"But he had a plan?"

"I say the nigger is genius," Obinna said, starting to be animated. "He is a genius nigger!" he exclaimed, exploding in personal glee.

"What did he do?"

"We bought some gold, you know, other precious stones," he said mumbling to himself. "This is the brilliant part, we'll send some email saying we need to get rid of these things," he was beginning to mumble, he was the only one smoking now and he was in his own world where he was brilliant. "Well, they send small money, we send small stuff; they send big money, we send nothing." He tried to laugh and let out a long cough and sank into the couch.

"My guy, it was real," I said in a sudden hurry to leave. My glass and bottle sat there neglected, my head was fuzzy. I wondered how I would get home.

Suddenly, Obinna jumped up, "Yes, yes," he mumbled. We went to the room with the computers; a couple of guys were still busy.

"Uche, take am go stadium," Obinna said, throwing the car keys to him. "No forget tomorrow."

Obinna grasped my hand and followed it with a clumsy hug. I knew without a doubt I would never see him again or forget that night and I was fine with that.

Uche spoke often and nervously. He was ambitious but I was barely listening, my face was pointed out the window hoping to get some clarity for my journey home. Uche had his first catch the following day. There was a man from San Francisco who was arriving in the morning to save Uche from persecution because he was gay in a third world, repressive country. Uche was to pick him up at the airport, take him to a motel, strip him of all his property and drop him off at the American embassy.

I wondered if I should tell Aisha about my night; I wondered if I could. But I knew one reason why next summer, after my graduation, I was not going to return.

II

Fear Not For Man (Washington, DC, USA and South Western Nigeria, 2007 – 2009)

ONE

The rest of my stay went by quickly. It was mostly spent in the rocking chairs beneath Uncle's balcony talking with Aisha. I was surprised to discover I cared more about her and home than I expected. And I realised that all the excuses I gave for not returning had dried in my mind with the brilliant heat of the African sun. I was almost relieved to head to the airport, because rather than being plagued by ghosts from the past I was haunted by visions of a future I was reluctant to accept.

Uncle, Emeka and Mrs Folayo said their goodbyes at home, so I could share the sort of intimate goodbye with Aisha only possible in the open glare of an airport terminal. After a long, comfortable hug I turned before she could see the tears in her eyes reflected in mine. Suddenly, she repeated again, "You'll be back."

To this I replied, "And why is that?"

She responded too casually, too flippantly, too nonchalantly, "Because you love me."

And it came across exactly as she hoped it would not and implied exactly what we were both afraid to admit – that I was in love with her and she with me. And worse still, we both knew. The impassionate words so casually said would throw my mind into such a state of turmoil that I would not notice the turbulence of the flight. By the time the plane landed, I would feel guilty; because I was going to betray my heart and return to a girlfriend I barely loved anymore.

The first time I met her, she was staring at me with the bold nonchalance one reserved for someone they found attractive but rather beneath them. The contemptuous glare some Europeans reserved for the McDonald's golden arches, like they understood why some people could want to eat there, but certainly not them – an attraction that fell short of being tempting. I returned the gaze intrigued and amused. She had one of those rare beauties often overlooked, but once noticed was all consuming and became all that she was – an intoxicating beauty. She had extremely honest eyes, which belied her brilliance and her innocent habit of perpetually lying lips. However, I would soon learn to discern the imperceptible shrugs and incomprehensive sighs to know when she was being truthful. Her eyes were a dark brown and although the opaque green eyes of the other girls that became a pale blue when fatigued often dazzled me, hers reminded me of all the women I had loved. And the next day when I saw them as a dark army green, I thought of all the women I had unsuccessfully tried to love. She was the only daughter of a rich father and an uncaring mother and had developed the petulant luxury of always having her way. I was realising that my relationships were falling apart with alarming regularity and my disinterest in engaging in a new one was what seduced her to vie for my attention.

In the classroom, I was brilliant, but I soon noticed that my exotic status absolved me of most social conventions. It was a revelation I found enchanting as I realised people were very indulgent of an 'ignorant' foreigner with patient ears. So, when I spoke, I did it with such careless attention to my words and speech that one sometimes wondered if I purposely hoped to convey a bad impression. But when you left my presence, it was with a lingering question, which you could never put into words. I was tall and attractive but my features were cold and reserved and my dark complexion gave me the inkling of a captured statue.

This was the view I left with everyone upon first meeting. But the second time around I always came off as warm and engaging like a refined volcano and all the haunting notions of the previous meeting were melted away. The strangest part of all this was that I seemed to simultaneously affect these contrasting feelings. And people meeting me for the first time would say, "That kid was coarse and rude," while their colleagues would argue with equal vehemence that, "He was the most charming and interesting guy they had ever met."

In The States, like most Africans, I had been thought to be black, then savage, then exotic. I remained with these varying identities with different groups and liked the plurality of supposed personalities. With the first group, I soon learned to play basketball and discuss football. With the second, I alternated between barbaric stories that informed their biases and profound opinions that shocked their prejudices. In my quiet way, I tried to push the impression of the third image because it was that I most enjoyed. I knew different things from most of the people around me, so some thought I knew everything and others thought I knew nothing.

An arrestingly handsome face meant I had many acquaintances and my reserved personality ensured few friends. With these few, I would often revert to my most natural self – which was a young African student trying to learn in a foreign country. I enjoyed some romance, but it was often fuelled by mere curiosity and usually timidly puttered out when the parties discovered we had more in common than imagined and were unwilling to indulge our paltry differences. I impulsively sought out the exotic. I listened to the Beatles, Bob Dylan and only added Fela, whom I had grown up listening to, when I finally felt some yearning for the familiar African sun during a blind winter dawn in my second year.

It was one of those days that conspired to repeatedly remind me that I was miles away from home. One of those days that I realised I could not describe snow to Aisha, that the songs on my playlist had more guitars than drums, that a nurse and a teacher innocently assumed I was an athlete because of my colour. One of those days that reminded me that I was living in borrowed space and asked the purpose for my presence. One of those days when I did not want to hang out with Leke but needed to.

Leke's father was a Nigerian and his mother, British and he was probably the first and only half-caste to know how to play that to his advantage. He was not riddled with the usual insecurities, but instead exhibited a confidence that was humbling to behold. The best of both worlds would not surmise to describe him. His effeminate face proudly sat astride an athletic body to dazzling effect. He knew how handsome he was, but worse still was the power of his eyes. His eyes were a curious blue-green. They wavered between the lazy blue of the Atlantic and the refulgent green of the Pacific and when he looked at you, he seemed to harness the power of both oceans. He had the lazy eye of a haughty stare but rarely bothered to use it. When he did look you in the eye, more often than not you wished he had not. This was because every man felt uncomfortably intimidated and every woman fell hopelessly in love. He was the sort of friend you were permanently suspicious of but unable to untangle from. He never spoke about his colour, but when it seemed like he was about to be denied something, he gave a look that plainly asked, 'Is it because I am black?' to whites; and 'Is it because I am half?' to blacks and none ever saw the look of amusement that swiftly followed as they always turned away in shame and acquiesced to his demands.

He spoke Yoruba like he was from the village, Pidgin like he was from the gutters of Surulere and English with the polished tone of an Oxford scholar. It is a rare and startling thing to meet someone you instantly disliked, but despite eventually becoming close friends, it was exactly how I had felt the first time I had met Leke.

"You don enter funk again," Leke said taking one look at me. "Don't sweat that Daisy issue, she was not meant for you," he said, casually referring to my recent ex.

"It's not that," I countered, "it's just I've not been home since I left about four years ago."

"There's nothing there," Leke replied comfortingly, even though he visited Nigeria every Christmas and returned with the biggest smile and best stories.

"Perhaps I'll go next Christmas," I said.

"And what is wrong with this one?" Leke queried with obvious mirth.

"I'm not quite ready," I replied defensively.

"Well, I know what you are ready for," Leke said with a big smile.

And it was at that party I met Emma for the first time. It was at that party I returned her stare with one of detached amusement. And despite swearing off girls indefinitely just a few moments before, I found myself ensnared by her subtle aura.

I pointedly ignored her for the rest of that night and she did likewise. The next day we ran into each other and she struck up a conversation like we were childhood friends. Banter would be a more accurate description, as she never really conversed. She spoke in quick witty sentences that gave one the impression of being in a fencing match. She would switch topics in rapid succession and suddenly settle on one of seeming insignificance, squeezing out interesting facts until she finally stopped with a wink that seemed to cry, 'Touché!' She stimulated my mind in a way none had since I left the shores of my homeland without ever using the, 'How come you don't know that?' phrase that I found rather irritating and was common among others of similar intellect. 'People of your kind,' I used to teasingly say to Emma when I referred to other white Americans with an obvious north eastern breeding. It was on this languidly provocative foundation that we built the relationship I forgot in the recess of my mind the moment I had seen Aisha again.

She was one of those that erroneously thought that love was made for romance instead of the other way around. So, she ignored my brooding silence upon my return from Nigeria and tried to paper over the cracks that were appearing in our relationship with romantic dinners and spontaneous lunches. But in the rare moments when she remembered to be vulnerable, her eyes would turn amber and I would remember why I believed I was in love with her.

The mind of the guilty assumes the haughty stance that everyone else is similarly afflicted. So, one day, when I asked her, "Can you be in love with two people at the same time?"

Her response given with terrible cynicism, "You can fall in love with as many people as you let yourself," would thoroughly haunt me.

It created a feeling of guilt that ate at me for a few days and as always is with the culpable, it would make me suspicious of her every move.

It was the last semester of our college career and I had finally begun to slowly ease back to my life in DC, mostly banishing the voices from home that now only whispered to me occasionally. We sat in the underground metro on our way to see the cherry blossoms that were the temporary cure for faltering relationships. We carelessly flopped into the orange seats, our laughter cocooning us in a private chamber. My suspicions still took occasional nibbles at my mind and I suddenly noticed that Leke's arm lay on Emma's thigh in the careless way that betrays a familiarity with the naked flesh beneath. It would have been a passing suspicion that I would have regretted later but as I looked away, I caught the eye of Erin.

Erin was Emma's best friend and I was sitting next to her and opposite my girlfriend. Erin was one of those girls who when she was younger, could afford to be the best-dressed little girl in the room and since she went to a school where that mattered she became confident. As she got older and her nose continued to grow until even her clothes were not sufficient to make her attractive, it was this confidence that became her redeeming feature. However, I had noticed her reticence in the past few days and when I caught her eye and she quickly averted her gaze to a point of interest that did not exist, I knew.

While my indifference for the relationship had been recent, Emma's interest had gradually diminished after the initial stages when I had been aloof and participated in the relationship like an observer. And it was only a matter of time before I lost out to my friend who had the permanent habit of nonchalance, because it was a necessary trait in Emma's understanding of affection.

Perhaps if I had told her about Aisha, I would have cemented her love for a while longer for it was only in the last few days of my melancholic musings that she had felt for me as deeply as in the earlier days of our relationship.

That night, neither felt any grief when we broke up, except for the sad realisation that our discussions would be no more.

Just before she turned away for good, she put on a brave smile that lied and said, "What time of the day do you think you'd be?"

I did not really understand the question and was not in the mood for our usual repartee.

"You should be noon … but you're sunset" she said before I could respond.

"What does that mean?" I asked finally.

Then her smile became sad. It was a real smile. She kissed me on the cheek and walked away.

I spent the last three months of my college career in quiet seclusion applying for jobs. When Uncle and Mrs Folayo showed up for my graduation, I happily took them to all my favourite spots as I tried to convince myself that it was not that I did not want to return to Nigeria, but that I wanted to stay in America.

I quickly forgot about Emma's final statement until almost a year later. I had found a job I tolerated and I shuffled to and from work with the distracted gait of a man who worked simply for his pay cheque. Every other day, I went by the same Chinese restaurant two blocks from my house to pick up chicken fried rice. A mostly quiet, old couple manned it and the husband saw it as his duty to furnish me with the occasional words of wisdom.

I walked in that day with a heavier burden than on most days. Emeka's sentencing date was fast approaching and I could not decide if I wanted to go for it. I was getting daily requests on the phone from Uncle to move back to Nigeria permanently and I noticed Uncle's cough had finally overshadowed his laugh.

"I return home in two months," Tao said in his abrupt, unrequested manner as he handed me the bag.

"Why?" I asked. "You have a great thing going here and Mrs Tao seems content." I cast a suspicious eye at Mrs Tao who never spoke but efficiently sat behind the teller adding up the cost of the orders faster than the machine.

"Because I am great man, a man is never great outside home … not truly," he added. I wondered if everything old Chinese men said always sounded wise because of their staccato accents and abrupt words, but this made me remember Emma's line. As I marched home, I felt my past and my future were beginning to merge and point in the same direction and the present began to seem suspiciously transient.

My heart cried and I wondered for whom, my newly discarded lover, or for Aisha. I was lonely in a way I had not felt since my first month in the UK. I thought of those I had left behind in Nigeria. I sat before my computer and began to collate their stories, as slowly, evenly and chronologically as I could muster. I started with Uncle's because his story was mine as well and I realised in the banal documenting of his tales, I was trying to find myself. I was going to create an identity for myself. 'I am …' I wrote. My head said, 'a Nigerian man', but I could not put that down. What was that? I knew too little of my country. I wanted to write Uncle's tale but I was stuck at October 1, 1960. It was the day of Nigeria's independence, but he was already fifteen. I tried to imagine what the day must have been like. I got lost in my own revelry and was finally awakened by a particularly pensive blast of a trumpet. Emeka had given me Fela Kuti's entire discography. He had purchased it sentimentally, but never learned to enjoy music. I felt sorry for him. The song was called 'Black Man's Cry'. I thought it was apt for telling Uncle's story, so I wrote down:

Black Man's Cry (South Western Nigeria 1945 – 1967)

I liked the look of it in the centre of the page. I began to record what I could recall of Uncle's memories.

I wrote uninterrupted for five hours then remembered my meal. I went to the bathroom, studying my face in the mirror as I washed my hands. I suddenly began to laugh because I realised that what looked back at me would never truly be mine, because in my mind I was always better or worse than my reflection. It was an image for strangers, people who had never met me and wondered if I got the scar on my left eyebrow from a fight or a tackle – making short bios based on programmed stereotypes. As I sat in my lonely living room contemplating my life, I understood that yesterday was gone and yesterday was twenty-two years, six months and fifteen days ago. My head fell into my hands without my consent as I was momentarily buried by the insignificance of all my achievements as Tao's words hit home. I sat frozen in that pose pondering my next steps; the excitement of recording the first words had dulled like an unattended winter fire. Then the monotonous ring of the phone interrupted my musing.

Aisha's voice was almost frantic.

Fate had decided for me.

TWO

Perhaps it was something in the boiled, filtered water and the smoggy air. But a few days after I returned to Nigeria, my voice was louder, my actions more aggressive; my emotions came more freely – quick with a frown, quicker with a laugh. What I liked the most was that my mind seemed sharper; maybe it was because everyone was a philosopher, a coach, a comedian and a politician.

It was a desolate but necessary time to be back. Everyone seemed old and withered, the only bright spot being Aisha's presence. Uncle was dying slowly in his bed, the tissues of his lungs atrophying into blood and mucus as he stubbornly refused to go a hospital. "I'll rather die in my own home," he would say with mirth that was not contagious. He had tuberculosis and he barely had much longer to live. Emeka's trial was in a couple of weeks and he refused to change counsel despite the obvious fact that it would be impossible for Uncle to defend him. 'The trial is a sham,' he would say without emotion, but he had a serene smile like he was privy to information withheld from others.

One day as I sat in the mild comfort of the rocking chair, trying to shield my ears from the coughs that spilled off the balcony above me, Emeka appeared and sat silently in the other chair. We rocked wordlessly for an hour before Emeka said the first word and his final sentence came fourteen hours later, by which time we had both forgotten our stomachs, as even Mrs Folayo had known not to interrupt.

Emeka told me his life story in the toneless detachment of an airport announcement. Occasionally we would deviate to tease out a point, an argument, or a clarification and Emeka's reasons for his decisions often had the cold recital of a roll call. When I asked why Emeka left his home to follow Father Grey, he had said matter-of-factly, "It is a terrible legacy to die poor because fate and destiny often conspire to give your children a similar burial."

And I had known there was no point inquiring why he left Father Grey. I had always wondered about Emeka's attitude to faith. It was not obvious and stubborn like Mrs Folayo or irreverent like Uncle's, it was a simple, unassuming faith that seemed unshakable like the smile of an old wife who had said 'I do' fifty years earlier. It was more confusing because Emeka was the biggest proponent of science and I had been taught to believe they disagreed. When I asked him about it, Emeka had paused for a few minutes, remembering his old cellmate who still prayed assiduously in the pale light of their gloomy enclosure.

"Seun," he said tenderly, "there are some things you must discover on your own, but I see God as the why and science as the how. Look at that tree for example," he said pointing to the rowdy head of the orange tree next to them. "The gravity that will pull that ripe orange down is science, but the process that makes it mature is a miracle."

"But all that has been explained, it has to do with photosynthesis," I was beginning to chime in, drawing on my dim memory of agricultural science, when Emeka's gentle palm on my arm silenced me.

"My dear boy, that is the how, not the why. We often mistake the two." He let that sink in for a while then continued, "The clouds that collide to form flashes in the sky is science, the feeling in the heart of the farmer after he hears the long awaited thunder is thanksgiving. The heart pumping blood through the body is science; the skipping of your heart at the touch of one that you adore is love. Science is interesting ... God is beautiful."

Darkness had fallen and we lay in it like under a warm blanket. Rather than get up to switch on the light, Emeka finally lit the candle that sat on the stool between us.

"The beauty of life is that you're already dead before you're born," he said, lighting a match that flared brightly and fizzled out before it could light the candle. "Sometimes we achieve our purpose, sometimes we don't," he finished with a coy smile, lighting the candle with another match.

"He that sees God in everything sees beauty. When beauty is revealed in all, love abounds. Science is one-dimensional. God is everywhere. The people who tell you that the world appeared from a big bang will tell you you were crazy if you told them the car you drove was the result of a chance explosion. Do not let anyone's doubt infect your faith and do not let anyone's faith initiate your doubt. Don't let anyone confuse you into deciding matters of the heart with your head," Emeka said the last sentence with a pointed glance and I knew that it went beyond our current conversation.

"My dear boy," Emeka said again, "genius transcends vocation and you are brilliant, you will be fine. Everything connects in the horizon, but beware the lenses you use to spy it; remember beauty is deceptive and love is treacherous. Make your choices carefully, regret is a man's worst legacy." And with that Emeka was silent and I wondered what ate at his proud heart.

Emeka said, "A man's ambition must simply be to be the greatest man that ever lived." He paused and then said, "But a man's greatness is only measured in the eyes of those that love him."

And I thought I saw a golden tear reflected by the candle in the eye of my old companion.

The only day Emeka entered Uncle's room would be to say goodbye to his friend. The doctor made us file in one after the other, beginning with a brief teary encounter with Aisha. Mrs Folayo's was much longer and noisier. Her wails seemed to reverberate around the room, out of the door and down the road. Emeka sat quietly by his bed; they held hands for half an hour, sharing a smile without words. When I walked in, the room was dim like the day I last walked in, when Uncle told me about my family. Uncle managed to sit up a little bit, he hugged me and we both shed silent tears. Finally, Uncle said, "Akpokio," it was the only time Uncle had ever called me that, "I selfishly changed your name ..." a long harsh cough interrupted his words. "I'm sorry just ... just make us all proud." They were light words that carried a heavy responsibility. The doctor hurried me out when Uncle collapsed into another round of fitful coughs.

That evening we all sat around his bed, watching him alternate between a pained smile and harsh coughs that rattled his bony shoulders. "Open that window please, I want to see clearly," he said finally to Mrs Folayo and although he did not add the words 'One final time', we all watched his last sunset with him. His eyes stayed fixed outside and he said in a voice that promptly floated out of the window, the words I had often heard Mother use, "Life begins afresh in the morning." And he seemed to sink peacefully back into his pillow, a placid smile on his lips. It took almost thirty minutes before I realised what Emeka had known twenty minutes earlier, that the peaceful smile was the mask of the happily dead.

It was inexplicable. I sat in Uncle's study at his big desk with unfinished work. My thoughts were overshadowed by unanswered questions. I wondered what next, I knew Uncle's view – return home – it was as unwavering as the finality of his death. And as I sat at the desk, I heard a faint drumming, which confused me for it had no source. Suddenly, it got louder and overwhelming and I was sure it emanated from somewhere in the room, but from whence I could not tell. And then I saw them. They danced in, in their inchoate serenity: the stillborn dreams of 1960. Potential unfulfilled, they swirled, trapped and free, they floated in the captured heat of Uncle's study. Was this his legacy? Was this my destiny? I watched them dance to the tunes of my past and future. I watched them sway in the insecurity of today. I watched them and witnessed the rebirth of my life.

We heard Emeka coming towards the room and they danced away before him. I must have looked startled when he came in for he gave me a knowing nod and smile, like he knew. He told me all the remaining tales. I realised it was a beautiful story, one I wanted to be a part of.

Emeka was only two years older than Uncle, but after our conversation, he seemed as frail as a centurion. He seemed like he had been relieved of a great burden. For the next few days, he sat silently, wilting away in the rocking chair beneath Uncle's balcony, but we were all too swallowed in our personal grief to notice. We did not realise that Emeka suddenly seemed to be hovering above the grave and that his eyes had the unfocused look of a baby. But he still refused to talk about his trial. Aisha worked for Uncle's firm now. Mr Adedoja and Aisha would sigh in frustration at his unwillingness to corporate. Instead, he begged that they delay reading Uncle's will until the day after his trial and they write up his as well.

It was with frustrated resignation that they finally agreed to his demands. In the faded sky, a bright sun battled with thick clouds and Emeka's countenance seemed to reflect the weather. He was back in his habitual rocking chair and failed to hear the bell ring. Even Major had begun to show the signs of ageing and it was with some difficulty that the women at the gate managed to convince him that they were harmless.

Aisha opened the door and the face that greeted her with a nervous smile triggered something in her memory that she could not quite place.

"Is Emeka Ogbonna here? The one from the news?" The woman rushed out nervously.

"Yes," Aisha said hesitantly, "is he expecting you? Who should I say is looking for him?" she continued trying to regain her composure.

"No, he is not expecting us ... umhhh ... tell him," Nneka paused for a long moment, "Tell him some people from his past ..." she finished finally.

Aisha wanted to ask more questions, but the woman's demeanour silenced her and she politely led her and her older companion to the living room. She went through the library to where Emeka rocked in his chair with many questions in her mind.

Once she told Emeka he had two female visitors, he arose with a bright smile and asked shyly, "How do I look?"

It was then that she noticed that although he had aged over twenty years in just a few days, his face was cleanly shaven, his shirt neatly pressed and there was a whiff of cologne that battled to keep away the smell of old age.

"You look fine," she said tenderly, wondering what the women meant to him.

And finally, he felt peace. The peace he had sought when he pulled the trigger, the elusive peace that did not come when he gave up his wealth. The peace that had stayed away during the lonely nights in his little shed. He realised O.C had been selfishly wrong because it was a peace born of reconciled love. He placed a small black sweet with white stripes into his mouth and followed her back to the living room doing his best to march uprightly.

The minty smell of the tomtom preceded his entry and Nneka staggered to her feet, her head reeling between the past and present. As soon as she saw him, she exclaimed, "Oh my God! It is you! It was you! It is you."

Her words jumbled by the impact of many revelations. She broke down into tears and fell into his arms realising he was the man that had dropped her at the train station that night many years ago, a fact that also dawned on Aisha a few seconds later as she realised why the woman seemed familiar. And Nneka also realised he had been the gateman that lived across the street from them for those years who always waved from a distance and never said a word. Aisha stumbled out of the room in tears, leaving no witnesses to the long awaited reunion between Emeka and his family.

Dinner that night was joyous and bizarre. It was to be a meal between strangers but it seemed like Emeka was finally breaking bread for his entire family. He spent most of it staring at his wife, as they clutched hands beneath the table like teenagers protecting a secret crush. Mrs Folayo was too overwhelmed to talk. Nneka apologised to Aisha for never returning to check up on her, but it was an unnecessary apology because it had been better for all involved that things happened exactly the way they did. At the beginning of the meal, Emeka had blessed the meal but at the end, he pointedly looked at me and asked that I say grace. And I finally understood that the strange feeling that had sat in my stomach the entire meal was not from Mrs Folayo's cooking but the gradual realisation that I had been handed the keys to a door I could not locate quite yet.

As we sat happily in the living room after the meal, Emeka called his daughter, Nneka, aside. "I have only one request," he said, "That you stay for the rest of the week, but leave the day before my trial."

The sincerity of his tone made Nneka agree before she could object and she did not have time to be displeased with her decision because Emeka's smile suddenly became as the moon under which he used to tell her stories as a child.

Four days later, they said goodbyes with tears and smiles; only Emeka's wife wept with sorrow because only she understood. The next day when Mrs Folayo slowly ambled to his room to rouse him for his sentence, his lids were still wet, his lips still parted but his soul was gone to rejoin his friend.

THREE

Dolapo Odukoya's life ended beneath the cool, fragrant shade of a guava tree. He had not actually died there, but had requested his body be buried there, in the solitary security of his own compound. Of course, at this point he was known simply as Uncle.

I had searched my mind for the right words to say at Uncle's funeral but instead my memories had opened to me like a shy girl after her first kiss. Events long forgotten, dreams washed away, fantasies practically ignored, they haunted and accused me. I was not a failure, I was rather successful, but I had vowed to take the right way and had stuck to the one I knew. In the miracle of today, we often forget about the promises of yesterday.

Uncle had died on June 1, requesting that he not be buried until June 12, 2009, to mark the fifteenth anniversary of the event that claimed his wife's life and in mockery of the court case that was to hold that day, sentencing Emeka for the death of Governor John O.C Abari. To further complicate issues, Emeka had happily joined his friend and the only person who had known to get a casket was his wife. That morning when I opened the gate for the hearse to come and pick up Uncle's body, I saw it would be futile. A vast crowd sat outside the gate and at the front of it was Nneka and her mother with a coffin. Nneka had been weeping since the coffin had been delivered a few hours before until she saw the peaceful face of her father mirrored by his friend in the one next to his.

Aisha, Nneka and I did not know how long it took, but we marched with the coffins from Ikeja to Ikoyi and back, aided by a crowd that swelled continuously throughout the day. We dropped the coffins in front of the courthouse, which was mysteriously empty and I gave a farewell speech that made a nation weep.

In the oral tradition that is the Nigerian way, a person's life is remembered by his most recanted achievement, which is always the one moment when a mundane action has an eternal result. It is one of cupid's most lethal tricks for it deceives many into love as they replay that instance and retell it many times, blurring the magic of the moment with the doer of the action. It is a first kiss or a perfect compliment timely delivered. But it is not only a trick for love, it is also a tool for hope and it was during the retelling of my speech in barber shops, offices and decrepit rooms in exhausted slums that the nation realised that a new Nigeria had been born, a few months before she was to turn fifty. It was then they began to recant the magic of independence, to remember the hopes of freedom, to recall what should have begun to happen fifty odd years ago in 1960. It was then they exhumed the stillborn ghosts of 1960.

The sky wore a gray mask and our emotions had many faces. Both wills had been read and I sat next to Aisha in the compound that was now mine. We sat between the two graves that rested under the reassuring shade of the guava tree. The first fruits were beginning to ripen and their scent filled the air. I was strangely comforted by the death beneath me and life around me, the past beneath me and the future beside me. We had not said a word since we sat but gazed lazily at the gray sky. Suddenly a faint breeze blew and a guava fell into Aisha's lap. She picked it up in surprise. I was looking at her with an odd smile. She took a bite and handed it to me.

EPILOGUE

The Lost Tapes (Nigeria, 2010)

It had been nine months and six days since Emeka let out a contented sigh and went to join his friend. For a few weeks the country was electrified, the inhabitants of the slums in Ajegunle realised they were citizens; and those in the expansive mansions of Ikoyi remembered they were Nigerians. But slowly, the realities began to mock both and though the embers of hope still smoldered in forgotten corners of their hearts, the country went back to business as usual – almost.

In Lagos, a new government was in power, a man on a mission. His mission was simple – to save a city decaying from the rot at its centre. Despite his efforts, despite the support of the people, despite the tangible improvements in the lives of the citizens – the cabal was still displeased, choosing to place politics above governance; except for a couple, his peers were unfazed by the winds of change; and the presidency was still regarded as a toy to be passed around amongst overfed children.

The country had run rudderless for days as an unrepentant woman had held the people hostage with the flaccid power of her husband's deathbed. Old leaders attempted to once again seize power or pass it to their stooges. The ancient guard that should have long been relegated to the back pages of history refused to let the pages turn.

The death of John O.C Abari was regrettable but manageable and Mr Sukonmi, his personal assistant, quickly occupied the vacancy. The Assistant Governor was to take over the position, but

Mr Sukonmi had made the right friends; he allied with Alhaji and everyone else that aspired to the position found himself arrested or dead. Everything was going smoothly; Mr Sukonmi began to imagine he would run for two more terms and be the longest serving Governor in history. He began to settle comfortably into the Governor's mansion and quickly added the runway that even O.C had hesitated to build. Then the elections came around and he received a shock that set him in a panic, because the masses saw the light and he and his patrons were forced to realise they could no longer hide the destiny of a nation in the shadows of personal ambition.

Mr Sukonmi was distressed; elections were not supposed to be decided at the polls and everyone knew that. He had bribed all the right people and had the blessing of Alhaji and the rest of the cabal. He had remained a faithful party member and done everything necessary to ensure that the elections would not be decided at the polls. But that was exactly what had happened and the same group now had their sights on the presidency. If they were successful, it would mean an early demise to his lucrative career; a long awaited end to business as usual.

When she had initially appeared on the stage, Mr Sukonmi had spent the first few months trying to find the godfather that sat behind her movement and when he realised there was none, he had been cocky enough to publicly state that his opponent did not know anything about politics. "After all, she is tailoring her campaign towards the voters instead of those that actually hold the reins of power," he had said this with contempt when his opponent had finally been revealed. For a year, no one had known who the challenger was, but everyone was talking about it. All over the state, billboards had begun to appear, with detailed statistics about the condition of the state and that of Mr Sukonmi's account. Mr Sukonmi had branded them all cheap slander with an arrogant wag of his corrupt hand. Then the next wave of billboards appeared, showing the possibilities of the state and the people began to stir a little. Mr Sukonmi remained unfazed until blown up 'before and after' photographs of remote parts of the state that had been renovated began to appear on buildings and along the roads, with a soaring eagle and courtesy of the 'Progressive Party of the Masses' stamped at the bottom.

At this point, Mr Sukonmi's composure began to slip. He began to snap at reporters, turn down invitations to parties and take fewer trips to London. The public was elated and confused because they had only known a politics of sycophancy or disinterest: and this demanded neither as the actual candidate remained a mystery. The announcement that Nneka Ogbonna, the daughter of the man that killed his predecessor would be his opposition ignited a silent revolution that no one was conscious of until they got to the polls and saw all their neighbours standing patiently in the long lines. The officials were terrified; they had received exorbitant amounts to rig the elections, but once the votes were all cast, the patient crowd became an agitated mob that made it impossible to tamper with the outcome. The people asked that the votes be promptly tallied and for fear of their lives, they obliged, announcing an overwhelming victory for Nneka. The irony was that at the two polling stations where the hired thugs had been able to take control, they found their thumbs staining the box next to the PPM and each thought it was a private sacrifice until they counted the votes and saw that their devious colleagues had done likewise.

Initially Alhaji had been amused – he teased Mr Sukonmi for losing to a woman and said the youth were incompetent. Alhaji decided the time had come for him to run for presidency and he was going to show his protégée how it was done. Alhaji was old but he attempted to assuage the people's fears by indicating that he only intended to run for one term [to properly show the next generation how to influence politics and manipulate power]. He was confident in his arrogant assumptions until an unforeseen challenge began to emerge. A challenge he had initially brushed aside as 'manipulations of the evil ones'.

The manipulations of the evil ones had begun beneath the green branches of a guava tree under a grey sky.

Aisha handed me a guava fruit, I took a pensive bite and we remained there, silent for many hours. I had an unrestrained smile, which happens when my thoughts brew into clarity behind my dark impassive stare. Suddenly I knew. Her lips were a medley of clouds – thick black thunderstorms, inviting sunset red, soft sunrise pink – reflecting the moods of my unsettled soul. They parted with their knowing grace and settled my destiny forever.

The wedding was small and quick. Afterwards, we travelled to Abia to visit Nneka and then decided to go to Bayelsa because it was so close. We ignored the threats of kidnappings and visited the place I had called home in my nascent years. Standing by the black streams, I realised that a scar is the most beautiful tribute to a wound and a glance at Aisha confirmed it was inevitable we journey up to Jos as well. Six months later, we had been to every state in the country. We saw the courage of the impoverished fuelled by the ignorant hope that the next day would magically be better. We tasted the simple dreams of people with uninformed visions. We heard tales of happiness and hardship that had been treasured in heavy hearts waiting to be told. We realised that many lives sat in obscurity, waiting … waiting for us.

Aisha had been given Uncle's share of the firm and I had been given everything else. No one had guessed at the vast sums Emeka had stashed away until his bank was visited. He had split his wealth into four between Aisha, Nneka, her mother and I. My bride and I returned from our trip animated, like a blind man whose eyes are finally opened. We had the luxury of a retinue of brilliant minds available to us and Nneka and Prof were the only people that needed convincing. With the help of the rest of the FoN group, we planned excitedly and executed quietly. Nneka wresting Bayelsa State so effortlessly from Mr Sukonmi had been the test ground for the validity of our plans and the readiness of the people. Then we attempted the much harder job of influencing the presidency.

We utilised the same tactics as used for the state, yet the opposition continued in their nonchalant corruption. Alhaji began knocking off his competition, ignoring the PPM and our optimistic inexperience. He went from state to state refusing to talk policies or ideas, instead parading his wealth with unabashed opulence, intoxicated by the adulation of hired flatterers. The FoN group waited until he had practically anointed himself the next president and then we released the tapes. The initial reaction was muted and I began to fear our strategy would be ineffective, but Alhaji became too arrogant. He mocked our actions publicly, pointing out that the ignorance of the vast populace ensured indifference and he forgot he was old. Old enough to have made many enemies over time: so that when Mr Adedoja filed a suit against him for the wanton loss of life and property due to the Jos massacres initiated by him, there was a judge willing to prosecute and enough senators willing to bar his candidacy.

The elections in 2010 were strange because they were democratic. Nigerians had never known what it was like to have a president elected by the will of the people. Prof stood under the banner that proudly proclaimed 'Golden Jubilee'. He pushed his glasses up his oily nose and proceeded to give his first State of the Union address.

APPENDIX
Book Club Questions

1. How did you like the book? Did you like the gradual transition or would you have preferred to be thrown straight into the story?

2. Which was your favorite of the main characters— and what made them so: Each character was allowed 'to tell' their story, through choice of language, sentence structure. Did you notice this and did it help you appreciate the book better.

    *   What did you make of the specific interactions between the characters particularly: (Dolapo & Ranti; Dolapo & Emeka; Dolapo & Seun; Seun & Ranti; Seun & Aisha; Emeka & OC)
    *   Was the conclusion of Emeka and OC's relationship justified?
    *   Did it carry across that Seun was to be a summation of the other characters?
    *   Do you admire or disapprove of the characters?
    *   Do they remind you of people you know?

3. Did you get the parallel between Emeka and Dolapo, i.e. Emeka's life is a closer mirror of the reality of Nigeria with its ups and down, while Dolapo is what Nigeria could have been, i.e. a lot of potential harnessed properly.

4. Emeka was the only character in all parts of the book, yet he was introduced differently in every part, was this evident? Emeka loses all five senses at one point throughout the book, was this noticed?

5. Did you enjoy that it was broken into separate parts that synched in the end?
    Although there was an overarching voice telling the story, it was written like each character had told Seun their story at

separate times. Was this evident? Could the reader notice the subtle use of alliteration, sentence length, grammar complexity, vocabulary depth to differentiate voice?

6. What main ideas does the author explore?
   Stillborn
   Scent: Guavas
   Feel: African sun
   Sight: Fire
   Foresight: Often the events that are to unfold are told, yet as in Nigeria [the place setting] it seems the most obvious things are unpreventable despite the obvious negative consequence

7. Was the passage that most encapsulates the book, innocuously placed right before a shower evident?
   What other passages stood out for you with relation to the book, its theme, or just life issues in general?

8. Would you have preferred the end with or without the epilogue?

9. If you could ask the author a question, what would you ask? Feel free at @diekoye on Twitter.

10. Has this novel exposed you better to Nigerian history in an approachable way and broadened your view on the simple complexities of life and their unknown consequences?